Dedication

In loving memory of my sister, Fatma Louati.

Like Cathy, she was relentless, full of life, stood up to bullies,

and left us too soon.

But she lives forever in our hearts.

To my mom, Habiba. Like Julia, both mother and father.

She worked hard and raised three children on her own, and

we never went without.

To my sister Raida, who always inspired me to chase my

dreams and who shared many of the same ones. Film making.

Writing. Acting. I can't wait to see you bring your own stories

to life.

To my wife and kids. You make me want to be a better

person every single day. Because of you, I've learned to accept

love and happiness.

Contents

Captives

Chapter 1

Body In an Alley

Brooklyn. January.

He leapt over a puddle, landed clean, then jogged a few paces

to recover his balance before settling into a brisk, deliberate

walk. He held his trench coat above his head with one hand

in a vain attempt to shield himself from the downpour.

He glanced both ways and crossed the street, flashing the

universal traffic thank-you gesture, a flat palm raised toward

a slowing driver. The car's headlights lit up his face for a

moment.

He looked seasoned. Handsome in his own rugged, unapproachable

kind of way. A scar slashed through his left

eyebrow where hair refused to grow. His signature, some

might say, especially when paired with his deep brown eyes.

His beard was a couple of days old. A few gray strands on

either side gave him away. He was almost forty now. That

mattered to him. He was almost the same age as his mother

had been when she died. There was something unsettling

about that.

He liked to walk the city early in the morning. Before dawn.

Before most people woke.

There were always a few out. Bodega guys rolling up

metal gates. Stragglers stumbling home from an after party.

Homeless men waking in doorways, lining up in front of the

liquor store that sold cheap black coffee in Styrofoam cups.

The city was raw at that hour. Real. He liked being part of

that. Before the fancy business men and finance guys flooded the streets, rushing to get their morning lattes from corporate conglomerates that wouldn't even let the homeless use the bathroom unless they bought one of their chemical filled drinks.

That early, the city felt honest.

This morning was different.

He turned into a narrow alley, cutting through the concrete maze of the city. It stank like old grease and piss. There were crates collapsed in corners. A dumpster overflowing with soggy cardboard and day-old restaurant trash. Two small restaurants had black grease trails leading up to their back doors. An abandoned pushcart sat off to the side, piled with what looked like a homeless person's belongings… **And a body.**

Yellow tape cordoned off the scene, flapping in the rain. Officers stood in silence, while the forensic team, faceless in white hazmat suits, moved with quiet urgency. Blood had mixed with rainwater, forming a diluted crimson stream that crept toward the storm drain.

His heels clicked against the wet concrete as he approached. He flashed his badge to the officer on duty, then ducked under the tape without a word.

"Hope ya didn't have a heavy breakfast," said the officer who greeted him. He had a thick Brooklyn accent and a mustache to match. Big, bristly thing that looked like it could block bullets. His voice came out rough, like someone who'd smoked too much, yelled too often, or just naturally sounded like sandpaper. the kind that flattened vowels and gave every word weight.

The detective ignored the remark. "What do we got?"

The officer exhaled "Ain't never seen nuttin' like it," he said, voice dropping. "One'a da kitchen guys from da Chinese joint came out to dump da trash, saw a trail'a blood. Followed it, found da body, called it in." The detective looked past him toward the curb.

"Poor guy can't stop t'rowin' up," the officer added, nodding toward a hunched figure sitting on the sidewalk. A skinny Asian man, knees tucked close to his chest, face buried in his hands, shoulders shaking.

The detective stared at the body, rain dripping from the edge of his coat. Horror written all over his eyes.

He scanned the corpse and the scene slowly while forensics worked in silence around him. He didn't know what to make of what he was seeing. His brain couldn't compute it. His gaze kept flickering back and forth. Female. Arms and legs severed, sewn back on wrong. Arms where legs should be. Legs where arms belonged. Throat cut clean, ear to ear. Sewn shut again. Thick stitches. Wide gaps. Crude. The string looked like rough twine, the kind used on old potato sacks. Mouth split at both corners. Stitched back into a grin. Eyelids removed entirely.

She was naked. And judging by the amount of blood at the scene, it all happened here. The cutting. The stitching. The posing.

Brazen.

Then something cold crawled up his spine. It wasn't because of the horror of what he was seeing. That alone would have shaken him for days. Even with his hardened eyes, he had never seen anything like it. But… No. It wasn't that.

Next to the body was something shiny. Out of place. Exactly where it was supposed to be. Exactly where the killer wanted it found. A bracelet maybe. Or a necklace.

He froze, staring at it for a second. Then finally moved.

Stepped closer. Slowly, in disbelief. Rain still hammering.

Loud against a piece of cardboard laid to the side and the

restaurant's metal awning. His thoughts racing faster than he

could follow. "No, it can't be." He thought to himself.

The M.E. stood from a crouch as he peeled off his examining

gloves. Flat-voiced, he mumbled. As if to himself. "Victim's

deceased."

The detective, still staring at the shiny object as if it could

vanish, mumbled back, "No Shit."

Her eyes, lidless staring up at the sky. That forced, stitched

smile. Eerie. He didn't scare easy. But this was different.

Knees cracked as he crouched. Another lovely gift from his

fast-approaching forties.

A necklace.

No mistake now. The thin silver chain lay in the dirt, dull

except for one stubborn glint catching the alley light.

He stared at it, heart thudding harder with each beat, blood

rushing so fast it felt like it was paralyzing him.

His ears buzzed, pressure building like they might burst.

He knew what it was, even before he let himself believe it.

Reached into his chest pocket. Drew out a pen, clean,

precise. Slid the tip under the pendant like a surgeon then.

Froze.

Jaw clenched. Chest hollowed out.

"Did you take a picture of this yet?" he said, voice cracking just a little, not looking back. Just his eyes, cutting sideways like a blade.

Forensics guy jogged over, nodded. "Yeah. Got it."

He lifted the necklace slowly, careful not to let it slip as rain slid down his wrist. The pendant turned, catching a flash of light.

Someone's initials were carved into the back.

His frown deepened. His grip tightened. Heart racing. He stared. "How the fuck is this possible?"

Chapter 2

Missing

Nineteen Ninety Something.

Frank Jr. Good kid. Bad neighborhood.

Well… bad for outsiders.

His parents split early. His sister, Cathy, was two years older.

A lifetime wiser. She looked out for him. She had the heart of

a lion. Mouth like a switchblade.

Frankie, like she called him, was a quiet kid in a loud

neighborhood. And that could get misread as soft.

When the older kids teased him, patched-up pants, holed up

sneakers, Frankie didn't care.

He kept walking. Head high.

They were poor. But proud.

Cathy, on the other hand, never stayed quiet.

Not for a second.

She had a mouth on her. Knew how to use it too.

Clapped back hard.

Frankie would smile to himself.

The comebacks she'd fire off… she was too sharp for those

dumb kids. Too fast.

If it ever came down to it, he could throw a punch, though.

Take one too.

So could she…

Their apartment was small but cozy. Mom was always

rearranging furniture to make more space. You had to get

creative when you were poor.

They grew up tight on money. No vacations. Nothing extra.

But they never wanted for anything, even if debt had to be

piled on.

Their mom, Julie. Miss Silva, like the kids' friends used to

call her, was young. Beautiful. Married too fast. Divorced too

soon. She put herself through nursing school while raising

two kids in a city that didn't give handouts.

The guys on the block respected her. She helped them out

once, years back, when the kids were still small. Hid a couple

of them from the cops. No questions asked.

She never got involved in anything criminal, but she was

from the block and she looked out for her people when she

could.

She worked hard as a night nurse. Always on her feet.

Always tired. Almost never home.

The kids got used to it. They had their own routine.

When they were younger they built pillow forts out of couch

cushions, flashlights in hand, whispering stories until they

passed out. Anything to fill the silence. Anything to make her

absence smaller.

As they got older the forts disappeared. Homework. TV.

Bed. Routine.

By then the absence wasn't something they tried to cover.

It was just the way things were.

Sometimes their mom would surprise them and leave her shift early. A co-worker would cover for her and she'd come home with food and pastries. She didn't do it often, but when she did the place lit up. Those nights stuck.

It was a happy home, even through the rough times.

A happy family, even if it was broken.

Happy.

But not for long.

Christmas 1997

It was a cold one. The type that made your bones shudder. Unusual.

Frankie woke up early. He always did. Annoyingly loved being up before anyone else.

He passed by the Christmas tree and the wrapped gifts with a flutter in his chest. He was seventeen. An older teenager. But Christmas always brought him back to being a little boy.

He made himself some breakfast. Turned on the TV. Sat on the sunken couch with a bowl of cereal, hoping Mom and Cathy would wake up soon.

Mom came out first. Wrapped in her oversized sweater, makeup smeared, eyes half-shut. She pulled him into a hug.

"You up already?" she murmured.

"Yup," he said. "Merry Christmas, Mom."

"Merry Christmas, baby." She smiled, still half-asleep. "Is Catherine up yet?"

"No. Haven't seen her yet," he replied.

She yawned and looked around. Then spotted something on the floor. A small gift box already opened.

"She couldn't wait, could she?" Frankie said, smiling.

"You know it," Mom said with a grin.

Catherine had to open one gift on Christmas Eve. That was the rule. Been that way since she was two. She couldn't sleep otherwise.

"She went out with Inez last night after opening it," Mom said, heading for the kitchen. "Some Christmas party up in the hills. Don't know when she got back. I was knocked out cold."

"Yeah, you were," Frankie said.

She smiled, returned with a mug of coffee and nodded toward the gift.

"Go on. Open that small box while we wait for her. It matches the one she opened. I got you both the same thing."

Frankie grinned. Picked up the box. Gave it a little shake by his ear. One eye closed.

"Hmm… a bicycle?"

Mom laughed hard. He always made her laugh. He loved making her laugh.

Life had made her cry more than her share.

He opened it.

Inside was a thin, shiny necklace.

She started talking as he lifted it out of the box.

"I passed by this store near Chinatown. Saw these two necklaces in the window. Went in. The guy told me they were the last ones. I couldn't afford them, but he agreed to put them on layaway for me. I've been paying him slowly for months."

She stepped closer.

"The pendants are Saint Nicholas of Myra. Patron saint of

children. I thought it was fitting."

"Thanks, Mom," Frank Jr. interrupted her gently. He knew she could go on forever.

"I love it."

"Look in the back. I had it engrav…"

A loud phone ring cut her off. Startled her.

It felt wrong.

Christmas morning.

Who the hell would call.

Another loud ring. Frankie started to get up, but his mother put a hand out.

"I got it."

She shuffle-jogged toward the receiver.

A half-ring as she grabbed it mid-sound.

"Hello?" she answered, a little concerned.

"Hi, Miss Silva. This is Inez. I'm sorry to call so early."

"Oh, hi Inez. Merry Christmas, sweetheart."

Inez. Catherine's best friend. Another good kid. Rich, but not snobby. Surprisingly grounded. Total stand-up gal. She spent more time at the Silvas' place than in her own mansion. There were always rumors about abuse in her family. Her father was very rich. Before he died, the whole family was closed off from the world, except for a few other rich families they vacationed with. The boy who hosted the Christmas party was from one of those families.

After her father passed, the grip loosened. She had more room to breathe. More freedom. Still, if money had not been an issue she would have left for good.

She loved Miss Silva like a mother. She loved Catherine like a sister.

They met at dance camp. Back when Catherine's dad was still helping with money and they could afford such luxuries.

"Merry Christmas," Inez replied.

Not her usual warm self. There was a hesitation. A tightness. Like she was afraid to ask what she's about to ask.

"I'm just calling to make sure Catherine made it home okay last night."

"Oh. I thought you drove her home. Was everything okay?" Ms Silva asked. She wondered if the girls had fought. They never did, but you never know.

"Yeah, everything was okay… but no, I didn't end up giving her a ride."

Ms Silva felt a little annoyed. Inez was supposed to drive Cathy home. That was the deal.

Her tone shifted. "Yeah, she's fine. She's still sleeping."

"Oh thank God. I don't know… I just had a weird feeling." Inez said.

"What do you mean?" Ms Silva asked.

"I dunno. She wanted to leave early.

My car wouldn't start.

My brother David tried to fix it, but it wouldn't.

Which is weird, because later that night it worked fine…" Inez kept

blabbering.

Ms Silva cupped her hand over the receiver and stretched

her neck toward the couch.

"Frankie!" she called. "Cathy's in her room, right?"

Frank Jr. looked up from the couch.

"I think so. I haven't seen her."

Inez was still ranting on the line.

"I don't know… I just wanted to make sure she's okay. She

promised she'd call me when she got home, but she never did.

I called last night, but no one picked up. I didn't want to keep

ringing and wake you guys up."

"Hold on, Inez," Ms Silva cut her off, put the phone down

and headed down the hall.

It was a five-second walk to Cathy's room. She had walked

to that room countless times. Never once was she conscious

of the distance. Now she was. She felt a vortex open in her

gut, a pit that would never close. She ignored it. She could

see the door knob.

"Please be there. Please be there. Why wouldn't she? Of

course she's there. Of course…"

She opened Catherine's door. Her hand was shaking.

Dark room. Only a thin ray of light slipping through the curtains.

She reached around the wall and flicked the light on.

Room was quiet.

Bed untouched.

Outfits that hadn't made the cut the night before were still

laid out.

No Cathy.

Her heart dropped.

She searched her mind for a logical explanation.

Woke up early and went out for something?

No. The bed wouldn't be made.

She never made the bed in the morning.

Not impossible… but very unlikely.

And the outfits on the bed — the ones that didn't make the

cut.

If Cathy had left early, she wouldn't have put them back

there.

Something was wrong.

Very wrong.

Her hands went cold.

Her heart started pounding, like it wanted out of her chest.

"No. No no no. What the fuck!"

She turned and ran back to the phone, snapping her fingers

at Frankie. A signal that meant *come here, now*. Something

was wrong.

Her eyes were wide. Panic clear in her voice.

Frankie jumped off the couch, heart racing, confusion written all over his face.

"Inez… she's not here… She's not here!"

Miss Silva had seen some shit in her lifetime.

She knew how to be calm and collected in the worst moments. She didn't flinch when things went bad.

She had seen it all. Abuse. Physical and emotional. Neglect. Gaslighting. Harassment. She dealt with it. All of it.

Tough lady.

But this was different.

This would break her.

She just didn't know it yet.

She asked Inez to walk her through the night. Every detail. From the moment Catherine left to the moment she should have called.

Then she begged her to come over.

Inez agreed without hesitation.

Stand-up gal.

"Mom? What is going on?" Frankie asked, feeling like his mom was over-dramatizing something.

Miss Silva hung up and immediately started dialing 911.

Flustered, she replied, "Your sister. She's not here."

Frankie was about to say something, but the voice on the

other end interrupted him.

"911. What's your emergency?"

"Yes, hello. My daughter. She's missing," Miss Silva replied.

Frantic. Voice shaking. Hands colder than before.

"How old is your daughter?"

"Eighteen. Nineteen," she corrected herself quickly. "She just had a birthday." She explained.

"And how long has she been missing?"

"She didn't come home last night. About eight or nine hours."

"Ma'am, you need to call your local police department. This line is for emergencies only."

Miss Silva's heart dropped. It was the first time she felt how lightly this would be taken. Not the last.

"What? This is an emergency."

"Call your local station and file a missing report, ma'am," the dispatcher said. Flat. Impatient.

Click. A busy dial tone.

Miss Silva, still frantic, pressed the switch hooks to get a dial tone back and dialed 411 for the local police station number.

Each interaction felt like a lifetime.

She motioned to Frankie for a pen.

Wrote the number down.

Finally, she called the local station.

They weren't helpful. Not surprising. Catherine was

nineteen. An adult. Went to a party and didn't come home.

Not a priority for cops. No obvious indication of foul play.

Girls her age spend the night at friends' houses all the time

after partying. It is not out of the realm of possibility that she

didn't call home. Fell asleep on someone's couch.

Except… it is.

Ms Silva knew it. Cathy would never fail to come home

on Christmas Eve. She left the party saying she was coming

home. Inez was at the party. She had nowhere else to go.

Something was definitely wrong. But the cops don't know

that.

And cops don't believe moms.

Not enough time had passed for the police to treat this

as a missing person. So they gave her the same gaslighting

remarks they always give.

"She's probably with friends."

"Call us in the morning."

"She'll show up when she wakes up."

"She's probably sleeping it off."

"She'll be hungover and embarrassed."

"No," Mom said. Firm. "Not Cathy. Something's wrong."

Inez showed up not long after.

Still in her sweats. Hair undone. Makeup from last night.

Worry all over her face.

She found Miss Silva slipping between two states.

Frantic. Weeping. Shaking like she might come apart.

Then focused. Clear-eyed. Locked in. Asking all the right

questions.

"My baby. My baby," she would cry out. Then suddenly

snap back.

"Walk me through it again, Inez. Where was the party?

What time did she leave?"

She kept going like that.

Feeling powerless. All she had were questions.

Hours passed. Felt like years.

Cops still were not helping.

Still were not believing.

When the sun started going down, a patrol car finally pulled

up in front of the Silvas' apartment building.

A uniformed officer stepped out. Walked up to the door,

looking around like he didn't like what he saw.

Poor neighborhood. Cracked pavement. Loud kids. Probably

already forming his opinion.

Another missing girl from the wrong zip code.

Miss Silva opened the door.

Her face was swollen. Eyes raw. She hadn't stopped crying

since morning.

The officer stepped inside. Took out his notepad.

Started asking questions. Cold ones.

What was she wearing. Who was she with. Had she been drinking.

Any history of running off. Trouble at home.

His voice stayed flat. His face, smug.

Like he already knew the ending.

Like they were wasting his time.

"She'll turn up," he said, almost bored. "We even got an officer missing now at the precinct."

Then he laughed. Loud. "Probably partied too hard."

He caught himself and cleared his throat.

Obnoxious prick.

Oakland's finest.

He left the Silvas' house and headed to the place where the party was held.

Big house. Gated. Rich neighborhood.

Respectable family. Own a meat plant out in East Oakland.

Boy who threw the party just turned 20. Good kid. Spent his summers learning the ropes in the plant. His dad made sure of it. Said it built character.

Bright future.

He interviewed the parents. Seemed like a nice couple.

Polite. On the up and up.

Didn't want to trouble them.

Didn't press.

Didn't ask to speak to the kid.

They said he was sleeping. He left it at that.

Didn't ask to see where the party happened.

Didn't poke around.

Apologized for the inconvenience.

Said he was sorry for bothering them on Christmas.

Then left.

The dad was a major donor to OPD. Close friends with the mayor.

That might've had something to do with it.

No report.

No photos.

No walk-through.

Didn't need to.

Rich family.

Lazy prick.

Oakland's finest.

Back at the Silvas' home, Miss Silva and Inez sat on the couch.

Calling anyone who knew Cathy. One name after another.

No answers. No news.

Frankie stood off to the side. Cold sweat clung to his neck.

Pit in his stomach like a lead weight.

He kept running every scenario in his head.

What could've happened?

An accident?

She would've been taken to a hospital.

But no. They would've called by now.

His mom had already called every hospital in the area.

No one had been brought in matching Cathy's description.

An accident, but she hadn't been found yet?

Shit.

She could be out there. Alone.

In that kind of cold that needles your joints and works its

way inside.

The kind that turns minutes into hours.

Not the kind of cold this city was used to.

It felt unnatural. Like something was off.

"I gotta go look for her," he muttered to himself.

He grabbed his heavy coat and slid his feet into his boots.

His mom was on the phone, holding it to one ear while

keeping her eyes locked on him. Piercing. Frown deep. Voice

low but sharp.

"Where do you think you're going?"

"I'm going to look for Cathy," he said. Determined.

He turned to Inez.

"I'm walking to your friend's house. The one who had the

party. I need the address."

Inez blinked.

"It's far from here, Frankie. Up in the hills."

"I don't care," he said. "I'm going. If she's on the side of the road… I gotta go look for her."

Inez started to respond, but he cut her off.

His voice rose, just a little.

"I need to do this. I can't just stand here."

She paused. Then nodded.

"Okay. I'm coming with you."

She grabbed her coat and headed for the door.

Stopped.

Turned back and ran to Miss Silva. Wrapped her in a hug.

"Don't worry," she said. "We'll find her. She'll turn up."

Frank Jr. looked at his mother.

"Stay here, Ma. In case she comes back. Or someone calls.

Keep calling people. Keep trying."

She stared at him.

When did he become such a man?

Just a few hours ago, he was a boy in pajamas, eating cereal,

waiting to open his Christmas gifts.

And now he was walking into the bitter cold.

Hiking toward Oakland Hills. Looking for his sister. The

one who had protected him. Looked after him his entire

childhood.

There was no real plan. No clear direction.

They had no clue what path Catherine would've taken.

Would she have called a cab? Walked? Gotten a ride?

Deep down, Frankie knew this was useless.

But he couldn't stand still.

He had to move.

Had to feel like he was doing something.

They walked in silence for a while. Sniffling. Breath fogging

in the cold air.

On the way, Inez started recounting everything that happened

at the party.

Step by step.

Trying to remember something.

Anything.

Chapter 3
The night before

The Silvas' apartment was inviting. Warm in a way that wrapped around you and put you instantly at ease. The kind of place where you felt safe. Loved.

Small rooms packed with furniture, and framed photos lining the walls. Christmas decorations filled every corner. The kind of cozy 90s apartment we're all nostalgic for now. The tree was manicured, lights wrapped neatly around it, with presents spread across the floor.

Oldies Christmas songs played low on the radio.

Catherine and Inez were helping Miss Silva prep for Christmas dinner, like they did every year.

Inez didn't care much for her own home. She never felt loved there. She found every excuse not to be there.

In fact, she and Catherine had been talking about moving in together after the holidays.

Inez's family didn't want her to leave, so they weren't helping financially. She'd been saving.

Same as Catherine.

Outside, the cold pressed in.

That piercing kind. Like a thousand needles working into your bones.

Unusual for Oakland.

Felt wrong.

Felt like a warning.

After they finished prepping and cleaning the kitchen, Miss

Silva made everyone hot chocolate. They plopped down on the couch, tired but happy.

Catherine's gaze drifted to the presents under the tree and she smirked.

"What?" Miss Silva asked.

"You know what," Cathy replied, laughing.

Miss Silva smiled and pointed to two identical small boxes. "One of those is yours. You can open it."

Cathy jumped off the couch and lunged for the boxes. One had her name on it. She sat by the tree and tore it open.

"Aww! I love it! Thanks, Mom!" Cathy said while holding the necklace up and turning it in the light.

"You're welcome, baby. Let me help you put it on."

Cathy crawled over and sat between her mother's legs while Miss Silva fastened the clasp.

"I got Frankie the same one," Miss Silva said, fixing her daughter's hair once it was on. "The pendants are Saint Nicholas of Myra. Patron saint of children. I thought it was fitting. I had them on layaway for months…"

Miss Silva kept going on about the pendants.

Cathy stood up and turned around, shot Inez a look. *Here we go.*

"Do you know how much I love you?" she cut in, slipping into a baby voice. She knew her mom could go on forever

Miss Silva looked up, eyebrows raised. Suspicious.

Cathy let out half a smile.

"Oh no. What do you need?" Miss Silva breathed.

"What?" she grinned. "I can't tell my mom I love her?"

"Out with it, girl. What do you need?"

Cathy smiled. "Well… there's this party, and I was really thinking…"

"Yeah? You were thinking? That's a first," her mom shot back, joking.

"Hey!" Cathy laughed. "I am *very* good at thinking, I'll have you know."

"Alright, alright. So there's this party and you wanna go. What day is it?"

"Well… that's the thing. It's tonight."

"What? It's Christmas Eve!"

"I know, but even Frankie isn't here. And I really wanna go. All my friends are going."

"Frankie's literally down the hall. Two apartments away. And I took the night off. You know how hard it is for me to get nights off. Especially holidays."

Miss Silva was a nurse. Long shifts. Crazy weeks. Never had a say in when she worked. Holidays were a luxury.

But her daughter just turned 19.

Asking for permission at this point was more of a courtesy, and they both knew it.

She was an adult now. She was allowed to want a night with her friends.

Miss Silva told herself that.

Still. She didn't like it.

"Alright, girl. You can go. But please be careful. And don't stay out too late. Inez, you driving her home?"

"Yes, Miss Silva!"

"Alright… get outta here. Where's that remote? I'm gonna watch the Christmas special."

"Love you, Mom!"

"Yeah, yeah. Love you too."

The girls disappeared into Cathy's room, buzzing with excitement.

They started getting ready.

Giggling. Dancing to the tunes of NSYNC or whatever boy band was playing on the radio.

Inez had a walk-in closet bigger than Cathy's whole bedroom.

She hated it and hated her whole castle.

She'd rather be here.

With her best friend.

Borrowing her clothes.

Laughing.

Getting ready together.

"What do you think of this one?" Inez held up a short red

skirt, shaking it by the waistband.

Catherine glanced over from the mirror, finishing her eyeliner. "Nah. Try the ripped Levi's."

Inez raised an eyebrow. "Seriously?"

"Ooh yeah," Catherine grinned. "With the leather jacket. Total rebel angel."

"My mom would die," Inez said as she sifted through the clothes, hunting for the jeans. "'That's not proper attire for a young lady,'" she added, mocking her mother's voice with a stiff, uptight flair.

"She already hates me," Cathy said.

"Don't worry. She hates me too," Inez replied.

They both laughed as Inez pulled on the jeans, smoothing them over her hips.

"What about you?" she asked. "Wearing that little plaid skirt again?"

"Nah. I'm gonna be twinning with you tonight," Catherine said. "Ripped jeans, black boots, leather jacket."

"Boys won't know what hit 'em," Inez said, grinning as she tugged the jeans on.

Cathy burst out laughing. Her laugh was contagious. Inez followed.

They laughed. Always.

Inez grabbed a brush as the laughter faded, sat on the edge of the bed, and began running it gently through her brown, curly hair.

The bedroom was small but warm, fairy lights around the window, a soft hum of Christmas music drifting in from the living room.

"Who's gonna be at the party?" Catherine asked, reaching for her lip gloss.

"Not sure," Inez replied casually. "I know David's going."

Catherine groaned. "Your brother is a creep. I hope he doesn't try to flirt with me again."

Inez froze. Just for a second. Her hand stopped mid-brush. Her face fell, just a little.

Catherine turned. "Hey. I'm just joking."

Inez blinked, snapped out of it, forced a smile. "Yeah. I know."

Whatever had crossed her face was already gone. Like it had never been there.

"Come on," she added, standing up. "Let's go raise some hell."

They walked out of the room laughing, looking like twins. Cropped leather jackets with too many zippers.

Acid-washed ripped jeans. Pointy boots. Long dark brown curls bouncing behind them. Wide smiles. So wide you could see their back molars.

They called out a final "Bye!" to Miss Silva, who was half

asleep on the couch, then headed out the door.

It didn't register at first. Then Miss Silva sat up on the couch and turned towards the door. "Be careful!" She shouted.

Too late. They were already gone.

Whenever her kids went anywhere, it was always the last thing out of her mouth. "Be careful. Make good choices." It didn't sit right with her that she said it too late. Maybe superstition. Like breaking the habit might bring bad luck. Silly. She hugged the throw blanket, staring at the TV, convincing herself everything was fine. She's a big girl. She always makes good choices.

Her thoughts drifted, the way they always did when she was alone. Back to when the kids were little. The struggling years right after her husband left. Unpaid debt. No money for food or school supplies. They somehow survived. She somehow provided. Now the kids are grown and they both helped whenever they could. She was proud. They were her prize.

She slowly drifted off to sleep under the comfy blanket. Christmas lights flickered around the tree, their reflections soft on her face, mixed with the glow of the TV still playing in the background. The delicious smell of baking still lingered. This was her last blissful sleep. After tonight, she would never know peace again.

Frankie was at Mo's apartment, same floor, just a few doors

down. It was another Wednesday night there. Mo and his family didn't celebrate Christmas. Their apartment was calm. Neat. Almost barren.

Mo's family spent a lot of time back home in Yemen. They ran the corner store. Six months here, six months there. That's how they did it.

One branch of the family held down the business in Oakland while the others went back home. Then they switched.

It was common. Most Yemeni store owners Frankie knew did the same.

Frankie didn't usually like going to other people's homes. Made him uncomfortable when he was little. Most homes had a dad. That was strange to him. Different. But he always made an exception for Mo.

They'd been friends since preschool. Their moms were acquaintances from Frankie's mom shopping at the corner store Mo's family ran. Later, both families ended up in the same building.

Mo was quiet. Probably on the spectrum.

Back then, there wasn't a whole list of diagnoses for neurodivergent kids.

They were just called weird. Shy. Different.

Frankie took a liking to him right away.

They'd been inseparable ever since.

Lately though, things had started to shift.

Mo was pulling away. Getting more closed off.

He was always himself around Frankie, but now something
was different.

Angrier.

Bitter.

Tired of the world.

Started talking more about how unfair everything was.

How he was invisible.

How the world didn't see him.

Didn't want him.

Frankie stayed level-headed. Always tried to calm him
down.

Tried to anchor him.

But Mo was spending too much time online.

This new thing. The internet.

Chatrooms. Forums. Message boards.

Hours in front of a screen, locked into a world that wasn't
real.

Frankie could feel it happening.

Mo was finding his people out there.

People who got him better than Frankie did.

That was fine. Frankie wasn't jealous.

He just didn't want him going down the wrong path.

That night, Mo snapped.

Foaming at the mouth about the cool kids.

How they'd never give him the time of day.

How girls wouldn't even look at him.

"I'm tired of it," he said. "I'm fucking tired of it."

Frankie tried to calm him down.

"Fuck them, man. We don't need them."

Mo took it differently.

Way differently.

"YES. Fuck them all. All of them. I'll show them."

Frankie let him cool off. Waited. Then said his goodbyes

and left.

Went back to his apartment.

His mom was passed out on the couch. He turned off the

TV, unplugged the Christmas lights, and headed to his room.

He peeked into Cathy's room, thinking he might hang out

with her if she was still awake.

She wasn't.

The room was messy, clothes the girls had tried on still laid

out on the bed. He closed the door and went to his room.

Plopped onto his bed. Read a few pages.

Drifted off. Still in his day clothes.

Something woke him up in the middle of the night, startled.

Thought he heard a scream. Not unusual in this neighborhood.

Then the unmistakable sound of an apartment door closing

down the hall.

Then quiet.

Maybe he was dreaming, he thought.

He changed into his pajamas, brushed his teeth, and sleep

took him again.

Woke up. Christmas morning.

Ate cereal.

Mom got up.

Opened his gift.

Phone rang…

Everything changed.

Chapter 4
Missing. Part 2

Now he was walking uphill through Oakland with Inez.

His sister was missing.

No one was doing anything about it.

They walked in silence for a while.

Their breath fogged in the cold air. No plan or clear path.

Just motion. Motion for the sake of it. He knew, deep down,

this was useless. But stillness was too painful.

Inez was recounting details from the night before in a low

voice, careful not to miss a single thing.

"We got to the party around ten," Inez said. "We were the

last ones to get there.

We danced. Hung out in the basement. Watched *Home

Alone*."

Inez's voice was shivering, her eyes kept shifting.

Trying to hold it together.

"Cathy, uh… she got tired. Said she wanted to head home

early. My car wouldn't start. My brother David tried looking

at it but he couldn't fix it so Cathy said she'll just take the bus.

We offered to walk her to the bus station but she refused. She

didn't want to pull me away from the party. Bus station wasn't

that far.. She said." Inez shook her head. Like regret is settling

in. "I should have never let her walk alone…"

Frankie didn't answer… He didn't have it in him to console

Inez. Not right now. He can't be worried about her too, right now.

"She felt bad, you know… leaving Miss Silva alone on

Christmas Eve." Inez continued.

"Told me not to worry. That she takes the bus all the time.

It's Christmas Eve. She'd call me the second she got home…"

Inez paused then softly

"So… I let her go."

She wiped her eyes with the back of her gloved hand,

sniffled, then cleared her throat.

Frankie kept his eyes straight ahead.

"She didn't… Call." Inez whispered. Fighting the tears.

Frankie's voice came out low. Flat.

"Do you know who she went with?"

"No. I really don't. She left alone as far as I know."

She rubbed her hands together. Looked down the street.

Then her eyes lit up, sharp and sudden.

"Wait."

She grabbed his arm.

"Your friend. He was there. Out on the porch. Maybe he

saw her?"

Frankie stopped walking.

"Wait. What friend?"

"The kid you're always with. What's his name…"

"Mo?" he said.

"Yeah. Him."

Something cold crawled up his spine.

And it wasn't because of the weather.

Inez kept talking.

Frankie wasn't listening.

He cut her off.

"Did Mo stay the rest of the night?"

"I'm not sure. I didn't even know what he was doing there.

I think he was friends with some dude who was invited.

I saw them talking on the patio.

They seemed… intense."

"We need to go back. Now."

When they got to the building, he was already charging up

the stairs, leaping over steps, taking them three at a time.

Third floor. He didn't stop.

He rushed to Mo's apartment and knocked hard.

No answer.

He knocked again. Louder.

Then again.

Across the hall, his mom's apartment door opened.

"Frankie? What's wrong? Did you find anything?"

Frankie didn't turn around. Still knocking.

"Mo. We need to talk."

Miss Silva stepped into the hallway.

"Mo's not there. Malika's with me. She's been taking care

of me. What an angel."

Malika, Miss Nasser, was Mo's mother. A Middle Eastern

immigrant. Overprotective. Fiercely loyal to her friends and neighbors. Over the years, she and Miss Silva had grown close. They knew they could count on each other.

Miss Nasser peeked out from behind Miss Silva:

"What's going on?"

Thick middle eastern accent. Heavy worry.

"Hi, Miss Nasser," Frankie said, catching his breath, backing away from Mo's door. Inez was right behind him now.

"I need to talk to Mo. He was at the party. The one where Cathy went missing."

"I know," Miss Silva said. "He told us he was there. Said he didn't see her leave."

Frankie shook his head.

"He was out on the porch. How did he not see her?"

"I don't know, honey," his mom said. "But that's what he said. Why would he lie?"

"I heard his door slam late last night. Maybe even early morning. Did he come home late?"

"No way," said Miss Nasser. "He came back around eleven thirty. Which is late for him, yes, but not early morning. No. We would never let him. He's eighteen now, but still…"

Frankie cut her off, gently. "I'm sure there's an explanation. I'll speak to him when I see him." Like his mom, she could go on forever.

They went back inside the apartment. Sat down. Said nothing.

The silence pressed in.

Time dragged like a limp body.

Poor choice of words.

It was almost 8 p.m.

Still no sign of Cathy.

There were officers in the apartment now.

It was a missing person case now.

It was real now.

Cops were at the party house too.

Taking statements.

A list of attendees was compiled.

Names. Numbers. Calls were being made.

Search parties were forming.

Yeah.

It was real now.

Mo finally came back.

Awkward as always. Didn't know where to look.

Honestly, who would…

There's no handbook for how to act when someone goes missing.

No etiquette guide for behavior during crisis.

Frankie shot up from the couch.

Tried to talk to him.

But the cops got to him first.

.They brought him into his apartment.

Sat him down on the couch.

Started taking his statement.

Cops found him strange right away.

Wouldn't look them in the eye.

Kept scratching the back of his arm.

Repeating words.

Circling sentences.

He could tell. They suspect him.

But he couldn't help how he acts.

Never could.

They decided to take him to the station.

Frankie came out of his apartment.

Saw them walking Mo down the hall.

His mom behind him.

Both faces locked in disbelief.

Confusion all over them.

Frankie whispered,

"What the fuck, Mo?"

His voice cracked.

"What'd you do to my sister?"

Then he yelled,

"What'd you do to my sister, Mo!"

Miss Nasser was already following the cops.

Her eyes wide. Her voice sharp.

"He didn't do anything!" she shouted back.

"My son would never. This is all a misunderstanding."

The hallway was dim and damp.

Walls yellowed with time. A smell of wet drywall and old

smoke clung to everything.

Above them, the ceiling light flickered.

Cheap neon. Loud buzz. Half-alive.

The cops walked Mo down the hall.

Their faces dipped in shadow. Lit briefly. Then gone again.

Flash.

Dark.

Flash.

Mo's face flickered in and out.

Expression flat. Eyes low. Nothing new there.

Then, one flicker. One frame.

A shift.

A smile?

Couldn't tell.

By the next flicker of light, his face was flat again.

Just for a second.

Barely there.

Could've been a shadow.

Frankie saw it.

Or thought he did.

Didn't matter.

It lodged in his chest like a nail.

pulled him back into the apartment.

The place was bustling with cops. Voices low. Radios

crackling.

Cathy's bedroom was being torn apart for clues.

Drawers yanked open. Closet emptied. Flashlights scanning

under the bed.

A woman in her early fifties walked toward them.

Earth-tone pantsuit. Hair pulled tight into a ponytail.

Seasoned face. Eyes that had seen too much.

Tough. You could tell before she said a word.

She reached out and held Miss Silva's arm. Firm but gentle.

"I'm Detective Shaeffer," she said. "I'm sorry you're going

through this. I have a daughter myself. 13-year-old. I will do

everything in my power to get to the bottom of it."

A warm break from the cold stares and empty words.

Finally, someone who can relate. Someone who gave a

damn.

"I know you've been through this a few times, and I'm sorry,"

Shaeffer said. "But I need to get up to speed, and I don't want to miss anything. Is it okay if I ask you a couple questions?"

Before Miss Silva could answer, Shaeffer turned her head

toward an officer leaning against the wall.

"Can you make Miss Silva some coffee?"

Her tone wasn't a suggestion.

The officer blinked, caught off guard. Tried to say something.

Shaeffer didn't give him the chance.

"Kitchen's over there. You're a smart guy. You'll figure it

out."

She turned back to Miss Silva.

"You want milk?"

Miss Silva shook her head. No. Still in disbelief.

In awe, really.

This woman. This detective. was something else.

A tough gal like her. Probably been through hell to get here.

Didn't flinch. Didn't fold.

Not like the others.

Detective Shaeffer led Miss Silva to the couch who was still

holding onto Frankie's arm.

Wouldn't let go.

He was protective of her. Always had been.

But something about this detective…

He felt like he could trust her.

They all sat down.

Shaeffer leaned forward. Elbows on knees. Eyes locked in.

She listened to every word. Asked a question here and there.

Never interrupting. Never wasting time.

"Does she have a boyfriend?"

Miss Silva shook her head.

"No."

Then looked at Inez, just to be sure.

Inez nodded.

"No. Not that I know of."

"Anyone who might hold a grudge?"

All three answered at once.

"No."

Cathy was loved.

By everyone.

That smile. Huge. Impossible to miss. The kind that stuck with you. The kind that forced you to smile back.

Even the older guys from the block looked out for her. The ones always working some quiet deal at the West Oakland docks. Crime passed down like property for generations.

Loyal to their blood.

Bad news to everyone else.

They had seen her grow up. Seen her scrap.

She wasn't afraid of anybody. Stood up to bullies, no matter how big they were.

Once, a football jock slapped her.

She got back up.

Kneed him in the balls, landed a clean hook to his jaw, then spat on his fucking face while he was down clutching his crotch. Spit mixed with blood.

His own friends were rooting for her.

She was fourteen.

They respected that.

Respected her.

And now she was missing. Did someone take her?

If someone tried something, one thing was certain.

She would have given them hell.

Speaking of older guys from the block.

While Detective Shaeffer kept asking questions, the neighborhood tough guys showed up.

Word had gotten out. Cathy was missing. That meant something.

They walked in like they owned the floor.

Tracksuit jackets half-zipped. Chests out.

Silver chains. Tight jeans. Simple tennis shoes.

Even in this kind of cold.

Stand-up guys.

The kind who lived on the other side of the law but still showed up when it counted.

They were family.

They had Miss Silva's back whenever shit hit the fan.

They stepped into the apartment like they belonged there.

Didn't say much. Just called her name.

They looked like they didn't have time for bullshit.

Miss Silva saw that.

She stood up without thinking.

Her face shifted. Serious. Like something inside her

snapped back into focus.

She moved toward them.

Shaeffer followed. Instinct.

Two of the guys casually stepped in the detective's way.

Not rude. Not aggressive.

Just enough to slow her down.

One of them, Tony, leaned in, whispered something in Miss

Silva's ear, then stood tall, looking her dead in the eyes like

a dog waiting for the command: "Attack!" She shot a side

glance at Detective Shaeffer, raised an eyebrow while looking

down at her feet, then looked back up at Tony. The eyebrow

resettled. She gave him a very subtle nod. That set Tony off.

He gave a half-whistle to his guys, and they were gone, like

they had somewhere urgent to be.

Miss Silva walked back to the couch.

Slower now.

Something on her mind.

She sat down without a word.

"Who were those guys?" Shaeffer asked.

Miss Silva didn't answer.

Her mind was somewhere else.

"Miss Silva?" the detective said again.

"Hm?" Miss Silva looked up.

"Oh. They're just the neighborhood guys," she said.

"They were just checking in. Seeing if we needed anything."

Shaeffer kept her eyes on her.

"Miss Silva… I'm here for you. So is the OPD.

Please don't let them do anything stupid."

Miss Silva didn't respond.

Didn't have to.

Her silence said it all.

Don't tell me what to do and what not to do.

I'll do whatever the fuck I need to do to get my kid back.

Detective Shaeffer double-checked her notes.

Left her card with Miss Silva.

Gave quiet instructions to a couple of officers before

heading out.

No wasted movements. All business.

Meanwhile, the neighborhood had already mobilized.

A search party. Spontaneous. Word of mouth. No questions

asked.

They didn't wait for orders.

They didn't need them.

One of the neighborhood ladies—old school, headscarf
tight, face all worry and grit, asked Miss Silva for a recent
photo of Cathy.

Miss Silva handed it over without a word.

Her hands were shaking.

The woman's teenage son helped her make posters.

They printed as many as they could.

Black and white. Cheap paper.

Didn't matter.

What mattered was getting Cathy's face on every wall, pole,
and corner store window.

They started plastering them everywhere.

Bus stops. Bodega windows. Chain-link fences.

Anywhere someone might look twice.

By now, it was late.

Quiet.

Still fucking cold.

The kind of cold that pierces your ears and stabs your brain.

The clock was ticking.

First forty-eight hours are crucial.

Everybody knows that.

Half of that was already gone.

It had been twenty-four hours since anyone had seen Cathy.

Under Detective Shaeffer's direction, the police organized

a search of their own. More structured. Better resourced. Detective Shaeffer led it.

They started at the property where the party had taken place. A huge estate. From there, they worked outward toward a wooded patch in the hills. Not large, but dense enough to hide things. Things no one wanted to find.

They moved in grid formation.

Volunteers and officers advanced step by step. Sniffer dogs out front.

Silent. Focused.

Every sound meant something now.

Frankie and Inez searched together. Inez's brother joined them. They fanned out across the estate. Flashlights cut through brush and low branches.

Inez's brother knelt near the bushes by the driveway.

Frankie and Inez hurried over.

"What is it?" they asked.

"Nothing," he said, handing over a dime. "Thought it might be an earring."

Frustration built with every false find.

They moved on. Out of the estate and into the wooded patch. They checked every inch. The scent dogs found nothing there.

Detective Shaeffer was certain of it. Nothing in the woods. But the dogs had gone wild at the estate. The scent was strong there.

So where had she gone?

Back at Miss Silva's apartment, everyone was gone.

The police. The neighbors. The welcomed noise.

The quiet returned.

Frankie and Inez sat with Miss Silva, trying to comfort her.

It didn't help.

Eventually, Inez passed out sitting upright on the couch.

Head tilted. Arms crossed. Like she hadn't meant to fall asleep,

but her body had given up.

The silence crept back in. Dense. Deafening.

Miss Silva pulled Frankie aside. Her voice low, careful not

to wake Inez.

"We need to go meet Tony."

Chapter 5
Lead

Frankie looked her in the eye.

"What did he whisper?"

"There's someone. Someone they think knows something."

Frankie didn't blink.

"Let's go," he said. Not a shred of hesitation.

They went down to the building's basement, where a few storage units lined the walls. It was dark and musty, the air thick with mold. Exposed cables ran like veins through old brick walls, and the paint, faded and sickly gray, looked like it belonged in an early-century mental institution. Puddles on the floor from some slow, constant leak.

You could smell the rot.

Tony and the guys were already inside one of the units. They had just gotten there and they had someone with them. The guy looked scared shitless. They had grabbed him from a nearby bar.

They had waited for Miss Silva's nod back at the apartment. That's how much they respected her. If she wanted to go the police route, they'd back off. But if she gave the word - and she had, with one sharp nod - they'd grab the fucker.

He had been running his mouth at the bar.

Drunk. Loud.

Talking about a "gorgeous broad"

Drunk out of her mind

In the back seat of some old station wagon.

Driver was "soliciting her," he said.

He had a turn.

What a piece of ass.

Young thing. Curly black hair. A beaut'.

Drunk?

Or drugged.

Miss Silva and Frankie walked in just as the guy was

dropped into a chair in the middle of the storage room.

Dark. Moldy. Echoes off the concrete.

They had always stayed away from this kind of shit.

Miss Silva made sure of it.

Even if they saw something, they stayed out of it.

No cops. No snitching.

That was the code.

And everyone respected that.

But this was different.

If this fucker knew something…

He better start talking.

Miss Silva's first name was Julia.

She was only thirty-seven at the time. Still so young for all

this shit.

Beautiful in a way time couldn't erase.

Life had tried.

It failed.

Long wavy hair like Cathy's.

Pointy nose. Big brown eyes.

Italian features. American grit.

She didn't wait.

Stormed straight up to the guy.

Grabbed him by the collar.

Spit flying.

Voice raw.

"Where is my daughter?"

"I… I had nothing to do with it. I swear."

The man was slurring his words. The kind of guy who's in

a perpetual state of drunk.

"Where is she?" insisted Miss Silva.

He was dying tonight.

He knew it.

Tony stepped forward.

Pulled a Glock from under his jacket.

No words. No need.

He cocked it, calm.

"Okay, okay…"

The guy looked to the side, head down like he couldn't keep

it up. Like it was too heavy for his skinny body…

"I don't know man… There was this chick.. I told these guys

here" Waving his hand like it was dead hanging by the wrist only.
"I'm pretty sure she was a hooker…"

Miss Silva's face tightened like she wanted to slap him but

kept listening.

"… This dude was pimping her in his car out in the woods

so you know I did my thing and was on my way.."

Miss Silva pulled out a photo.

Held it inches from his face.

His expression dropped.

Color left his body.

Gone like someone pulled a plug.

"Look, this dude said she was a hooker. Said she was out

cold in the back of his station wagon. I… I had a turn. I didn't

know…"

Miss Silva clenched her fist.

Frankie got to him first.

One punch. Clean.

Knocked him out cold.

Blood hit the wall.

He went for more.

Tony grabbed his arm.

"Leave it, kid. We got this.

You don't want this shit getting back to you."

When the guy came to, he was tied up.

Cinder blocks near his feet.

He knew where this was headed.

The lake.

Miss Silva stepped in.

"Guys. We need to stop this. Now."

Tony looked at her in disbelief.

"We take him to the cops," she said.

"No fucking way, Julia" Tony snapped.

"Yes," Miss Silva said. Firm. Still shaking, but clear.

"I trust this detective. She can get more out of him.

They can draw a sketch of the driver. Look for the car.

Trust me. I'll take him. This won't get back to you."

The guys looked to Tony.

Nervous. Angry.

The guy saw his window.

Eyes darting. Voice shaking.

Swearing left and right.

"I won't say shit. I swear. No harm done, right? Just a black

eye. That's nothing. What's a black eye between friends, huh?"

No one laughed.

Tony took a breath.

Looked at the guy tied to the chair.

Then at Miss Silva.

"If the cops can help find Cathy…

Fuck it."

He nodded towards the drunk.

"Untie him. You're going for a ride."

They threw the guy in the back of an SUV.

Frankie and Miss Silva rode with them.

They pulled up to the station and dropped them off.

No words exchanged.

They disappeared into the night.

Miss Silva and Frankie walked in. Drunk guy wedged

between them. Wobbly.

Asked for Detective Shaeffer.

"We've got someone with information," Miss Silva said.

A minute later, Shaeffer came down the hallway.

Took one look at the three of them.

Clocked the guy's black eye before anyone said a word.

"What do we got here?"

"He has something to say," Miss Silva said.

Shaeffer raised an eyebrow.

"oh, yeah? Nice of him to volunteer. That's some shiner

you got there."

The guy looked away.

Frankie rubbed his knuckles.

Red. Swollen. Didn't say a word.

"I got it from here," Shaeffer said.

She grabbed the guy by the arm and walked him down the

hall toward the interrogation rooms.

"Go home, Miss Silva," she called back.

"We'll let you know if we find anything."

She paused. Looked at Frankie.

"And no more trouble."

"I'm not going anywhere," Miss Silva said.

She found a bench and sat down.

Frankie followed.

Slumped next to her.

Leaned into her. Sideways.

She hugged his arm.

Kissed his shoulder.

Her eyes were half-open. Puffy.

She hadn't cried in hours. Still looked like she had.

One memory kept looping in her head.

Wouldn't stop.

Cathy was four. Her father had just left them. Miss Silva
was wrecked, barely holding it together. And Cathy, sharp
even then, walked up, wrapped those tiny arms around her,
and said, "I would never leave you, Mamma." Then came the
question. "Are we going to be okay, Mamma?" And Miss Silva
had answered without thinking, without knowing, "Of course,
baby. I will always protect you."

Protect you.

Like an echo. Haunting.

Fuck.

That memory.

Go away.

Not now.

Faintly at first, then louder, "Miss Silva?"

Miss Silva stirred. Detective Shaeffer was gently nudging her awake. Miss Silva rubbed her eyes, looked around, trying to piece it together. For a moment, she forgot where she was. Forgot the fluorescent lights. Forgot the coffee stench and the ache in her bones. For one second, she forgot her daughter was missing.

One second of bliss.

"Did you get anything out of him?" she asked, voice dry, rubbing her eyes.

"Yes," said Shaeffer. "We got a sketch and put an APB out on the car. You should get home. It's almost light out."

Frankie walked up from the vending machine, handed his mom a power bar. Sat down next to her. Frowning.

"What about Mo?" He said, barely looking up.

"Mo left earlier with his mom" Shaeffer replied. "We took his statement. Poor kid's just… different. He doesn't know anything."

"He was at the party," Frankie said, voice rising. "Claims he didn't see her. How the hell is that possible?"

Shaeffer shrugged. "Maybe he wasn't paying attention."

Frankie shook his head.

Even if *he* wasn't.

There's no way Cathy wouldn't have noticed him.

And knowing her…

As soon as she saw him she would've said something.

She always did.

Cathy didn't do quiet. Didn't do invisible. Not when people she loved were near.

Detective Shaeffer stepped outside with them, exhaustion settling into her shoulders. She waved down a patrol car, gave a few quiet instructions, then opened the back door herself. "They'll take you home," she said. Miss Silva nodded her thanks. Frankie didn't say a word. Just got in.

Sat in the back seat, arms folded, eyes fixed on nothing. His jaw clenched tight. He wasn't letting this go. Mo knew something. Maybe he didn't mean to. Maybe he didn't even realize it. But he knew something. And Frankie was going to get it out of him.

Miss Silva sat beside him, hands in her lap, staring out the window as the cruiser rolled down empty streets.

Where are you, Cathy? she thought. *How does someone vanish like that?*

She knew her daughter. Tough. Smart. Responsible. Not the type to run away. Not the type to be lured away. But in her heart, she knew. Something was wrong.

Terribly wrong.

They walked into the apartment with a weight they couldn't

shake.

Inez was stretched out on the couch, a throw blanket pulled
up to her chin. Christmas tree lights flickered faintly across
her face.

Under the tree the gifts were still unopened. All except one.

Frankie's eyes landed it on it. The necklace.

He moved toward it slowly. Picked it up. Turned it over. On
the back, engraved in delicate, looping script: FS. His. Cathy's
had CS engraved. Same style. Same font. Same saint.

Same Cursed Christmas.

That was the necklace. The same one the detective was
holding twenty-two years later.

Lifted with a pen.

In an alley. Rain sliding down his wrist.

Jaw locked. Heart racing.

Initials. CS. Fancy font.

How the fuck is this possible, thought the detective.

Detective Silva.

Frankie Silva.

Chapter 6
The Investigation Begins

January 2019

"Fucking traffic," she said under her breath as she pulled on her latex gloves.

Mid-thirties. Pantsuit. Blonde hair in a ponytail. Striking features. Detective Rimler. Emily Rimler. Detective Silva's partner.

She stepped up behind Detective Silva, took one look at the body,

and gagged.

Covered her mouth with the inside of her elbow, turned, and walked off fast.

Stopped a few yards away, hunched over.

Almost threw up. Didn't.

Detective Frankie Silva followed.

Gently touched her back.

"You okay?"

She held up a single finger.

She'd seen bodies before. Plenty.

Five years in homicide doesn't leave you soft.

But this… This was different.

His hand lingered on her back, rubbing slow and gentle.

You could tell they were familiar. More than just partners.

"I'm good," she said at last.

Then, quieter, raw,

"What the fuck."

"You don't know the half of it," Frankie said.

"Shit," she breathed as she was standing upright.

Rain kept falling. Relentless.

A crowd was gathering behind the yellow tape. Faces

blurred by umbrellas and streetlight glare.

Drawn in by the horror. Can't help it.

People slow down for tragedy. Always do.

"Keep them away from the scene," Silva barked at a patrol

officer, nodding toward the line.

He looked back at his partner. Studied her face.

"You sure you're good?"

"Fuck off," she said, without looking up.

"How'd you get here so fast, anyway?" she asked, walking

back to the body, putting latex gloves on.

"I walked," he said.

"In this rain?" she exclaimed, crouching low beside the body.

"Yes." He said. Firm.

She didn't respond. Her eyes scanned every inch of the

corpse, in disbelief.

Frankie stayed back.

Watching her. Watching the body.

His eyes locked on the pendant.

It was being bagged in an evidence bag now.

He didn't know how to process it. Not yet.

"What do you make of all this blood?" she asked the M.E., who was taking notes just past the victim's body.

She nodded at the pooling beneath the torso. Dark. Sticky.

"Think he chopped her up here?"

He looked up at her over his glasses. Didn't like the phrasing. Looked back down.

"I don't see any arterial spray," he said. "No blood spatter either."

Cold. Matter of fact.

Frankie stepped in. "You saying it was staged?"

"Could be. Or the rain washed away all our evidence."

Frankie's eyes followed the bag holding the pendant.

"Not *all* evidence," he said to himself.

Emily stood up, took off the gloves, and slipped them into her pocket. She scanned the alley left and right, eyes sharp, searching for cameras. Then she pointed.

"Bingo," she said.

A camera on the south wall, pointing straight at the body.

Frankie looked at the thick-mustached officer with the sandpaper voice and gave a nod.

The officer walked over, holding some kind of cardboard above his head, trying to shield his already-wet police cap from the rain.

"What can I do ya for?" he said.

Frankie pointed at the camera. "Need that footage. Fast."

"On it," the officer replied. No jokes. No sarcasm.

Frankie raised an eyebrow, half curious.

"Need anything else? Get you some cwaffee or some such?" The officer added sarcastically.

"There it is." Frankie gave a half-smile.

"You have officers going door to door?" Frankie asked, watching the officer head toward the restaurant with the CCTV.

"As we speak," he called back, not even turning around.

"What's with the straight-out-of-an-eighties cop show vibe?" His partner asked, smiling.

"He's alright," Silva said as he was walking back.

She turned serious, following him. "Ever seen anything like this?" she asked, rhetorically.

Of course he hadn't, she thought to herself. Where would he have seen something this horrible?

"Yes," Frankie said. Firm.

She stopped cold. Shocked. He looked at her. She blinked, eyebrows raised as she scanned his face, waiting in disbelief. He finally looked away, then back at her.

"Cold case. Dismemberment. Similar."

"Serial killer?" she breathed as her feet started moving again

"Maybe," he said. Stared at the body as camera flashes lit it, then the alley around it.

Brief bursts of light.

He turned toward the crowd at the end of the street.

"He's probably watching," he said.

She stepped beside him, followed his gaze.

"Or she," she said, half a joke. "Don't discriminate."

"Fuck off," he muttered, half-joking.

"Shit," he added under his breath.

"What?" she asked, suddenly alert.

He shook his head.

"He was right."

"Who?"

"Mustache. I need coffee."

She rolled her eyes, smacked his arm.

"Asshole. Thought you saw something."

"Let's go," she added.

They rounded the alley and ducked into a corner bodega, brushing rainwater off their coats.

At the counter, steam rose from a glass coffee jug. They poured two cups and wrapped their cold hands around the heat.

Small comfort.

Frankie's eyes wandered towards a uniformed officer who stood by the counter, notepad in hand, interviewing the young Hispanic kid working the register.

Frankie watched the kid shake his head. No. Didn't see a thing.

"How the fuck do you dump a body and no one sees it?" He said.

"Bystander effect," Emily said. She paused, took a sip of steaming coffee, then went on.

"Even when something feels off, people talk themselves out of it. They don't see what we see. Someone dumping something? Probably a delivery. Probably nothing. Move on."

"Yeah," he said.

Agreed, but it still made his stomach turn.

They reached the door just as the officer wrapped up his interview, sliding his notepad into his back pocket.

Frankie pushed the door open with his foot and held it as the man stepped outside, Emily right behind him.

"Nothing, huh?" Frankie asked.

"Nada," the officer replied.

Frankie nodded, then walked back toward the scene with his partner, sipping the last of his coffee.

"We're gonna need the feds on this." he said.

"No shit," she replied.

He picked up the pace, reached a small dumpster, and tossed the empty cup. Emily caught up, and together they turned into the alley.

The body was being carefully loaded for transport under the relentless pounding rain. Headed to the forensics lab, then the M.E.'s office.

This one would need to be studied. Meticulously.

"Let's head back to the precinct," Emily said. "Labs will take a while. Maybe we pull that cold case file. FBI probably has a profile on this guy."

"Yeah," Frankie said, staring off.

The past was creeping in.

"Hey," she said. "You good?"

"Yeah." He blinked. Refocused. "I need a ride."

"I figured," she said.

They ran to her car in the rain. Coats over their heads. Stepping on puddles. Soaking through and through.

Once inside the car, Frankie shook his head like a wet dog.

Emily flinched. "What the... Watch it, boy!"

"Sorry," he said quietly. Unlike him.

She gave him a sideways look. "What's wrong with you?"

"What do you mean?" he said.

She raised her eyebrows, eyes still on the road through the sheet of rain covering the windshield. They hit a red light. She glanced at him, eyebrows still raised.

Silence.

He looked back at her, weighing what to say. Then he let out a heavy sigh.

"It's Cathy," he finally said.

"Who?" Emily asked, turning her eyes back to the road as the light turned green.

Silence.

She glanced at him again.

"My sister," he said.

Emily blinked. She'd forgotten.

Hadn't heard that name in a while.

Not that Frankie ever really got over her.

But it had been a long time since she'd heard it out loud.

Did the victim remind him of Cathy? she wondered.

She looked forward. "Of course, Cathy… Your sister." she said. Then softer, "Sorry…"

"The victim had her necklace," he said, voice flat. "Laid beside her."

A chill crawled up Emily's arms. Sharp. Electric. Goosebumps.

She knew what losing his sister had done to him. From the little he'd shared. And from her own digging.

Still unsolved. The kind of case that ends up on true crime podcasts and online sleuth forums.

She glanced at him again. "That doesn't make any sense. How do you know it was hers?"

"Because I know."

"Frankie, it's been decades. It could be a similar necklace.

Think about it."

"No." He cut her off. "It's hers. No doubt."

"How can you be sure?"

He hesitated. Took a beat. "Because… it's the one my mom

gave her. That night she…"

He stopped. Couldn't finish.

"She gave me one too," he said quietly. "Matching. Engraved.

It's hers."

Another chill ran straight up Emily's spine.

"What the fuck," she thought.

Or maybe she said it out loud.

"Captain's gonna take you off the case," she said.

"Yeah," he muttered. Looking to the side out the window.

Still raining. Still looked like night at Ten in the morning.

Windshield wipers working overtime…

They pulled into the station lot.

Neither had said a word.

Frankie's mind was racing.

Emily didn't know what to make of the information.

Seemed unreal. She was really worried about Frankie.

The station sat inside an old brick building. Classic bones.

Thick doors. The kind of place that creaked when you walked.

Inside, it looked more like a warehouse than a precinct. Desks

packed in tight, neon lights buzzing overhead. Hustling.

Bustling. Phones ringing. Statements being taken. People

waiting.

Frankie and Emily walked through the chaos and made it to their desks. They faced each other. Always had. Easier to work that way.

Captain McLaughlin called them in before they could even sit. They looked at each other.

"Here we go," Emily said.

The captain didn't waste time. He was waiting outside his office door.

Ex-military. Looked like a walking relic. Flat-top haircut, buzzed tight on the sides. Mostly gray now. Dark patches hanging on. High-waisted pants held up by suspenders. Mustache like it was still 1985. Thick eyebrows, almost as thick as the mustache. Face locked in a permanent frown. Sounded like an old Texan farmer.

The kind of guy who'd seen it all.

"This is gonna be a high-profile case. We do this by the book. No fuckups," he said, turning and leading them inside. All three stepped in.

Rain hammered the office windows overlooking the concrete jungle.

Distant car horns cut through the room, background noise no one noticed anymore.

Mixed in with the occasional phone ring.

And the steady clack of keyboards.

He continued toward his desk, muttering, "The mayor's gonna be on top of me like white on rice with this one."

He paused. Rubbed his face. Looked down at the stack of freshly delivered crime scene photos.

"Fuck. You ever seen anything like this?"

He pointed at the photos.

Emily looked like she was about to gag again.

She sat.

Frankie stayed standing.

"I think there are similar cases," he said. "I remember one cold case in particular."

He paused.

Before anything else, he had to bring up the pendant.

"Cap'n," he said, tone shifting. Serious now.

"The pendant. Next to the victim. I think it belonged to my sister."

The captain raised his bushy eyebrows, glanced at Emily, making sure he'd heard that right.

"Say what now?"

"My sister. Cathy. You remember her case?"

The captain had heard about it. Dug into it deeper when Frankie went through his psych eval, after that shooting. He had been shot at, returned fire, hit the suspect.

Policy. Anyone who shoots or gets shot must go through it.

Cathy's case had come up often in those sessions. The captain had to be informed.

"Yeah… shit. I remember." he said, eyes locked on Frankie, waiting impatiently for what came next.

"Her pendant was never recovered," Frankie said.

"I think it's the same one they found next to the body."

"What makes you say that?" the captain asked, looking at Frankie like he'd lost his damn mind. His expression was hard to describe, but it read something like:

"What the fuck would a fucking necklace from a twenty-two-year-old fucking case be doing all the way across the fucking country, from Oakland, California to Brooklyn, motherfucking New York?"

Fair question.

Frankie pulled the necklace he was wearing from under his shirt, undid it, and set it on the desk.

"Because our mother gave us the same one. Only difference is the engraving. FS for me. CS for Cathy."

The captain leaned forward, eyebrows still raised. He pawed through the piles of papers on his desk, found his reading glasses, slipped them on. Grabbed the crime scene photo folder from and flipped through it fast. He landed on the full-body shot and winced involuntarily.

"Fucking A…"

He kept flipping until he found the photo of the necklace, yellow evidence marker next to it.

Held it up beside Frankie's.

Identical.

"Well, shit," said the captain.

Next photo, necklace flipped over, engraving.

No mistake.

CS. Same font. Same design.

"I'll be damned," the captain muttered, leaning back hard in his chair and slamming the stack of photos down on the desk.

"You're too close to this, Silva. I can't let you lead the case."

Frankie knew this was coming. He didn't look surprised or overly emotional. Just calm.

"Don't bench me," he said. "I'm good. You know I'm good."

"The fuck you are…" Captain cut him off.

Emily tried to step in but didn't get a word out.

The captain cut her off too, leaned forward, and pointed at her like he already knew exactly what she was about to say.

"You'd just let him run it if I made you quarterback, and you know it."

She didn't argue. He wasn't wrong.

"Fuck," he muttered, leaning back hard in his chair. Rubbed the back of his neck.

That don't-fuck-with-me look was written all over his face.

Frankie and Emily knew it well. They both backed off. Waited in silence for what was coming next.

"You two are my best detectives. I don't want O'Malley to fuck this up."

Frankie saw an opening. Tried to speak, something like *I won't let you down.*

The captain cut him off without missing a beat.

"Shut the fuck up."

Frankie swallowed it. Stayed quiet. Staring down at his shoes, still soaked through.

The captain turned to Emily.

"You're running point on this."

Frankie looked up. Emily leaned forward off the back of her chair. Ready.

"Do not make me regret this," Captain said, locking eyes with her.

Then turned to Frankie.

"*You* can consult. Since the necklace belonged to your sister, you might have some insight."

"Alright," Frankie said.

Emily stood.

"Where do we start?" Captain asked.

"Cathy's case files," Frankie said.

Captain snapped.

"You're not fucking running point, Silva!"

"Oh, I was just consulting," Frankie replied.

Captain's glare hit hard. Sharp enough to push Frankie back a couple steps.

Then he turned to Emily, waiting for her answer.

"Cathy's case files," Emily repeated, calm. Unshaken.

Captain exhaled. Loud.

"Get the fuck outta here," he muttered. Then added, "Who am I even kidding…"

He knew he'd be running it, no matter what. Still, he would keep a close eye.

One misstep and they were off.

They headed for the door. The captain was rearranging papers on his desk when he suddenly stopped and called out.

"Wait."

They both stopped short and turned back.

The captain grabbed a sheet from the stack and held it out.

Emily hurried over and took it.

"You are invited," it read.

She skimmed it, angling it so Frankie could see as the captain explained. "Tonight's the retirement party. Meredith's been planning it for months."

"Oh yeah," Emily said. "She invited me."

"Me too," Frankie added.

The captain was retiring this week. A sad moment for everyone.

He would pretend he could not wait to get out of the place.

Say he was tired of dealing with these dumbasses. Joke about freedom.

But deep down, he did not want to go.

This was his purpose.

And without it, life felt like it had ended without warning.

Maybe, as a parting gift, he could help Frankie solve his sister's case once and for all. He thought it quietly.

"Wouldn't miss it for the world," Emily said.

Frankie stayed silent. He did not know what to say.

He genuinely loved the captain.

"Alright, alright. Get outta here and do some work," the captain said, breaking the tension.

They walked back to their desks in silence.

"It's still too early on the West Coast," Emily finally said.

"We can call Oakland later. Try to get access to Cathy's case files."

Frankie nodded.

Cathy's necklace.

Found at a fresh crime scene.

That changed everything.

New evidence.

The case wasn't cold anymore.

It was officially active.

That got Frankie's blood moving again.

Something real to chase.

"Let's check on the body at the morgue," Frankie said.

"Fun," Emily muttered.

They moved down the dark hallway, walls painted a dull gray, flickering neon buzzing overhead. The kind of place that stayed cold no matter the season.

They reached the elevator. Pressed the down button. Waited.

"We need to call the FBI," Emily said.

Frankie exhaled. "Yeah."

Ding.

The doors slid open. They stepped in. Pressed B. Waited again.

She glanced at him. "We can use all the help we can get."

She's right. He hates it when she's right. She's always fucking right.

"Help," he muttered, "not a takeover."

"They probably already have suspects," she added.

Ding.

The doors slid open.

A darker hallway stretched ahead, until it opened into blinding white.

Subway tiles. Stainless steel. Harsh neon lighting overhead.

The morgue.

"Captain will call them," Frankie said.

Emily nodded as they stepped inside. The M.E. was already at work, gloved hands steady as he weighed an organ on the steel scale.

"Heart… two eighty-three grams," he said into the recorder. "No abnormalities on visual inspection."

He didn't look up.

"Hey, Doc," Frankie said.

"Hey, Silva," the ME replied.

"Anything?"

He stood upright, adjusting his glasses with the back of his wrist, careful not to touch them with his gloves. Still staring at the body.

"Umm… this'll take a while, as you know."

"But?" Emily asked, reading the hesitation.

He took off his gloves and paused the recording. "But I can tell she was starved. No food for at least three days. Tortured, also…"

He walked slowly around the stainless-steel table.

"No insects."

"What's that mean?" Frankie asked.

"Kept indoors for most of the postmortem," the M.E. said. "She was probably discovered not long after she was placed there."

"Time of death?" Frankie asked.

"Around midnight," the M.E. replied. "Based on the progression
of rigor mortis. It had set in, but not fully. That gives us
a pretty tight window."

"Okay," Frankie said. "Anything else?"

"Yeah," the M.E. said. "See this?"

He pointed to patches of skin peeled off in rough, uneven
circles.

Frankie leaned in, pulling his tie over his nose. "What is
that," he said, muffled through the fabric.

"Not sure," the M.E. replied. "Some sort of circular tool
ripped the skin right off."

"Sanding disk?" Frankie asked.

"No. Softer," the M.E. replied, heading toward a stainless
steel tray on the counter.

Emily hovered closer behind Frankie, covering her mouth
and nose with one hand. As if his body could shield her from
the smell. From the sight.

She leaned in just enough to see the marks, then gagged.
Turned. Ran out.

Frankie raised an eyebrow in her direction.

The M.E. glanced at him while changing gloves and grabbing
something off the tray. "She okay?"

"She's fine," Frankie muttered. Then back to the table.

"What's circular, softer than a sanding disc, and can rip skin off?"

"I don't know," the M.E. said. "But we found this."

Frankie looked up, eyes narrowing. "What is that?"

He stepped away from the table, moved around it, and came in closer.

"A bristle?" he asked.

"Yeah. Like… uh… like a brush," the M.E. replied.

Frankie got it.

"A circular brush. Like the kind they use at car washes. Fast motion, high pressure. If it's hard enough, used long enough…"

He shook his head.

"What a sick fuck."

"What'd I miss?" Emily said as she walked back in.

"I'll fill you in," Frankie replied, already heading for the door.

"Anything else, Doc?"

"That's it for now."

"Keep me posted."

"Yep," the M.E. said, pulling on a fresh pair of gloves and hunching back over the body.

hey walked toward the elevator, Emily glancing at Frankie for an update like a pup waiting for a treat.

He glanced back, then looked forward.

"She was tortured. Some sort of circular object. They found a bristle. Most likely a car brush—the kind that connects to a water hose."

They reached the elevator, pressed the up button, and waited.

"Anything else?" Emily asked.

Ding. The elevator opened.

Captain was inside.

"Cap'n," they both said.

"Bruce in there?" he asked, nodding toward the morgue.

He stepped out. They stepped in.

"Yes," Frankie replied. "Working on our vic."

Just before the doors closed, Captain turned around, walking slowly backward.

"FBI's looped in. They sent you some files. Want Bruce to share his findings. They're sending an agent..."

He turned forward, voice fading down the Hallway. "Something Kitteridge."

The elevator doors shut. Frankie pressed 1.

"How did he..."

"I texted him," Emily cut in. "When I walked out of the morgue."

"Captain texts?" Frankie asked.

"Only people he likes," Emily replied, smiling.

"Figures," Frankie muttered.

His jaw clenched. Tight.

Emily noticed.

"It'll be fine," she said. "We need to learn to share our ball."

He didn't laugh.

His sister vanished in 1997. And for the first time, there was a connection.

Ding.

The elevator doors opened into the chaos of the precinct's main floor. A symphony of loud laughs, angry shouts, ringing phones, radio chatter, and distant car horns.

They cut through it all, heading straight to their desks.

The FBI files were waiting.

A potential serial killer was at large. Just dumped a body in their jurisdiction.

And there was a connection to Cathy.

Frankie was already ahead, brow furrowed, walking fast.

Emily lagged behind, chatting with a female patrol officer.

"How was your date?" Emily asked.

"Girl, I'mma tell you later, but he was fiiine," the officer laughed.

Emily laughed too. "Can't wait to hear all the dirty details."

The patrol officer kept walking, glancing back. "I'ma hit you later. Bye, baby. Be safe."

Emily raised a hand. "Bye."

She jogged to catch up with Frankie.

Unlike him, she had friends. And everyone loved her.

They got to their desks. It was in a small separate office dedicated to homicide. 4 desks. A small couch against the wall. A big corkboard on wheels..

Emily sat down and started typing at her desktop. Frankie wheeled his chair over next to her.

She logged into her email. "There," she said.

She double-clicked the message.

Federal Bureau of Investigation

Behavioral Analysis Unit

INTERAGENCY BRIEFING MEMO

Re: Serial Homicide Pattern – Linked Cases

Emily skimmed past the unnecessary introductory language, mumbling under her breath. Only speaking aloud what she deemed important.

Summary:

Following the January 21 discovery of a mutilated female body in Brooklyn… bla bla bla… cause of death, postmortem staging, and offender signature.

"Okay…" she muttered.

The presence of a pendant necklace matching that from the 1997 Cathy Silva case strongly suggests the disappearance of Cathy Silva in 1997 is connected.

Frankie's nostrils flared like he needed more oxygen. He leaned in, locked onto the reports. Looking for answers.

FBI Case File: FBORE-1999-4483

Victim: Melissa Romano

Age: 21

Location Found: Wooded area, Eugene, Oregon

Reported Missing: December 24, 1999

Date Recovered: December 27, 1999

Cause of Death: Blunt force trauma to the head

Reporting Party: Civilian campers

Condition:

• Body located approximately 15 feet from trail

• Badly beaten

• No clothing on body

• Jewelry recovered near left foot: one silver bracelet

Note: Bracelet not identified by the Romano family as belonging to victim

Further Review: Bracelet cross-referenced with prior missing persons cases

Identified as belonging to: Valery DeLuca, FBI Case File: FBSEA-1998-3121

FBI Case File: FBSEA-1998-3121

Victim: Valery DeLuca

Age: 22

Last Seen: Seattle, WA – March 1998

Recovered: December 31, 1998

Location Found: Green Lake Dog Park

Cause of Death: Blunt force trauma to the head

Condition:

• Badly beaten

• Jewelry recovered at scene: one pair of silver hoop earrings

- Earrings did not belong to the victim

Update (2010):

• Missing item from DeLuca case, silver watch, recovered

at scene of 2010 Rachael Cohen homicide

• See linked case file: FBNYC-2010-8847 (Cohen, Rachael)

Emily clicked the linked file. Rachael Cohen. 2010.

"Look at this one," she said, pointing at the screen. "Rachael

Cohen. Went missing here. Brooklyn. I bet her evidence box

is still local."

Rachael Cohen

Age: 19

Last Seen: Brooklyn, NY – 2008

NYPD Case File: NYPD-2010-1102

FBI Reference: FBNYC-2010-8847

Status: Deceased

Details:

• Body recovered December 25, 2010 in Prospect Park wooded area

• Victim's limbs severed and reattached post-mortem

• Sutures crude and uneven

• Clothing removed. Scarf found near body. Stained

• No foreign DNA recovered

Note: Jewelry (earrings) left at scene near left shoulder, linked to DeLuca. Now part of multi-jurisdictional review.

Frankie grabbed a pen, scribbled the case number on a scrap of paper, and took off.

"Uh… I guess we're going," Emily muttered, scrambling to follow. She came back two steps later, grabbed her coat.

"It's freezing down in the archives."

They headed down to the basement below the basement.

B2.Concrete floors. Low ceilings. Fluorescent lights buzzing like they wanted to die.

"This place gives me the heebie-jeebies," Emily said.

Frankie didn't hear her. Or it didn't register. Not at first.

He was focused. On a mission.

Then it did.

"Oh yeah?" he said. "And the morgue doesn't?"

"Oh yeah, the morgue does too," she said. "Actually, probably the whole precinct." She smiled.

Frankie half chuckled.

"Sometimes I wonder how you became a detective."

Her face changed.

Silence. Unusual for her.

He caught it immediately.

"Shit. I'm sorry," he said quickly. "I didn't mean it like that. You're an excellent detective."

He paused. Tried again.

"It's just… the shit we see. It hardens you. You know? And you're kind. Happy…"

He stopped. Thought for a second.

"Unbroken."

"All right, all right," she cut in. "Nice save." She smirked.

"And I'm not that kind," she said, punching him lightly in the shoulder.

They reached the mesh window manned by Gladys. Early 60s. Thick glasses. Recently quit smoking, so more pissed than usual.

Didn't even look up.

"Badge and case number," she croaked. Thick New York

accent. The kind where they say couwaffee instead of coffee.

Already out of breath. And pissed.

Frankie held out his badge and checked the note he had

scribbled.

"NYPD-2010-1102"

She glanced up, just over her glasses. The attitude shrank a

little.

She knew Emily. Everybody loved Emily.

And for Gladys, not being outright rude was the closest

thing to niceness.

"Hi, Miss Gladys," Emily said. "How's your granddaughter?"

"Fine, I guess… Don't get ta see her that oft'ten, ya know?"

Gladys said as she got her old-school computer fired up. "Her

ma'… I told my son he shoulda never married that girl, but

does he listen? Nah. Now they're divorced, she's got custody,

and…"

Frankie exhaled hard.

Gladys stopped talking and stared up at him. Paused just

long enough to make sure he knew she didn't appreciate that.

"Anyway," she continued, tapping a few keys on her keyboard,

then squinting at the screen. "I don't see her as oft'ten as

I'd like ta. …" Pause. More squinting. "Uhh… looks like ya

evidence is in Cold Case. Sunset Pawk, off Foist Avenue, near

Fifty-eighth.

"I know where it is," said Frankie.

"Come on, let's go."

"Whey ya think ya goin'?" Gladys said, almost smirking.

"Dey ain't gonna let youse check out the evidence box dhere widhout permission. Ya crazy? Ya put in a request wit me, Dey'll deliver it here."

"When?"

"When dey get to it."

"It's urgent." Said Frankie.

"It's always urgent," Gladys fired back, not even looking up.

Emily stepped in before it turned into something.

"We'll keep sifting through the digital files now, check the physical evidence when it gets here. Captain can put a rush on it."

"Yeah, dhere ya go," Gladys nodded. "McLaughlin can do that fo' shuwa."

"Thanks," Emily said.

They turned and headed back to their desks.

"I don't think she likes you very much," Emily said.

Frankie was caught off guard. Let out a short, involuntary chuckle.

She always knew how to make him laugh.

"No…" he said. "I don't think she does."

He yawned as the words left his mouth, then shook his head like he was trying to wake himself up.

"Let's get you some coffee," Emily said, tapping his shoulder like she was comforting him.

They stopped at the kitchenette on the way to their office.

Same shitty machine. Same burnt smell.

As Frankie poured a cup, another officer walked in, O'Malley.

The obnoxious type. Walked with his chest puffed out like

a prize rooster. Shirt half unbuttoned. Always had something

to say.

"Frankie," he said, already smirking. "Heard you found a

Frankenstein this morning."

Frankie didn't react. Still pouring. The comment didn't

register right away.

Emily clapped back without missing a beat.

"Frankenstein's the doctor, you dumb dumb. Not the

creature."

"Oh, how fitting," O'Malley said, grinning.

"Frankie. Frankenstein."

Then he started laughing at his own joke, loud, wheezy,

annoying.

Frankie stopped.

Stood there, still facing the counter.

Coffee in hand. Burning hot.

His jaw locked. His eyes drifted down.

Running through scenarios.

Mug to the face?

Overhand to the nose?

Elbow to the throat?

He was about to sip the burning hot coffee when one final thought hit him.

Hot. Burning. Perfect choice.

Emily saw his face. She knew that look.

Stepped in. Quick.

Again.

"Get the fuck outta here, O'Malley," she snapped. "You're so fucking dumb."

O'Malley raised his hands, fake surrender.

"Sorry. Just a joke. Jeez… what crawled up *his* ass today anyway?"

He walked out still chuckling to himself.

Frankie shook his head. Took a sip of coffee.

Spilled some on his shirt.

"Shit," he muttered, stepping back, wiping at it with his tie.

"Come here," Emily said, pulling him closer.

She grabbed a towel off the counter, wet the corner, and dabbed at the stain.

Frankie watched her. Didn't say a word.

When she finally looked up, he looked away.

Fast.

He had feelings for her. Strong ones.

But everyone he's ever loved disappears.

That's why they keep circling back, breaking up, starting over.

Frankie never learned how to be loved without waiting for something awful to follow. So he pushes her away. Over and over.

But the feelings are still there.

Always have been.

Just… not now.

This wasn't the time for that.

Not yet.

She felt it too. Cleared her throat, tried to brush it off.

"Looks good. Looks fine. Come on, let's go."

"Thanks, Em," he said.

Em.

Her heart skipped a beat. She secretly liked it when he called her that.

If only he…

"Excuse me," someone said behind them, interrupting her thoughts.

They turned.

Old-school lawyer type. Pressed suit. Fancy fedora. Probably here to meet a client.

"Didn't mean to interrupt," he said in a whiny voice and a little smirk. Third-degree without trying.

They stepped apart. A little flustered.

"No worries," Emily said quickly.

They left the kitchenette and walked back to their desks in silence, not touching, but still too close.

Each dropped into their chair. Hers was angled just a little toward his.

Frankie logged into his desktop. Emily logged into hers.

She sighed. "Should we try to get ahold of your friend? From back in the day? See if he remembers anything?"

"Yeah," Frankie said, unenthusiastic. He wasn't too happy about the idea of reaching out to Mo again. Not after all these years. They hadn't spoken since that night.

But it had to be done.

Still, Frankie knew it couldn't be Mo. The timeline didn't fit. Mo was in Yemen during some of the murders.

Someone else needed to be called.

After all these years, he thought. *Inez.*

Emily opened the FBI email again and clicked on the unsub profile file:

FBI BEHAVIORAL ANALYSIS UNIT

UNSUBJECT PROFILE – ACTIVE INVESTIGATION

Subject: Unknown Male (UNSUB)

Case Classification: Serial Homicide with Sexual Component

Profile Status: Active

Profile Prepared by: Behavioral Analysis Unit, Quantico

"Listen up" She said to Frankie. "They sent a profile along
with the files."

Frankie leaned back on his chair staring at the ceiling while
Emily was reading.

Emily opened the FBI file.

"Male," she read out loud. "Mid-forties to mid-sixties now.
White. Or white enough to disappear."

She scrolled.

"Big. Strong. The kind of body that fills a room without
trying. Looks imposing. But not memorable."

Frankie stayed quiet.

"Above-average intelligence," she continued. "Not academic.
Tactical. Patient. He plans. He adapts. He learns."

Another scroll.

"He works with his hands. Something physical. Butcher.
Auto work. Maintenance. Lab. Somewhere tools and chemicals
are normal. Somewhere mess doesn't raise questions."

She paused.

"Probably works alone. Or answers to very few people."

She kept reading.

"He needs control. That's the core of it. Ritual after death.
Order. Precision. He doesn't rush. He practices. Takes breaks

when he has to. Moves. Lays low. Comes back sharper."

Emily glanced up at Frankie, waiting for a question. Or a reaction.

He was still staring at the ceiling. Rocking his chair.

She went back to the screen.

"He's emotionally detached. But not socially clueless," she read. "He knows how to talk. Knows how to calm people down. Gets submission before force."

She leaned back, eyes off the screen.

"These profiles can get pretty dense," she said.

"Yeah," Frankie said. "They can get pretty close too."

Emily rubbed her eyes, grabbed the mouse again, and found her place.

"Upbringing wasn't stable," she said. Then added, "No shit."

"Cold house. Domination. Mother ran it. Controlling. Possibly religious. Image obsessed. Father either enforced it or disappeared. Either way, no protection."

She scrolled.

Frankie shifted in his chair.

"Early rejection," Emily read. "Especially from women. That stuck."

She paused.

"Alright. We get the gist."

"No," Frankie said. "Keep reading. Every detail matters."

Emily sighed, exaggerated. Like a spoiled kid.

"Fine."

She continued.

"Victims are female. Eighteen to twenty-five. Brunette. Slender to average build. Not random. He's chasing one face. One memory."

She didn't say mother. Didn't need to.

"The assaults are deliberate," Emily said. "Repeated. Punitive. After death, he rearranges them. Reverses limbs. Stitches mouths. Makes them quiet."

"So the perpetrator is male. Forties to seventies. Smart. Good with his hands. Shitty childhood. Obsessed with one type of woman?" Emily said.

She added, "Like literally every man in New York?"

"Yeah," Frankie replied. "Pretty much."

She looked up, struggled to hold back a laugh. Covered her mouth. Looked down. Tried to stop. Couldn't.

Frankie glanced at her. Smiled.

Then they both broke. Laughed.

Nothing was funny.

Just the ridiculousness of it all.

His desktop lit up as the laughter faded. He looked at the screen.

Cathy's digital file had just come through. The Captain must have asked for it.

His face went serious in an instant. He rolled his chair closer and hovered the mouse over the main folder.

And froze.

"Cathy's file is here," he said. Almost a whisper.

Emily didn't say a word.

She let him take his time. Stood and crossed to the corkboard.

Time to work.

She began pinning crime scene photos, maps of recovery sites, cross-referencing them against last known locations.

Victim IDs. Jewelry logs. Dates of disappearance.

One line of evidence at a time.

Photos. Locations. Movement.

Building the profile.

Soon, the cork board would be filled with red yarn lines.

And the story would start to reveal itself.

Meanwhile, Frankie finally double-clicked. The folder spat out dozens of files. Reports, statements, photos.

And with that double-click, something split open in his head. Not a memory.

Something darker.

Older. Familiar.

Old grief crawling back in like mold under cracked tile.

It festers. Unwelcome. Unstoppable.

Memories he'd buried deep. Parasites.

Feeding on what little peace he had left.

He was back.

Back in the dark.

Back in the cold.

Back in the past.

Chapter 7
The Day After Christmas.

December 26th 1997

Frankie had just gotten home from the station, where he and

his mom had dropped off the drunk with the black eye.

They'd spent most of the night there.

Detective Shaeffer had come out, said they got a sketch and

put out an APB.

Then she flagged down a patrol car.

Told them to go home.

Except… She didn't tell them everything.

As soon as she shut the back door behind them, she turned

around jogging. Determined.

She'd gotten more out of the drunk than she let on.

Couldn't say much. Not yet.

It was still an active investigation.

The guy had lied.

Said he met the station wagon driver and the girl on the

street. Truth was, there was a house. A shack really.

Crack house, meth lab. Both.

The girl might still be inside.

SWAT was already suiting up.

Shaeffer and her partner, Detective Kim , Asian American,

no-nonsense, tough as hell, built like a body builder got in the

unmarked car.

SWAT tailed them.

Lights off as they approached the address.

No fuss.

Shaeffer popped the trunk.

Grabbed a Kevlar vest and tossed it to Kim. Put one on herself.

Then she pulled out a shotgun, handed it to Kim.

Checked her sidearm, cocked it one-handed.

Slick.

Routine.

SWAT leader jogged over.

"How you wanna do this?"

Shaeffer didn't blink.

"Finesse."

The leader smirked.

"Never heard of it."

"I mean it," she replied, whisper-yelling through clenched teeth.

"Potential abducted nineteen-year-old inside."

"Roger," he said, breaking into a sprint back to his team.

The station wagon sat out front. Just like the tip.

The yard looked abandoned. Creepy.

It was dark but you could still make things out.

A moldy bathtub on its side. An engine block. Busted furniture... Junk scattered everywhere.

SWAT flanked left and right.

Leader held up his hand: two with him to the left, three to the right.

Shaeffer followed left. Kim went right.

House was dark. Silent.

Shaeffer peeked through a busted window, half boarded.

Couldn't see much.

Then a light switched on.

She ducked fast.

Everyone froze.

Sweat formed on her forehead despite the freezing cold.

You could see everyone's breath, but under the SWAT kit and the pressure, they were all sweating.

SWAT leader raised a mirror, angled it in.

A man stepped into view. Matched the description.

White briefs. Dirty. Lit a bowl like it was just another Friday.

SWAT leader signaled the right flank.

Shaeffer motioned across her throat: **Don't!!**

They went in anyway.

SWAT. Bulls in a China shop.

Door flew off the hinges.

Flashlights and lasers sliced through the dark, catching dust in their beams as they cut across the room.

"LET ME SEE YOUR FUCKING HANDS!"

"ON THE FLOOR NOW, MOTHERFUCKER!"

"GIVE ME ONE REASON, I WILL BLOW YOUR FUCKING HEAD OFF!"

They swept the house.

"CLEAR!"

"KITCHEN CLEAR!"

"BEDROOM CLEAR!"

Then,

"I GOT SOMETHING!"

Shaeffer stepped in just as the last "ALL CLEAR" echoed down the hallway.

She holstered her weapon. Walked over.

A SWAT member stood over a filthy mattress.

Huge stain dead center.

Girl.

Late teens.

Naked.

Eyes glossy, barely tracking.

Shaeffer peeled off her jacket and covered the girl's shoulders.

"Call EMS!" she shouted.

The man was cuffed. Roughly.

"WHAT THE FUCK IS THIS FOR?"

"You got the right to shut the fuck up," SWAT leader growled, shoving him outside.

Shaeffer knelt by the girl.

"What's your name, sweetheart?"

"Vee," the girl mumbled.

Shaeffer leaned in.

"V?"

"Victoria… Everyone calls me Vee."

Shaeffer's face dropped.

Blood ran cold.

Not Cathy.

Fuck.

Still.

This girl needed help. Not a total loss.

"That's my girlfriend!" the guy shouted from the porch.

Shaeffer turned.

"Girlfriend, my ass, you ugly fuck." She looked at the SWAT member holding him. "Get him outta here."

"His 'girlfriend'… and anyone he brings over or takes me to," Vee mumbled. Eyes half-closed. High.

"You don't have to worry about him ever again. You're safe. I got you," Shaeffer said, voice steady.

"Right," V muttered. "Don't pretend you care. No one does."

Shaeffer didn't respond.

Words were cheap.

She'd show her. Like she'd shown many before her. She

cares. Truly.

Shaeffer helped her up and handed her off to a SWAT member, who walked her over to EMS for evaluation.

She'd be coming to the station.

Witnesses said there was solicitation.

They'll sort it out in the morning.

Once the girl sobers up, Shaeffer is getting her help. No way she's staying with this piece of shit, pimping her out.

Shaeffer stepped off the front porch, exhausted. Started undoing her vest. Peeled it off. Let out an unvoluntary sigh of relief. Kim followed right behind her, vest already in hand.

The sky was just starting to brighten.

That's when the call came in.

They found something.

Loud knock.

Inez woke up, startled on the couch. She had fallen asleep sitting upright. Rubbing her stiff neck, she looked around.

Frankie was also out cold, slumped in a chair beside her. Miss Silva sat nearby, clutching old photographs and a tissue. Her nose was raw from crying.

Miss Silva jumped, hurried to the door, and opened it.

From where Inez sat, she could only see part of her. But then, she heard a shriek and Miss Silva collapsed. Her body seemed to fall in slow motion against the side wall. As she hit the floor, her face came into view.

Horror, personified.

The kind of face a person should never have to make.

Inez jumped up as Miss Silva let out a raw, feral scream

"NOOOOOOOO!"

Frankie jolted awake, heart pounding, already running toward his mom. He saw his mother on the floor. Detective Shaeffer stood in the doorway.

He dropped to his knees beside her. Held her head in his hands.

Tears streamed down his face. Inez collapsed beside them, sobbing, clutching them both.

They found Cathy's clothes. Blood-soaked. Every piece.

That was the call Shaeffer had received right after the raid.

"Where… where did you find them?" Miss Silva asked, the words barely escaping her lips.

Frankie helped her to the couch. Inez sat close, arms around her. All three frozen. Breathless.

Shaeffer stood in front of them. Steady.

"We don't know much yet," she said, her voice even. Careful.

"Her clothes were recovered early this morning. East Oakland. Near the Coliseum. We sent them to the lab. We're canvassing the area…"

Miss Silva stared blankly. Like she hadn't heard a word.

"How do you know they're hers?" she asked.

"They match the description, but we need confirmation. I'm sorry."

Shaeffer opened her folder. Pulled a few photos. Slid them across the coffee table.

"Please take a look."

Inez leaned forward. Miss Silva beside her. The photos showed blood-stained fabric. Soaked. A leather jacket. Torn.

"That's hers," Inez said, her voice trembling. "She embroidered that flower herself. Bottom right corner of the back."

Shaeffer hesitated. Then spoke, voice low, confidence even lower.

You could hear it in the tremble.

"Miss Silva… we're doing everything we can. Let's hope the clothes lead us somewhere. Anything."

Frankie understood that loud and clear.

They weren't searching for Cathy anymore.

They were searching for her body.

He didn't move.

Couldn't.

A piece of him had just been ripped away.

Not just any piece. The one that kept him alive. His best

friend. His protector. His hope. His sister.

The world suddenly looked exactly as it was.

Cold. Brutal. Unfair. Rotten.

Cathy had been the filter that made it all feel bearable. Her

joy made things brighter. Her light softened the edges.

Gone.

Welcome to hell.

He hated that he was thinking about himself. Selfish. But

the thought came anyway.

Cathy. Was she Killed?

His mind couldn't bear the thought. It was all noise. Static.

He felt dizzy. Thought it was in his head at first.

But it wasn't.

Everything went black.

He collapsed, head cracking against the corner of the coffee

table.

A sickening thud. Then blood. Lots of it. Gushing from his

eyebrow, split clean in half.

Miss Silva screamed.

Detective Shaeffer rushed to his side.

He came to a moment later, blinking. Dazed.

His mother was holding a towel to his head.

"I'm okay," he muttered. "I'm okay."

"You need stitches," Shaeffer said, voice firm.

"I'm fine," he lied.

"Frankie! You need to be looked at," Inez insisted. "I'll take you."

It didn't feel real. None of it.

But he nodded. Stood. Followed her.

Miss Silva came with them.

Autopilot.

They drove to the ER.

Waited.

Inez filled out the forms.

Frankie sat still, staring through the walls, a bloody towel pressed to his eyebrow.

His mom leaned on his shoulder.

Still in disbelief. How could this be? Her daughter's clothes.

Recovered. Soaked in blood.

"Someone killed my daughter."

The thought lodged and stayed. Brain rot.

"Someone killed my daughter. Someone killed my daughter…"

"Frank Jr. Silva."

The name barked through a loudspeaker. It snapped her
out of it.

Frankie went in.

They offered painkillers.

He refused.

Just clenched jaw and white knuckles.

Five stitches. Right through the brow.

His signature look, from that moment on.

Born in blood. A forever reminder.

They headed back to the house in Inez's car. A quiet ride on
empty roads, except for the December wind howling outside.
Faint. Constant.

The city felt deserted.

Christmas lights lined the streets.

Everything looked different.

All the things they usually looked forward to this time of
year now felt eerie. Sad.

Back at the apartment, Frankie knocked on Mo's door. No
answer. He knocked again, harder.

A man opened. Looked familiar.

One of Mo's uncles. From Yemen.

Then it clicked.

Right, he remembered. Mo and his family were going back

to Yemen right after Christmas.

He greeted the uncle, asked about Mo.

The man nodded. Confirmed it.

Back in Yemen.

For the next six months at least.

Mo was gone.

He knows something. Even if he doesn't realize it.

Frankie could feel it in his gut.

Now he's gone.

Did he have something to do with this?

doubt creeps in when nothing makes sense.

Chapter 8
The Aftermath

Forty-eight hours came and went. After that, they say you're

no longer looking for a missing person. You're looking for a

body. And with all that blood on her clothes, the unfathomable

started to look like reality.

It's a strange thing, watching your worst nightmare take

shape in front of you. You think it could never happen. But it

could. You think you'll never get used to it. But… You do.

And just as something like routine began to settle in, the lab

results came back from the clothes found in East Oakland.

No fibers. No fingerprints. Just blood and a trace of organic

residue no one could identify with confidence. Bovine, maybe.

Or something close.

But the blood.

It wasn't Cathy's.

That gave Miss Silva the push she needed not to give up.

And she never did.

Miss Silva spoke to the police daily. Detective Shaeffer kept

her word and remained available. Always.

Then she was reassigned.

The new detective was not as available.

Not as… human.

The trail went cold. They couldn't match the blood on

the clothes. No one from the party could remember Cathy

leaving. The parents of the kid who threw the party were rich.

Influential. They wanted no more attention.

What are they hiding?

Miss Silva never stopped asking.

She tried to keep Cathy's case at the top of the pile. Volunteers helped raise reward money for any relevant information.

Calls poured in. None of it held. Most leads went nowhere.

The police didn't have the resources to chase them all.

Sightings came in anyway. Mexico, from someone fresh off a cruise. A gas station in San Jose.

A psychic called Miss Silva directly. Said Cathy was alive. Said she was within miles of their apartment.

She believed him.

Hope. A dangerous feeling.

She told the cops. They brushed it off. She argued they should at least try to trace the call. It could be the abductor. Could be connected.

They assured her they were following every lead. Doing everything they could.

Oakland's finest.

She called. She badgered. Did TV interviews. Pleaded. Held placards. Joined groups. Formed new ones.

It didn't matter.

Other cases slowly took priority.

Frankie eventually went back to school. A senior. People stared. Felt bad for him.

For someone who hated attention, it was torture. He felt exposed. Stripped.

Without his sister, the world felt unbearable.

He'd already been far ahead of his class. Smart kid. He graduated high school and moved to New York. He didn't want to leave his mom, but he had to.

Miss Silva visited him often. And for a while, they seemed to move on. Not really. But reality settled, and they laughed again. Weeks turned into months. Months into years.

But the not knowing gnaws at you. Hits when you least expect it. Like a dark cloud following you around, and you never know when it's going to open up and pour.

Four years passed since Cathy's disappearance. Frankie graduated college and joined the academy to become a police officer. He could've been anything. Rocket scientist. Engineer. He chose this.

His smarts helped him move up fast.

And just as suddenly as Cathy disappeared, Miss Silva passed away. Forty-one years old. Drowned in her bathtub. Maybe accidental, they said. But who knows.

Frankie couldn't say for certain that his mother wouldn't have taken her own life. He couldn't imagine the pain she'd lived with. As a parent.

But he knew how much she loved him. She would never

abandon him like that.

But again.

Who knows.

He was alone now. Completely.

Always thinking of Cathy.

He made detective. Studied cases. Scanned every report
that sounded remotely like her. No body. No clear M.O.
But he narrowed the pattern.

California. West Coast. Brunettes. Missing. Late teens to
early twenties. Hundreds of unsolved cases.

Then the shooting happened.

He emptied his clip. The suspect was already down.

Anger. Too much anger.

Therapy was mandatory. Cathy's case came up. A lot.

His captain took note. Benched him for a while. Cold case
rotation.

One file kept pulling him back.

One case in particular.

The victim reminded him of Cathy.

Six years later

A body in an alley. Limbs swapped. Cathy's necklace beside
the corpse.

Frankie and Emily going over Cathy's files. Pictures of blood-soaked
clothes. Statements. Mo's statement. Frankie leaned in.

Shit, he thought.

Mo.

Chapter 9
The Investigation Continues

January 2019

Frankie had always suspected Mo knew more than he let

on. He had also always trusted him. Something was off,

though. And Frankie knew Mo well enough not to mistake

odd behavior for guilt. He was used to it.

This was different.

Mo was different that night. Different even for him.

He must have seen something. Maybe he felt bad for not

doing anything about it.

Mo being at that party. That was not like him. And how did

he not see her.

Stranger things have happened. But to leave for Yemen the

very next day. And stay gone for years.

After Cathy went missing, the cops, the questions, the noise,

Mo's family got spooked. They were already heading to

Yemen for their usual six-month stint, but this time, they

decided Mo would stay. Indefinitely.

He needed something more conservative. Less trouble. It

did not matter that he was eighteen.

Frankie had always hoped he was wrong about him. Desperately

hoped. But nothing else made sense.

Until now.

If these killings were connected, then it could not be him.

It could not be Mo. He was in Yemen from December 1997

until 2003.

He clicked Mo's statement open.

The PDF loaded slow, like something ancient clawing its way out of a coffin.

His eyes scanned the document, hunting for anything that jumped out.

Then he started reading. Line by line.

Mo's voice was still fresh in his head.**Formal Interview Transcript – Mohammad Nasser**

Date: 12/25/1997

Time: 9:55 PM

Location: Oakland Police Department, Interview Room B

Interviewing Officer: Det. Kim

Present: Officer Berger

Subject: Mohammad Nasser

Age: 18

DOB: 03/04/1979

Frankie's eyes moved side to side, fast. Scanning the page. Processing as quickly as he could. Looking for something that mattered.

So far, nothing.

"Initial contact was made with Mohammad Nasser at approximately 8:30 PM at his residence, 3247 International Blvd, Apt. 3."

Yada yada yada.

"Mohammad appeared confused and nervous."

Skip. Skip. Skip.

He landed on the interview transcript.

Det. Kim: Mr. Nasser, where were you earlier tonight?

Mohammad Nasser: At a party.

Det. Kim: What time did you get there?

Mohammad Nasser: Around ten. A little after, maybe.

Frankie paused there. Stared off. Remembering that night.

At Mo's house. Mo angry, feeling invisible.

His gaze drifted back to the screen. He kept reading.

Det. Kim: Anyone else there you recognized?

Mohammad Nasser: I think I saw Inez. But I don't really
know her like that.

Det. Kim: What about Catherine Silva?

Mohammad Nasser: No. I mean, I don't remember seeing
her.

Frankie drifted again.

How did he not see her.

Maybe he saw something he didn't want to say.

He knew there was no point delaying it anymore. He had
to talk to Mo. The thought alone made his stomach turn.

He worried about what he might find out but… it was time.

He had already looked him up. Had his number saved.

Never brought himself to dial.

Not until now.

Frankie grabbed his phone and stood fast. He looked at Emily.

"I'll be right back."

She nodded, acknowledging him.

He stepped into the hallway, scrolled through his contacts, then dialed.

The ringtone lingered. No answer.

An unknown number from New York. No surprise he wouldn't pick up.

Frankie pressed redial immediately.

Ringing.

Then.

Mo picked up.

"Hello?"

Shit. It's happening.

"Hey, Mo," Frankie said.

"Hey. Who's this?"

"Uh… an old friend. From a long time ago. It's Frankie, Mo. From International Buildings."

Silence.

"Hello?" Frankie added.

"Frankie…" Mo said. Stunned. "Brother… fuck. I miss you. Where you been?"

Relief hit him harder than he expected.

"I missed you too, Mo."

He hadn't realized how much. Mo's voice alone pulled memories back. Rougher now. Still unmistakably his.

A beat.

"You in Oakland?" Mo asked.

"No. I left a while ago. I'm in New York. Brooklyn."

"Oh. Nice. Never been."

"Mo. I need to talk to you," Frankie cut in. "About Cathy."

Silence.

"I don't know what to say, Frankie…"

"Can you just walk me through that night," Frankie said. "I know you didn't have anything to do with it. I just…"

"Of course not," Mo interrupted. "I would never."

"I know," Frankie said. "But you were there. Tell me what you saw. Anything."

"It's been so long, man… I don't remember."

"Please, Mo. Anything might help."

"Why now?" Mo asked. "Why are you looking into it?"

"There's been a crime here. In New York. Might be connected. Did you see the kid who threw the party?"

Silence.

"Mo?"

"Look… it's nothing but—"

Frankie's heart dropped.

"What is it?" he pressed.

"That night, I went to the party to do something bad."

Frankie crouched against the wall. He needed to sit for this.

"Bad?" he asked.

"Yeah. Me and Salah decided to mess with the rich kids' cars."

Frankie's jaw tightened.

"Is that why Inez's car didn't work?"

"No. No, I swear. I knew Inez. She wasn't like them. We never went near her car. We couldn't really do anything to the other cars either. Too many people around but…"

A pause.

"I ended up keying the car that belonged to the kid who threw the party."

Silence.

"And I think he saw me."

Frankie stayed quiet. Let him continue.

"He came out of the bushes while I was doing it. So sudden. Saw me. I don't know if it was the host for sure, but I think it was. He looked messed up. Like he'd been in a fight or something."

Frankie pressed the phone tighter to his ear.

"He didn't say a word. Just looked at me. Then hurried back inside. I grabbed Salah and we left. I dropped him off and went straight home."

Another pause.

"When I got home, I saw the car I keyed pulling out of the lot. I thought he was coming to tell my parents or something. When nothing happened, I figured it was just a similar car."

That was it. Frankie thought to himself.

The moment Cathy was taken.

The host was in the bushes.

Mo saw the car again at the building.

Why was it there.

"Why didn't you tell the police?" Frankie asked. Flat.

"I didn't think it mattered," Mo said. "And I didn't want them finding him and him telling them I keyed the car. I was scared my parents would find out. I never thought it had anything to do with Cathy."

Frankie exhaled.

"I'm sorry, Frankie."

"It's alright," Frankie said. "I get it."

A beat.

"I gotta get back to work," Frankie said. "But it was good hearing your voice."

"You too, brother. Don't be a stranger."

"I won't."

He ended the call.

The call he had dreaded for years.

A weight he'd carried for decades finally lifted.

He stayed crouched against the wall, staring at the phone.

Mo's name still on the screen. Replaying the conversation in his head.

Then his eyes lit up.

He shot up and ran back to his desk.

Back to the transcript.

Times. Routes. The usual questions.

Then it hit.

Frankie leaned closer. Eyes flickering. Frown tightening.

Det. Kim: When you got home, anything unusual?

Mohammad Nasser: Not really.

Det. Kim: You sure? No one saw you come in. Maybe a neighbor. A store clerk. Anyone.

Mohammad Nasser: Uh… I mean, there was this white truck. An SUV. It was pulling out of the lot just as I drove in. Could've been a neighbor. Or someone visiting.

Frankie paused.

"There it is," he muttered. "White SUV."

Mo had said he thought it belonged to the rich kid. The host.

The car he keyed.

He exited Cathy's folder. Clicked on Melissa's.

Kept reading. Still muttering.

"Last seen near 13th Avenue in Eugene. Body recovered six months later in Hendricks Park."

Scroll

"Boyfriend had an alibi…"

More scroll.

"I saw it somewhere, I know I saw it…"

Emily glanced over.

"Saw what?"

He didn't look up.

"White truck. Mo mentioned it. Said he saw one pulling out of the lot the night Cathy disappeared. Right as he was getting home."

He kept reading. Clicking. Clicking. Fast.

"I just spoke with Mo," he told Emily.

She looked up. "How'd it go?"

He recapped the conversation, focused on the important piece. The rich kid's SUV. Then added,

"I heard a scream that night."

Emily froze.

"You what?"

Frankie kept scanning the screen with his eyes.

"I thought I was dreaming. Half-asleep. I heard something. Then I heard Mo's door close. I don't know maybe 10 min later…"

He looked up, finally met her eyes.

"I didn't know what time it was... But if that scream was real..."

Scroll.

"There. I fucking knew it. Look."

Emily rolled her chair beside him. Stood up and hovered over him. Leaned in. cheek almost touching his.

"Melissa told her best friend she thought she was being followed. White SUV kept showing up."

Frankie's jaw tightened.

"What if Cathy made it all the way to our apartment building but never made it inside?"

The silence pressed in.

Emily exhaled slowly. Let the pieces settle. She knew what that meant for Frankie.

That he heard it.

His sister being taken.

And went right back to sleep.

Dealing with that realization would have to wait. Somehow. For now, there was a thread. The white SUV. And it needed to be pulled until something gave.

Emily leaned back, grabbed her chair and started rolling it toward her desk when someone knocked lightly on the open door. Just enough to get their attention.

"You're gonna wanna see this," the analyst said, already turning.

Frankie and Emily looked at each other, then stood. Followed. Quietly. Except for the sound of their heels echoing down the long, narrow hallway.

"He's talking to us," Frankie said, finally breaking the silence.

Emily nodded.

"Alright. What's he saying?"

"Sliced eyelids," Frankie said. "He wants us to look. Maybe. And the pendant. From twenty-two years ago."

"He wants us to remember?" Emily cut in.

"I don't know. Maybe," Frankie said. "He's telling us Cathy was his. But why. After all these years."

"And why the limbs swapped?" Emily asked as they moved down the hallway.

"That's fucked up," the analyst chimed in. "Twisted."

They reached his desk. A few printouts were scattered across it—missing persons reports.

"Yeah," Frankie said. "He's unraveling, maybe. It's been decades. Maybe he wants more attention. Or maybe it's his way of saying it's fucked up that we didn't connect her to him."

"I was reading through the profile the FBI built," Emily said, pulling out a chair and sitting down. "Emotionally detached, but methodical and patient…"

"So everything has meaning," Frankie replied, dragging a chair over. "It may seem like the act of a butcher, but we're dealing with a surgeon."

The analyst stood between them, caught somewhere between fascination and awe. He didn't usually see this part, the thinking behind the hunt.

Frankie looked up at him. Held the glance for a second.

The analyst didn't take the hint.

"Alright," Frankie said. "What did you want to show us?"

"Oh shit, yeah. the analyst said, "sorry… We just got it sorted out. Come take a look."

He rolled his chair over to a video setup in the room, spun the dial back, and hit play.

"Watch closely, y'all gonna. Lose…Your… Shit."

Frankie and Emily leaned in, more serious now, if that was even possible.

"You got actual footage?" Frankie asked. Voice low. Eyes locked.

"One of the nearby restaurants had a camera pointed straight at the alley," the analyst said.

"Yeah," Emily replied. "We know."

"Wait for it…" he added.

And there it was.

A van reversed into frame.

A man stepped out. About 6 feet. Painter overalls. Full gas mask. Creepy. Calm. Too calm. Deliberate.

He walked to the back of the van, slowly, like a worker setting up for a job. No rush.

Opened both back doors, pulled out a white bucket, and poured it out.

Then he grabbed a tarp. Both ends. Started dragging.

A body. Face down.

Sliding out slowly with the tarp.

Once it was clear, the man stepped to the side and flipped the body over.

Right onto the puddle he had just poured.

Face up now.

Frankie didn't blink.

"What the fuck."

Gas Mask Guy pulled something from his front pocket and placed it next to the body. The pendant.

Then stood there. Just stood.

Staring down, like he was admiring it.

Then he turned around slowly and looked up.

Straight at the camera.

Held the stare. Then walked back to the van, closed the back doors. Climbed in, and drove off.

No big deal.

"Jeez," said Emily. "Wait… what did he dump?"

The analyst shook his head, starting to answer. "No idea…"

"Blood," Frankie cut in. Cold. Certain.

"Doc was right. He didn't cut her up in the alley. He did it somewhere else. Saved her blood. Then staged the scene." He shook his head.

"Sick."

Frankie continued, voice low and steady. "We need to share this footage with the FBI."

The analyst nodded.

"And loop in the Captain."

Emily stood. Nodded.

"I'll go talk to him," she said, grabbing her coat from the back of her chair and heading out.

Frankie stayed seated. Turned toward the analyst.

"Are we running analysis on the blood found at the scene?" he asked.

The analyst nodded. "Yeah. Standard procedure. We'll run a full panel. And push it through CODIS in case it doesn't match the vic."

"How long?"

"Few days. Depends on lab availability."

Frankie's jaw tensed. He gave a short nod, clearly not thrilled.

"Alright. Come get me if you find anything else. Or if a faster lab opens up."

The analyst nodded again but Frankie was already turning

back, walking away.

He headed back to his desk and started going over statements

taken that morning at the scene.

No one saw anything.

Typical New York attitude.

A guy in a gas mask parks a van in the middle of an alley.

Dumps a body. No one notices.

Just another Tuesday.

The fuck is wrong with us.

We see a homeless person passed out, we step over them

and keep walking.

A man grabbing a woman by the arm, yelling. She's clearly

in distress.

"Not my problem."

A Black man jogging in a white neighborhood?

Call the cops.

Shoot first. Ask last.

Where the hell are we headed as a species.

He glanced at the corkboard. The timeline had a gaping

hole.

Did he retire?

Was he in jail?

Or were there more killings no one had connected yet? He

sat on his chair. Arms crossed, eyes scanning every photo,

string, and sticky note like they might suddenly rearrange

themselves into an answer. The precinct buzzed behind him, but it barely registered. He was deep in it.

Emily stepped in, cutting through his thoughts.

"We got a meeting set up. FBI."

Frankie didn't respond. Just gave a slow nod, still staring at the board.

"When?" he finally said.

"Now," she said. "Let's go."

That got him alert. He stood up fast and ran after her.

They made it to the conference room. Oval table in the middle. Big screen on the wall. New tech just installed. Neither the Captain nor Frankie really knew how to work it. Emily connected her laptop to the casting device and changed the input.

"There," she said.

They logged into the video conference.

FBI Deputy Director.

OPD Captain and lead detective.

Seattle PD Captain and lead.

Eugene's Deputy Sheriff.

And SEA PD's top team.

FBI had gathered everyone to share the profile of the killer and get briefed on the latest murder.

The Deputy Director, Aja Shaikh, sharp-eyed, calm, opened

the meeting.

"Thank you all for joining. Each of you has at least one case linked to the same killer. So far, most of these murders have stayed out of the media, or at least the connection between them has.

We never disclosed the jewelry he leaves at the scenes. That detail is what linked most of these cases. It's also why no one in the press has caught on."

Pause.

"Another commonality is the timing. Around Christmas…"

Murmurs on the screen.

Whispers at first. Then louder.

Departments talking over each other.

"I know you all have questions," she said, raising her voice just enough.

"I'll get to them in time. Let's get on with the briefing." She waited a beat until the room quieted then continued.

"Our Behavioral Unit has already shared a preliminary profile. If you haven't received it, let us know.

We don't know enough. But we do know he picks his victims around Christmas. He goes dormant for long stretches.

We believe he keeps some of them captive. Not all.

So there's a method. A reason why some are held and some are killed right away.

I won't get ahead of myself. But we have our work cut out for us. And we're racing against time."

Frankie spoke up.

"Does the Bureau think this Christmas Killer will strike again soon?"

The Director nodded.

"Based on previous cases, he abducts someone and disposes of a body around the same time.

"So he either already took someone…"

She paused.

"…or he's about to."

Frankie stayed quiet.

He thought to himself.

No body was ever found when Cathy went missing.

Maybe she was the first. Or maybe there was a body that was never connected.

He made a mental note to check bodies recovered around that time.

"We are assigning a liaison from the BAU, Special Agent Kitterdige to the NYPD assisting Detective…" the Deputy Director glanced down at her notes…

"Rimler."

Emily nodded.

"Captain McLaughlin will ensure all findings from the most

recent case are shared across jurisdictions.

There are no turfs on this one.

Let's work together and catch this son of a bitch."

"Happy to answer any questions at this time."

Seattle PD captain cleared his throat.

"Captain Cheing here. Can you brief us on the most recent case?"

"I'll let Captain McLaughlin handle that. Captain?"

The captain leaned forward slightly, fidgeting with his reading glasses. He set them down on the conference table and started talking without pause. He knew the details by heart.

"Body was found near Chinatown by a restaurant worker around five a.m. Dismembered. Arms where legs should be. A pendant was left at the scene. Confirmed to belong to a missing person, Cathy Silva. Nineteen ninety-seven. Initial findings suggest torture. Possibly long-term captivity. Time of death estimated four to five hours before discovery. Body appears to have been kept indoors post-mortem. Medical Examiner is still conducting the autopsy as we speak."

He glanced at Emily.

"Did I miss anything?"

She shook her head. "No."

OPD Captain chimed in .

"Umm, Captain Kim here. Are we officially treating Cathy

Silva as one of the Christmas Killer's victims?"

The Deputy Director responded, quick and firm.

"I guess that's what we're calling him now…

Umm, there is a connection. But Cathy Silva is still

technically missing.

No body was ever recovered. That said, the killer had her

pendant. So yes, the case is now officially connected."

OPD Captain continued.

"We sent the case files to NYPD. Thin file, really."

"We'll fatten it up," Frankie cut in.

He recognized the captain. Older now, but the face was

familiar.

Shaeffer's old partner.

Captain Kim gave a small nod, glanced sideways at one of

his detectives. The line about fattening the file didn't sit right.

Sounded like a dig.

He'd been there in ninety-seven. Worked side by side with

Shaeffer.

They hadn't left any stones unturned.

At least, that's what they told themselves.

"Any other questions?"

The Deputy Director jumped in, cutting the tension before

it turned into a pissing match.

Low murmurs filled the screen.

Internal questions. Side chats.

A minute passed.

Then quiet agreement.

No more questions for the Deputy.

They'd reach out to one another if help or information was needed.

"Alright then. That's it for now," said the deputy, tapping a stack of papers against her desk to square them.

"I'll touch base with you offline, Captain McLaughlin. The rest of you…" She looked up at the screen over her glasses. Took a beat.

"Good luck. Let's catch this monster."

Feeds from the different departments went black, one after the next, as they dropped off the meeting.

Emily ended the call, closed her laptop and tucked it under her arm. She sighed. Looked over at the Captain, still scribbling in his notepad.

Then at Frankie, leaned all the way back in his chair, eyes on the ceiling. Swiveling slowly.

One hand over his head. Trying to figure out his next move.

"You coming?" she said.

"Ya" he breathed out, almost startled, sitting up straight.

Took a second. Gathered himself.

Then stood. "Let's go," he said.

Her phone rang. She picked up with a joking, "Yello." But

her face turned serious fast.

She snapped her fingers at Frankie getting his attention to follow her, then turned and started walking briskly down the hall.

Frankie jogged to catch up.

"Thanks. Be right there," she said, ending the call.

"What's up?" Frankie asked.

"Umm.. They…" she dragged the word, milking the suspense.

"…found a fingerprint."

"What?" His eyes went wide.

"Yep," she said, grinning wide. "On the pendant."

Frankie's eyes widened.

They hurried to the analyst's office.

Frankie stormed in.

"Any hits?"

"Not yet," the analyst said, half-annoyed. "This'll take a while, you know."

"I'll wait," Frankie replied, already pulling up a chair.

The analyst swiveled around, looked at Frankie, then at Emily.

"He ain't leaving," she confirmed.

He sighed, swiveled back around to his screen. Knew he'd lost that one.

"I already ran it through AFIS," he said. "No hits. Running

it through NGI now. It's a full, clean print. Beautiful, really.

If there's a record out there, we'll get it."

"You think it's his?" Frankie asked Emily.

The analyst started to answer.

"Honestly, it's hard to…"

Emily fake-coughed.

He got the hint.

"Sorry," he said.

She smiled.

"I doubt it," she said, turning to Frankie. "He's very careful."

"I agree," Frankie said. "A full, clean print. It feels deliberate. A message."

"If he left it on purpose," Emily said, "then he knows we can match it. There has to be a hit somewhere."

She sat next to him.

Both of them staring at the analyst's back as he worked, eyes locked on the screen.

Eventually, he left the desk, letting the search run while he handled other matters.

Frankie and Emily stayed.

They had nowhere else to be.

The autopsy report wasn't ready. And this was the closest thing to a lead.

An hour later, the screen flashed.

No match.

The analyst returned, glanced at it, and gave a dry shrug.

"No dice," he said.

Frankie grunted. "Are you sure you checked all databases?"

"We're not looking in the right place." Emily cut in.

She turned to the analyst.

"Where else would there be fingerprint records?"

"Umm… immigration, military," he said. "But all of those are synced with NGI."

She leaned forward, eyes locked on the digital copy of the fingerprint.

"What are you trying to tell us," she whispered.

Frankie stayed silent.

The Deputy Director's words echoed in his head.

"He abducts someone and disposes of a body around the same time."

"Missing persons," Frankie said.

"That's it!" Emily snapped.

"We need to check all reports from the past week," Frankie said, turning to the analyst, who was already spinning his chair toward the screen. Rapid typing. Eyes flicking between windows. Squinting.

He typed again.

"There," he said. "Two hundred thirty-three reports."

Frankie leaned in.

"Filter out the men."

"Okay… one eighty females."

"Now narrow it to those between seventeen and thirty."

More typing. Fast.

"Seventy-six left."

Frankie stared at the screen.

Behind him, Emily spoke.

"How do we know which one he has?"

"The fingerprint," he said.

Confident.

"How many went missing on Christmas Eve?" Emily asked.

"One," the analyst replied.

Her heart sank. "We start with her," she said, firm.

Frankie stood. "Let's go."

Emily followed.

They hurried down the hall into an open area where an old vending machine hummed beside the elevator. They passed it and turned down another hallway lined with offices. Frankie stopped at the second one, knocked gently on the glass door.

"Come in," a female voice called from inside.

Frankie and Emily stepped into an old office. The window looked out onto another building, no sun sneaking through. Detective Mendez sat buried in paperwork, looking up with curiosity.

"Busy?" Emily asked.

"Hey, Emily," Mendez said. "Ahh, you know it." She pushed a few files aside, lifted her glasses onto her head, and rubbed her eyes.

"How can I help you guys? Heard about your vic this morning."

"Yeah," Emily said. "Crazy…"

Frankie interrupted. "We need a missing person file. Might be connected."

Mendez's frowned, looked at Emily who handed her a piece of paper with the missing person's first and last name. Sophia Galanis. She took it and looked it over then sifted through the stack on her desk and pulled the file. It was fresh. Reported about 8 or 9 days ago.

"You think you've got a lead on my missing person?" Mendez asked.

"We don't know yet," Emily replied.

Frankie was already flipping through the file. It had a photo, last-seen location, home address.

"What can you tell us so far?" he asked Mendez.

"Sophia Galanis. Nineteen years old. Goes to college down in Florida. Came up for the holidays," Mendez said. "Last seen Christmas Eve. She went to the mall with some friends. CCTV caught her leaving around 9:30 p.m. We see her walk into the subway station and get on the train around ten. She

never leaves."

Frankie's eyes lifted. "How's that possible?"

"It's like she vanished," Mendez said.

"Any suspects?" Emily asked.

"None so far."

"Any suspicious activity in the station or on the train?

Cameras?" Emily pressed.

"There's a camera," Mendez said. "Someone was blocking

it. By the time they moved, she was gone."

Frankie glanced at Emily.

Mendez kept going. "No one suspicious. She sat next to an

older man. Nicely dressed. Fedora."

"Can we look at the footage?" Frankie asked.

"Yeah," Mendez said, reaching for her glasses on her head

and sliding them down onto her face. She typed a few keys,

squinted at the monitor, clicking through a few folders on her

desktop. The CCTV footage had already been uploaded by

Transit. She pulled it up. then motioned for them to come

around.

"There," she said, pointing. "That's Sophia."

Frankie and Emily leaned in, eyes fixed on the screen

following the brunette as she walked down the station stairs.

She glances over her shoulder once, then finds a bench and

sits.

"She looks nervous," Frankie said.

Mendez hummed, unconvinced. "I don't know…" She said.

"She's looking back. Clutching her purse," he added, sensing Mendez's doubt.

"It's New York," she said flatly. She was about to add something about how a girl alone on the subway would naturally be cautious. But she never got the chance.

"Still," Frankie cut her off. "I think she already crossed paths with her abductor. She seems uneasy."

Mendez studied the screen again. The theory made sense if she was abducted.

Then, almost to herself, she said, "We don't even know if she was abducted."

"It's been nine days," Frankie replied without missing a beat. "You think she's at a spa somewhere?"

Mendez leaned back in her chair, pushed her glasses up to her head, and sighed. She knew he was right.

Sophia wasn't back at college. No one had seen her. Her boyfriend hadn't heard from her. Everyone described her as responsible, grounded.

She'd never run away. After her father died, she and her mother had grown even closer. She wouldn't disappear on her.

And to vanish from the train like that made no sense.

"What should we be looking for?" she finally asked.

"We don't know if her disappearance is tied to our case," Frankie said. "But if it is, look for a tall guy. Six feet, maybe more. We don't have much else. Just watch for anything off."

He stepped back abruptly from the screen, closing the missing person file.

"Call us if you find anything on the footage."

Mendez looked up, surprised. "That's it?" she asked.

Frankie was already halfway to the door. "For now."

Then he looked at Emily, gave a short nod. "We gotta go."

Emily nodded back then turned to Mendez who was still looking baffled.

"We found a fingerprint. Might be connected. We need to run a comparison with your missing person." She explained as she walked out.

"Wait!" Mendez called out from behind her desk.

"Sorry, we gotta move! I'll call you as soon as we know anything!" Emily yelled back, already out of the office.

Mendez jumped up from her chair and hurried after them, stepping into the hallway just as they turned the corner.

She stopped, watching them disappear in disbelief, then shook her head and went back inside.

The detectives jogged out of the precinct into the parking lot. It was getting dark, though it had never really been light. A dark, gloomy day giving way to an even darker night.

The air was a lot colder now, too. They tightened their jackets, crossing their arms as they walked toward the car to get themselves warmed up. Their breath was visible in front of them. The sound of their heels echoed against the old parking walls, mixing with the screech of tires somewhere in the distance. Once inside, Emily cranked the heater to full blast and they peeled off, heading toward the missing girl's home.

Frankie held on tight to the file as he looked out the fogged up window. The rain had eased. City lights shimmered in puddles across the street. Buildings reflected in slick asphalt. Homeless figures hunched in corners.

Commuters moved fast, heads down, minding their own. Distant. Disconnected.

Any one of them could get abducted right this minute and not a soul would notice.

Eyes like magnets, sucked into the vortex of their glowing screens.

Captives of their own devices.

His thoughts were suddenly interrupted.

"Hello? Did you hear me?" Emily waved a hand in front of his face, palm up, moving it up and down like she was checking if he was still conscious.

"What?" he said, blinking, confused.

"I've been talking to you for the past five minutes," she said, exasperated.

"Sorry," he muttered. "Just thinking."

They turned into a quiet neighborhood, trees lining the smaller roads. Quaint houses. The kind of place where nothing bad ever happens. Hockey games in the street. Barbecue Sundays.

The car headlights swept across the front of the house as they pulled into the driveway.

It was fully dark now. Night had finally settled.

Frankie and Emily got out.

Footsteps crunching against the gravel driveway.

"Let me do the talking," Emily said.

Frankie glanced at her, then hopped up the steps to the porch and knocked on the door.

He looked down at his feet.

The door opened.

A woman in her late fifties, Mrs Ganalis, eyes puffy like she'd been crying.

Déjà vu.

"Ma'am, I'm Detective Silva, and this is my partner, Detective Rimler. Is it okay if we come in?"

"Did you find my daughter? Did something happen to her?" the woman pleaded, face full of worry. Vulnerable.

When someone you love goes missing, the not knowing is

hell.

Are they alive? Are they hurt? Are they cold?

Frankie knew the feeling. He looked at the woman and all he could see was his mother in 1997.

Triggering.

Emily stepped forward.

"We're still looking, ma'am. No new information yet, but we do need to ask a few questions to help with the search."

Mrs Galanis paused for a beat. Then opened the door wider and nodded them in.

They stepped into a warm, cozy home.

The heat was almost too much after the chill outside.

Photos were scattered across a round dining table.

Emily glanced at them.

Who has actual printed photos anymore, she thought.

"I always print them," Mrs. Galanis said, almost like she'd read Emily's thoughts as she led them to the table.

"I'm old-school like that. I like to hold them as I go through them." She paused to wipe her nose, then started gathering the pictures.

"Always have," she added softly, under her breath, almost to herself.

"You don't have to put them away on our account," Emily

said quietly.

"It's fine," the mother replied. "Can I get you two some coffee or something?"

"No thanks," Emily said.

Frankie stood watched her remembering how much it had meant when Detective Shaeffer was being kind with his mother.

Rimler had that same instinct. She made people feel safe.

The mother sat, slowly, sniffling. Tissue in hand, dabbing at her nose now and then.

"So, you said you had questions?" She said.

"Yes," Emily said. "Well, actually… we need to ask for a favor."

"A favor?" the woman repeated, surprised.

Emily nodded. "Yes."

"We need to take a couple of Sophia's personal items. Things she used regularly. To dust for prints."

"Why?" the mother asked. "Why do you need her fingerprints?" Then, as the thought hit her, her voice cracked.

"Did you find a body? Please… tell me the truth!"

"No. Nothing like that, ma'am," Frankie said.

"Then why?" Mrs. Galanis pressed.

"I'm sorry," Frankie replied. "We can't share that at the moment."

Emily jumped in, "But it could help us understand more

about what happened to Sophia."

The woman looked at Emily, then at Frankie, trying to piece together their thought process.

She sniffled, wiped her nose with a tissue, and finally said, "You can take her hairbrush. Her laptop's here too. She was visiting for the holidays."

"Thank you," Emily said, reaching out to gently touch the mother's arm.

Mrs. Galanis nodded faintly, turned, and went to fetch the items.

Emily followed, already pulling on her gloves. "I'll grab them," she said. "We need to be careful not to mess up any existing prints."

Emily walked into the girl's room.

Frankie followed.

The room was undisturbed.

Memories hanging from the walls.

Childhood stuffies lined the bed.

He looked at the mother's face as she scanned the room.

Pain with every glance.

Déjà vu.

She pointed to the items.

Emily moved carefully, bagging them one by one.

As the detectives made their way out, the mother's voice

cracked.

"Please find my daughter. Please."

Her face was pure agony. Crying, breathless.

Even tearless, the tears had dried up days ago.

Emily steadied her voice.

"We're doing everything we can, ma'am. This helps a lot."

As she lifted the bag holding Sophia's things.

They walked out the door and down the steps into the

gravel.

Each step crunching underfoot, sharp against the quiet.

Even without turning, they could feel her gaze towards them.

Her hope resting on them.

That kind of responsibility wasn't lost on them.

Back to the station.

Back to the forensic lab.

"We need prints lifted off these items and compared to the

fingerprint found on the pendant from this morning," Emily

said.handing the bag to the forensics tech.

They headed toward their desks.

The captain was coming their way.

"Where the fuck you two been?"

"Missing persons' home," Emily said.

"And?"

"We pulled a few personal items for print analysis."

Emily gave him a look.

"What are you still doing here?" she asked.

"Just about to leave," the captain said. Then added a grunt.

"Ugh." He took off his glasses and rubbed his eyes. Stressed

"It's gonna be okay," Emily sing-songed in a baby voice, like

she was talking to a kid headed to the dentist.

"Yeah, yeah," he said. "You know how much I love people."

She smiled.

"Anyway," she said. "We're trying to place the fingerprint.

Nothing on AFIS or NGI."

"Alright," he said. "Keep on trucking. You'll get him."

He nodded toward Frankie.

"How's he doing?"

Frankie cut in.

"He's standing right here."

Both ignored him.

"He's alright," Emily said.

"Let me know if he loses his shit."

Frankie again, louder, pointing at himself with both hands.

"Still right here."

Ignored again.

"Will do," Emily said.

"Alright. I better head out before the missus sends an APB.

I'll see you two there?"

"You bet," Emily said.

"Don't be too long," the captain added as he walked away.

"Ugh," Frankie let out, an involuntary grunt.

"It's gonna be okay," Emily sing-songed again, using the same baby voice she had used on the captain. She laughed.

"Yeah," Frankie said. "You know how much I love people too."

"We've got some time to kill," Emily said, glancing at her watch.

"Wanna grab something to eat?"

"Better not," Frankie said. "Mrs. McLaughlin will expect us to eat dinner there."

"Yeah, you're right," she said. "All the more reason to eat now."

He let out an involuntary chuckle.

"Her cooking isn't that bad," he said. Then added, "But yes. Better be prepared."

They walked across the street to the diner.

Windows sprayed to look like snow.

Christmas decorations crammed into every corner.

Everyone knew them there.

The bell over the door dinged as they walked in.

A waitress, sixties, sharp eyes, pen in hand, spotted them right away. She pointed with the pen to an empty booth in the corner.

Emily nodded, slipping off her coat as she headed over.

They plopped down onto the vinyl bench.

The waitress showed up seconds later, pitcher of coffee in hand.

She flipped their mugs right-side up. Poured.

Then she looked at Emily.

"Hi, hun. Usual?"

"Yes, please," Emily said.

"And Mr. Grumpy?" she asked, glancing at Frankie.

"Same," he said.

"Alright." She jotted it down, then added, "Coming right up."

She turned and shouted the order toward the kitchen without breaking stride.

The diner buzzed around them. Loud, warm, full of life.

Windows fogged from the heat.

Freezing just outside.

"Looks like it's about to snow," Frankie said.

"Surprised it hasn't yet," Emily replied.

Then, awkward silence.

Emily broke the silence. "What do you think?"

"About?" Frankie asked.

"Sophia," she said. "You think he took her?"

He took a beat. Sipped his coffee.

"She fits the profile," he said. "Greek. Mediterranean features. Early twenties. Went missing Christmas Eve."

Another beat of silence. Coffee sips. Staring out the

window.

"Here you go, dear," the server said, breaking the silence as plates clinked against the table.

She topped off both mugs from the pitcher.

"Anything else, hun?"

"No, we're good. Thanks," Emily said.

"Enjoy," the server said, already moving back toward the counter, gathering plates as she went.

They dug into their food. Starving.

"Why leave a fingerprint?" Emily asked. Mouth full. Barely understandable as she wiped with a napkin and kept chewing.

Frankie watched her for a second.

She always seemed so free. Free of trauma. Free of fear of judgment. Free of inhibition.

Maybe that's why he…

He stopped himself. Swallowed. Wiped his mouth.

"It's a game to him," Frankie said. "To show us he's smarter. To tell us he has her and there's nothing we can do about it."

He took the last of his sandwich. Finished it in two equal bites. Wiped again. Reached for his coffee.

"Could it be…" Emily started, then stopped.

Frankie looked up, hands wrapped around the cup.

"What?"

"Could it be Cathy's?" she said. "You know. From back then."

He stared at her for a second. Then looked down at his cup.

"I don't think so."

She kept watching him, waiting. He had always been a man of few words.

He looked up. Took another sip. Then explained.

"The pendant is the indicator," he said. "It ties him to Cathy. The clean print is different. A clue. A piece of the puzzle. Not overkill."

He paused. A poor choice of words. Then continued.

"We already know he's connected to Cathy."

She agreed quietly. Finished the last bite of her sandwich.

Frankie pulled some cash from his pocket and laid it on the table.

"We better go," he said, grabbing his jacket.

She followed. Craned her neck for the server. Gave a quick wave.

Then they stepped out of the deli and into the freezing cold.

They rushed back to the station, cutting through the city's hustle. Grabbed their things from their desks and headed for the parking lot. Peeled out as they exchanged small banter.

"Did you get him anything?" she asked.

"Yeah," he said.

She shot him a quick, surprised glance.

"What?" he said.

"Nothing," she said, smiling. "What'd you get him?"

He reached into the pocket of his coat and pulled out a clear box containing a signed baseball.

"Oh," she said. "You got him a baseball. Great." Pure sarcasm.

"He's gonna love that."

Frankie chuckled despite himself.

"It's not just a baseball," he said, holding up the clear case.

"It's from a 1995 game. Signed by his favorite player."

The captain liked to play the tough, no-bullshit role, but underneath it he was a softie. Especially with Frankie. He had looked out for him since his first days as a rookie. His training officer. A stand-in father all these years.

They bonded over baseball. Oakland A's fans. Both of them.

Frankie once told him about a signed baseball from a 1995 game. The one Cathy took him to.

She kept yelling at the player to throw the ball. For her brother. His biggest fan. Loud. Relentless. She did not know how to be quiet.

The player grew irritated. The crowd too.

She kept at it.

Finally, the player gave in. Threw the ball to her. Scattered applause. Half annoyed. Half amused.

She handed it to Frankie.

He was embarrassed. Secretly ecstatic.

She didn't stop there. When the game ended, she dragged

Frankie to the back. Where the players came out.

She kept yelling at them as they walked past, trying to get

the ball signed.

The same player noticed her again. Recognized the obnoxiousness.

Laughed, shaking his head, and signed it.

He looked at Frankie and said, "You're lucky to have a sister

like her."

He fidgeted with the case as he remembered that day. As he

remembered Cathy.

Emily reached over with one arm and squeezed his shoulder,

massaging it as she drove. A quiet response to what he was

going through.

Chapter 10
The Party

Emily pulled into a store on the way to the Captain's home.

"What are you doing?" Frankie asked.

"Grabbing a card," she said.

She jumped out and headed for the entrance.

Frankie stared ahead, lost in thought. He couldn't imagine

his life without her. If only he could allow himself to be happy.

That was part of why this case mattered so much. He owed it

to Cathy. To the victims. To his mother. But also to himself.

He deserved happiness too.

Emily hurried back with a small plastic bag. She pulled out

a card and handed it to him.

"Here. Write something."

"No," he said. "I'm not good with words."

"Just write happy retirement or something."

"No."

She snatched the card back, scribbled for a moment, then

handed it to him again.

"Fine. Just sign."

He signed his name.

Emily pulled out another card and started writing again.

Kept writing.

Frankie leaned over. "What are you still writing in there?"

"Mind your business," she said, joking.

"Jesus," he said. "You're writing a novel."

"I care," she replied.

She stacked the cards, buckled up, and pulled back onto the road.

The Captain's neighborhood was quiet. Quaint. Streets lined with overhanging trees and old brownstones. Tall windows glowing softly from inside. Just enough to imagine the warmth behind the walls.

They parked on the side street and hurried up the stoop to the door.

Mrs. McLaughlin opened it and wrapped them both in a hug.

"Let me take your coats," she said.

"Oh, I've got it," Emily said. She grabbed both coats and followed Mrs. McLaughlin into the next room.

"Where's the retiree?" Emily asked.

"Over there," Mrs. McLaughlin said. "Smoking a cigar."

"That's not good," Emily said.

"I know," she replied. "It's his last vice."

They entered a crowded living room full of officers. Handshakes. Laughter. Familiar banter.

They reached the Captain. More handshakes. A few jokes.

Frankie spotted a couch near the wall and dropped into it.

Emily found the officer she'd spoken to earlier. The one with the date. She leaned in, already fishing for details.

Food made its way around. Desserts followed. Toasts were

raised.

Then the chant started.

"Speech. Speech. Speech."

The Captain grunted. Looked over at Frankie.

Frankie shrugged.

The Captain stood and raised his hands. "Alright. Alright, you fuckers."

Laughter.

"I never thought this day would come," he said.

"Neither did I," Mrs. McLaughlin yelled out, without missing a beat.

The room erupted.

The Captain smiled.

"I don't need to tell anyone in this room how shitty this job can be," he said. "What it takes from you. The things you see."

The room quieted.

"We shove it down somewhere deep and keep going. Day after day. Year after year. We tell ourselves it matters. That the streets are safer because of us."He paused.

"After forty years of service, the only thing that kept me going was my wife," he said. "Find yourselves a partner who gets you. Who balances the evil out of you. Keeps you grounded. Cleans your soul every night."

He raised his glass. The room followed.

"Thank you for putting up with me all these years."

She mouthed, *I love you.*

Then he added, "And if you think the last forty years were rough with me out of the house most of the day, wait until you see how it is with me in front of you all day. Every day."

The crowd erupted again.

"Here's to a pure heart and a clear conscience," the Captain said.

"Hear, hear," the room answered.

The Captain stepped away as people patted him on the back and congratulated him. He made his way through the room to the couch where Frankie was sitting.

"So," he said.

Frankie glanced over.

"When are you gonna man up?" the Captain asked.

"What do you mean?" Frankie said.

The Captain nodded toward Emily, who was laughing hard across the room.

Frankie looked at her. Then down.

"Working on it."

"Good," the Captain said. "No rush. You're still young."

Then looked at him and stared, making sure the sarcasm landed.

Frankie chuckled. Then reached for the clear case sitting beside him. The baseball inside. And handed it to the Captain.

"What's this?" the Captain said.

He examined it. Realized what it was. He knew the story.

Knew what it meant to Frankie.

He didn't say anything. Just tapped Frankie's leg. Gave it a

squeeze.

A subtle thank you.

People quietly started leaving. Emily helped Mrs. McLaughlin

tidy up a bit. Then she and Frankie said their goodbyes

and stepped outside.

They wrapped themselves in their coats, bracing against the

cold as they walked toward the car.

Fatigue and stress sat heavy in their necks and shoulders.

It was time to go home.

Emily got into her car, rubbing the tightness in her neck.

Frankie leaned down to her open window.

"You good?" he asked.

"Yeah. Tired. You?"

"Yeah," he said.

"You sure you don't want a ride?"

"I'm sure," he replied, straightening up. "Subway helps me

think."

"It stinks," she said.

He chuckled, involuntary.

"That it does," he said. "That it does."

"Alright." She shifted into gear.

"I'll check on you later."

He almost stopped her.

Almost said wait.

We need to talk.

But he didn't.

He just watched her pull away.

There's always tomorrow, he thought.

Now isn't the time.

He started walking toward the subway. It wasn't far from

the Captain's house. He rode it to the precinct stop and headed

up to his office.

His body was tired.

His brain wasn't.

He couldn't shut it off.

The CCTV footage.

The stitched limbs.

Cathy.

It circled him. Pulled at him. There was something there.

He could feel it. He just couldn't name it yet.

Killers get better with time. Cleaner. More careful.

But early on.

When they're just starting out.

That's when they make mistakes.

If Cathy was the first, there had to be something.

After about an hour, he couldn't keep his eyes open. He left the station and headed back down to the subway to go home.

Hard to believe it was just that morning he'd walked these same streets. Bodega guys rolling up metal gates. Stragglers stumbling home from after parties. Homeless men waking in doorways, lining up outside the liquor store that sold cheap black coffee in Styrofoam cups. Then the turn into the alley.

The body.

It felt like forever ago.

The streets were quieter now. Steam rose from sidewalk grates. Homeless people spread cardboard, settling in for the night. Partygoers moved between bars. Clubs. More bars. Oblivious.

He kept thinking about the Captain's words. The evil out there. The partner at home who helped cleanse the soul.

He needed that.

He descended into the subway. Same cracked tile. Same flickering light. Same piss-soaked air since 1974.

Someone bumped him coming down the stairs. Didn't apologize. Didn't even look.

He didn't react. Just added it to the list.

The city was wearing on him. The people. The noise. The decay.

He'd gotten so used to living on the edge of depression, he

didn't even notice it anymore.

He didn't remember the last time he slept without nightmares or sleep paralysis.

He didn't remember the last time he felt rested. Really. Most nights, he got home and couldn't remember how. Just there. On autopilot.

Just surviving.

He was turning into a shell of himself. A slow decline is always harder to notice.

This was his chance at redemption.

This was it.

He was helpless back then. He isn't anymore.

He got off at his stop. Walked the few blocks to his building. Up the steps, slowly, hand in his pocket for his keys.

Felt something else.

Paper.

Couldn't see it. Didn't care. Probably something from his desk.

Grabbed his keys from the other pocket, unlocked the door, dropped them and the mystery paper onto the dish by the entry table.

Locked up.

Shoes off. Coat off. Tie half undone.

He went to the bathroom. Washed his face. Stared into the

mirror. The lines on his face were deeper now, like trenches carved by stress, grief, and time. The scar above his eyebrow. Still there…

More gray showing. Multiplying by the hour.

He had lived more life without Cathy and his mom than with them.

It didn't feel that way.

But the mirror said otherwise.

He dried his face and went to the couch.

He opened his laptop. Back to the case.

Testimonies. Photos. Names. Over and over.

He had someone to focus on now. Based on Mo's recounting of that night. The rich kid. The host.

He remembered the parents. Cold people.

Why are you bothering us.

My son had a party.

It's not his fault if someone went missing..

He was twenty.

Home from college.

From UW.

Seattle. Hair rose. Connection to Seattle.

He opened a new tab. Googled the name.

Edward Allen Milton.

CEO. Milton Food Processing. Oakland, CA.

Married. Three kids. Picture-perfect. Articles with titles
like:

"The New Heir of the Milton Fortune"

"Milton Names New CEO"

Worked at the meat plant every summer since he was a

teenager. Charming. Went to college in Seattle.

Came back. Joined the family business. Helped expand it.

Took over when father retired in 2010.

Nothing on him. No dirt… Clean.

He double-checked every statement taken back in '97.

Again.

Everyone interviewed.

He could barely keep his eyes open. The room was dark

except for the blue glow of the laptop.

Edward wasn't on the list.

He was never officially interviewed.

How the fuck.

Did his father have connections at OPD?

Maybe.

But even with pull, Detective Shaeffer wouldn't let something

like that slide.

No way.

He called Emily. Just to double-check he hadn't missed any

statements.

It was late, but worth a shot.

The phone rang.

And rang.

No answer.

That wasn't like her.

But he didn't blame her.

Long day.

He went over the case notes again. From back then.

Nothing jumped out.

Drunk guy with the black eye was mentioned.

The raid on the crack house.

The girl they found on the dirty mattress. "Vee". looked just like Cathy.

She mentioned a guy. Wealthy. Dangerous.

Said the girls all warned each other about him.

Rough. Psycho. The kind you don't look in the eye too long.

"Wealthy…" Frankie said to himself.

Just like Edward.

Vee had never dealt with him directly. But she'd heard the stories.

No suspects.

No leads.

Just the bloodied clothes.

All of them.

Every item Cathy was wearing, down to her underwear.

Lab results didn't give much back then.

One detail stood out now.

A substance found on the right sleeve of her leather jacket.

"Bovine-based organic material…"

He stared at that line for a long time.

Bovine.

Meat plant.

His throat tightened.

No.

No way.

But it was right there.

Buried in plain sight.

And no one followed up.

"Edward… what are you hiding", Frankie muttered, staring

at the professional business profile photo on his screen. Wide

smile. Too wide. Almost fake. Empty beady eyes. Picture

perfect. By design?

Chapter 11
Brooklyn is Hunting

A loud ring pierced through the house, sharp and violent.

Frankie jolted awake, heart pounding. "How the fuck did I even fall asleep?" he thought. He was still fully dressed from the night before.

He stood slowly, careful, like any sudden movement might make his head detonate. Reached for his phone without looking and hit the side button to kill the sound. Rubbed his eyes, then squinted at the screen.

Captain McLaughlin, it read.

He answered. "Captain."

The voice on the other end exploded.

"What the fuck are you doing sleeping in, Silva? You on sabbatical or some shit? We got the FBI here waiting for you and Rimler. What the fuck are you two up to?"

Frankie pulled the phone away from his ear, wincing at the volume.

Whatever happened to the pure heart and clear conscience guy?

The rant kept going.

He waited for a tiny gap, then squeezed in, "I'll be right there. Leaving now."

He set the phone down. "Fuck". His head was pounding. He glanced at the laptop, screen dark in sleep mode. Tapped the trackpad. It lit up. There it was.

Edward's picture.

The first real suspect in twenty-two years.

He hopped in the shower. Got dressed. Autopilot. Barely

present. Thinking about the case.

Headed out. Still gloomy. Still dark. Drove this time. Called

Emily on the way. No answer.

What the fuck.

Pulled into the precinct parking lot. Walked in. Passed

O'Malley. Didn't say a word. Just grunted and kept moving.

Reached the captain's office.

FBI agent already there.

"Sleeping fucking beauty," the captain said, not looking up.

"So nice of you to join us. Face looks great. Very well rested."

It was only 7:30 a.m.

Frankie looked at the guy sitting across from the captain.

Young. Deer-eyed. Straight out of Quantico. Preppy.

Polished. Probably wore boat shoes off-duty.

Special Agent Kitteridge.

Captain still ranting in the background

Frankie grunted again.

Agent Kitteridge jumped up, eyes wide, carrying far too

much excitement and energy for that early in the morning,

and extended his hand.

"Special Agent Kitteridge. Nice to meet you, Detective Silva.

Heard a lot about you."

"Good to have you," Frankie replied politely. Flat tone.

Looking away towards the captain.

"I think I have a lead," Frankie continued. "The kid who

hosted the party…"

Captain cut him off and turned to Agent Kitteridge.

"Detective Silva is consulting on this case," he said. "Not

leading it."

He shot Frankie a look.

"Consulting."

Then, to Kitteridge, "What appears to be his sister's pendant

was recovered at the scene."

Agent Kitteridge smiled and nodded.

"Yes, you told me, Captain. Understood."

The Captain had already said it once to the agent. He only

made a point of repeating it to remind Frankie to act the part.

It went right over his head.

"The kid who hosted the party Cathy went missing from,"

Frankie continued, a little unhinged.

The Captain rested his head on his hand, just staring at him.

"His father owns a meat plant. He worked there every

summer. Knows how to butcher. And there was bovine

substance on the recovered jacket's left sleeve. No one looked

into him. Wasn't even interviewed."

Frankie paused, bracing for the usual pushback from the Captain, or whatever polished nonsense this preppy new agent was about to add.

The Captain was ready to jump in. Probably something like *You need to wait for your partner* or *That's it? His father owned a meat plant so he's a murderer?*

But he didn't get the chance.

Agent Kitteridge spoke first.

"I guess we better get moving then," he said. "Let's pull his records, see if anything pops. We shared the killer's profile with you guys. We'll cross-reference it."

Frankie looked at him. A flicker of approval behind his eyes.

"Alright," he said, almost hesitating. Caught off guard.

"Let's do it."

They started walking out of the office. Frankie glanced back.

"Any word from Emily?" he asked.

"Who?" the Captain replied, not even looking up from his paperwork.

"Detective Rimler," Frankie corrected himself.

The captain still didn't look up.

"What am I, y'all's fucking babysitter? She's a grown ass woman. I don't know where she is. Shit. Call her or send a patrol if you're so worried…"

Frankie smiled. The agent gave him a look. He kept ranting

as Frankie and Kitteridge walked off. The captain's voice still trailing behind them.

Agent Kitteridge made a quick call on the way to Frankie's office. Asked the Oakland office to send over everything they can get on Edward Allen Milton. As they walked into the office, Kitteridge ended the call and headed straight to the cork board.

He stood in front of it, studying the layers of photos and notes like it was a crime scene itself.

"Did you study the preliminary profile we sent you?"

"Yes," Frankie said, stepping closer to the corkboard.

"We're dealing with a highly organized offender," Kitteridge said. "He plans. He stages. This isn't random. It's ritual."

Frankie kept his eyes on the board.

"Did the FBI ever have any suspects?"

"No," Kitteridge said. "Not even close. We didn't connect the dots until much later. A lot of these cases weren't on our radar."

He pointed.

"The swapped limbs. When that pattern repeated, that's when we got involved."

"What do you make of that?" Frankie asked.

Kitteridge didn't hesitate.

"It's shocking. Grotesque. And that's the point," Kitteridge said. "He likes the reaction. The first person who finds the body. The family. The community."

He paused, thinking. Then grabbed one of the latest crime scene photos from the desk. Sat on the edge of it, eyes scanning the image. When he spoke again, his voice dropped.

"Schadenfreude."

Frankie leaned against the desk beside him.

"Pleasure in pain," he said, pointing at the photo. "That explains the torture. But these swaps are done post mortem."

Kitteridge looked at him, surprised.

"Yes!" he said. "Exactly. Pleasure in pain. But not just pain inflicted on the victim. Pain inflicted afterward. On the people left behind."

He turned back to the board.

"He runs on it."

Frankie agreed. He felt it personally.

The pain.

"Anything we can learn from his pathology?" Frankie asked.

Kitteridge slid the photos back into their folder.

"One abduction. One murder," he said. "One item left behind from the previous victim."

He tapped the stack.

"A cycle."

"Why leave something from twenty-two years ago this time?" Frankie asked.

Kitteridge nodded, acknowledging the break in pattern.

"I think he's closing the loop," he said. "Bringing it back full circle for a reason."

"The end?" Frankie asked. Not convinced.

"Maybe," Kitteridge said.

"Why now?" Frankie pressed.

Kitteridge shrugged. "Old age. Decline. Maybe he's dying." A beat. "Maybe he wants credit before it's too late."

"Oh shit!" Frankie cut in, sudden. "Speaking of the previous victim."

He leaned forward mid-thought. "I almost forgot."

His hand slid across the desk and closed around the photo of the pendant.

Kitteridge stopped talking. Watched him.

"He left a fingerprint," Frankie said. "On the pendant. Full."

"No hits yet?" Kitteridge asked.

"No," Frankie confirmed. "We think it belongs to the abducted victim."

"One murder. One abduction," Kitteridge muttered.

"Exactly," Frankie said. "We're running a comparison from a missing girl who disappeared on Christmas Eve, seeing if it matches."

He stood up, turned to his desk, and sifted through the files. Grabbed one. Opened it.

"Here," he said, handing it to Kitteridge, then continued as Kitteridge flipped through the notes in the file.

"Victims all fall within a narrow profile. Brunette. Mediterranean features. Late teens to early twenties. The missing girl is Greek. Twenty years old. She fits the pattern."

He paused.

"Same as Cathy…"

"His obsession started early," Kitteridge said. Eyes locked on the file of the missing person. "This isn't just preference. This is fixation. Somebody hurt him. Or someone he watched get hurt. Either way, it imprinted."

Frankie's voice dropped. "Mother."

Kitteridge nodded slowly as he dropped the folder back on Frankie's desk.

"Likely. Or a sister. Dominating. Controlling. Maybe abused too. Or just emotional suffocation. Whatever it was, he never processed it. He reenacts it now. Over and over."

"And every kill is an attempt to gain control over what he couldn't then," Frankie said.

"Nature versus nurture," he added.

"A bit of both, most likely," Kitteridge said. "But sex and violence got wired together early. First exposure to one came with the other."

"He needs space," Frankie added. "Somewhere private. Remote. Either lives near a rural edge of town or has access to something like it. Farm. Warehouse. Big property."

Kitteridge scribbled something in his notepad.

"He's strong," he said. "He carried bodies. Flipped them. Dragged them. He's comfortable butchering."

He looked up.

"He's not winging it."

Frankie exhaled slowly.

"I think he grew up in it. Around it. Meat plant. Fits Edward."

"Let's finish building the profile first," Kitteridge said, eyes scanning the board. "Stick to behavior. Don't bring Edward in yet."

Frankie leaned against the desk, arms folded. "Control. That's the thread. These weren't rage kills. They were orchestrated."

"Victims staged. Limbs swapped. Jewelry placed deliberately," Kitteridge added. "He's not just trying to shock. He's sending messages."

"He wants us to look. Wants us to notice."

He leaned back, thinking.

"Fit. Highly intelligent. Controlled. Narcissistic. And most of all…"

Frankie finished it for him. "Careful."

"Exactly," Kitteridge said. "Which is why he's been doing this for over twenty years, assuming Cathy was his victim, and no one's connected the dots."

He paused, then added, "Actually, I'm not familiar with Cathy's case. Not yet."

"Are you familiar with the other cases?" Frankie asked.

"I built the preliminary profile that was sent to you, actually. I know the previous cases by heart."

Frankie looked at him, semi-impressed.

"Alright then," he said. "Cathy. Nineteen at the time. Went to a party with her best friend. Left early. Never seen again. Bloody clothes were recovered the next day."

He stepped closer to the board.

"A neighbor was at the same party. Claimed he didn't see her. But saw a white SUV pulling out of our..."

Frankie stopped. Corrected himself. Kitteridge knew Cathy was his sister, but he needed to keep it professional.

"Out of the victim's building, as he was pulling in."

Kitteridge didn't look up. "Why is that important? The white SUV."

Frankie hesitated. "I heard a scream that night. Or I thought I did. I'm not sure. But it was a few minutes before the neighbor's door closed. Same neighbor who was at the party and saw the white SUV. So if I'm right, the scream happened just before the SUV drove off."

Kitteridge nodded slightly. "If a scream actually happened."

"Correct," Frankie said. "But there's another mention of a

white SUV."

Kitteridge's eyes lit up. "Melissa Romano!" he said, cutting
in, like the full picture had just hit him.

Frankie blinked. Impressed again. "Yes. Melissa Romano.
She told her best friend she thought she was being followed…
by a white SUV. Now if we can check what kind of Car Edward
drove in 97, we might close in on connecting him"

"Easy," said Kitteridge. He pulled out his laptop and nodded
toward an empty desk.

Frankie nodded back. "You can use that one."

Kitteridge opened the laptop, FBI seal lighting up the screen.
He typed fast, fingers moving with confidence. "Let's check
DMV records," he said.

A few seconds passed before the search hit. The screen
blinked, then filled with the details. Kitteridge read it aloud,
voice low but certain.

"There it is. White Lexus LX 450. Bought late '96. Registered
to Theodore Milton."

Frankie leaned in. Eyes narrowed. Heart pounding under
the surface.

"He used his father's car."

Kitteridge didn't look away from the screen.

"Or it's his. Registered to his dad. Maybe."

"He fits the demographic," Frankie said, eyes fixed forward.

"He was going to school in Seattle. Came home for Christmas break. Held the party. That was the last night anyone saw Cathy. Then two, three months later, Valery turns up dead. In Seattle. And now the white SUV…"

"We got him."

Kitteridge nodded once, closing his laptop and sliding it into his bag.

"We got enough to interview him."

Frankie knew. His gut was screaming. This was him.

He glanced at the time. Shit. He dialed Emily. No answer. Tried again. Straight to voicemail.

"What's wrong?" Kitteridge asked.

"Rimler's gone quiet. Not like her."

Kitteridge didn't hesitate. Grabbed his coat.

"Let's go check on her."

They walked out of the precinct, snow just starting to fall, still talking through the profile as their breath clouded in the cold air.

"Why did he go quiet all those years?" Frankie asked, blowing hot air into his cupped hands.

"I don't think he stopped," Kitteridge said. "Between '97 and '99, he was learning. Figuring out what he liked. Developing his craft. Then there's a gap until 2010. Maybe he didn't stop, just stopped leaving bodies. Started burying them. Somewhere close. His own garden of corpses. And now, another in 2019. Maybe there are more. Ones we haven't found. Or connected yet."

Frankie nodded while unlocking the car.

"A lot of serials do that," Kitteridge said. "Like Herb Baumeister."

"Who?" Frankie asked.

"Suspected I-70 Strangler," Kitteridge explained. "In the Mid-west. Bodies stopped showing up around '91. The same year he bought Fox Hollow Farm. Secluded property. Total privacy. He used it as a burial site. Quiet. Controlled. Just how they like it."

Frankie's jaw clenched. "That's what this guy needs. Control."

Kitteridge didn't reply. Didn't have to. They were both thinking it.

They got in the car. Frankie started it, grabbed his seatbelt, eyes still processing.

"Edward's family has a big estate in Oakland," Frankie said. "Maybe he's been doing this the whole time… But why dump a body in Brooklyn now? What's the motive?"

Kitteridge looked over.

"I think you are," he said.

Frankie froze mid-turn. Hands cold on the wheel.

"Me?" he asked, voice flat.

"Yeah," Kitteridge said. "He wants to see your pain. Wants to savor it."

Frankie looked up. Eyes dark.

Silence.

"Or he wants closure," Kitteridge added. "His version of it."

Frankie shook his head. "He's not done."

"Maybe not," Kitteridge agreed. Quiet. Uncertain.

Kitteridge's phone rang. He listened for a few minutes, then hung up.
His voice was flat.

"They found something of interest."

Frankie turned onto Emily's street. Jaw tight. Eyes forward.

Waiting for the rest.

Kitteridge exhaled, slow.

"His half-sister was murdered when he was eleven."

Frankie hit the brakes. "What?"

He threw the car into park and turned to Kitteridge,

stunned.

"They were at their lake house," Kitteridge continued. "His

sister was eight years older. Nineteen. Not a lot of detail.

They found her in the woods near the lake. Throat slit. Still

officially unsolved. But…"

They got out of the car. Frankie still stunned.

"What did his sister look like?" he asked Kitteridge.

"Brunette. Beautiful. Fits the profile. She was his half-sister

from a previous marriage. Mother was Italian. Died when

she was young. Father remarried."

Frankie stopped walking.

Kitteridge kept going for a few steps before glancing back.

Double-take.

"What's the matter?"

Frankie's voice was quiet. Flat.

"How did the mother die?"

Kitteridge's face shifted. He knew where this was going.

"I don't know," he said. "I'll find out."

"Shit."

They pressed the buzzer. No answer.

A tenant opened the front door on her way out. Frankie flashed his badge and held it open.

They climbed the stairs. Tension building with each step.

Apartment 2B.

He knocked. Nothing.

Again. Harder. Still nothing.

Frankie leaned in close to the door. Listening.

A door opened across the hall. He startled. Gun up.

An older woman stood there. A neighbor. Shocked.

Frankie lowered the weapon. Flashed his badge.

"Have you seen Detective Rimler?"

She shook her head.

"Not today."

He holstered his weapon, looked at Emily's door, then at Kitteridge, then headed downstairs. Faster now. Knocked hard on the superintendent's door.

The man opened. "Everything okay?"

Frankie showed his badge. "We need access to 2B. It's my partner. She didn't show. Not answering her phone."

The super grabbed his keys without a word and started up the stairs. Older guy. Moved slow. Each step a chore.

Frankie's patience was gone. He clenched his jaw, fists tightening with every creak of the stairs.

Finally, they reached the landing.

The super fumbled with the key, hands shaking. Click. Frankie and Kitteridge both drew their weapons. Frankie stepped in front of the door, nodded to the super.

"Move back."

The old man didn't argue. He stepped aside, eyes wide.

Frankie turned the knob. Pushed the door open slow.

They entered. Cleared each room.

Kitchen. Living room. Bedroom. Bathroom.

Nothing.

The apartment was pristine. Quiet.

Frankie scanned the room one last time as he holstered his weapon. Something was off. Too quiet. Too clean. No signs of struggle. No overturned furniture. Nothing out of place.

As a matter of fact, no signs of anyone living here at all.

No clutter. No dishes in the sink. No blankets tossed on the couch. No coffee mugs.

No life.

It looked like a showroom apartment. A set.

That's what didn't sit right.

Frankie's eyes narrowed. That's when he noticed the mirror.

Hanging by the entrance.

Upside down.

"This look upside down to you?" he asked.

"Yeah," said Kitteridge. "Looks like it."

Frankie pulled a pen from his pocket, gently lifted the mirror off the wall.

Something fell out.

A piece of paper. Cut-up letters from magazines and newspapers.

It read: **TOO LATE**

Frankie stared. "What the fuck…"

His heart dropped to his knees.

Feelings buried for 22 years came rushing back, raw and merciless.

The sick pit in his stomach. The static in his head. The dense silence where morbid thoughts thrive.

Someone he cares about, really cares about, is missing.

And he's been here before.

He knows how this ends.

He grabbed his phone. Called it in.

Frankie holstered his weapon. Turned to Kitteridge.

"He has her."

"She doesn't fit the victim profile. Why?" Kitteridge followed up. This doesn't make sense… He is not going to hurt her. He is after something else…"

"What the fuck could he be after?"

"I don't know. Yet. Walk me through the last time you saw her."

Frankie exhaled.

"We had the body. That long day at the precinct. The Captain's party." A beat. "We split up. She drove off. I took the subway."

"Anything out of the ordinary?"

"Besides the body in the alley with the limbs swapped?"

"You know what I mean. Think. Did he leave anything behind?"

Frankie shook his head.

"No. I just went home as usua…"

He stopped mid-sentence.

"What?" said Kitteridge.

Frankie bolted. Down the stairs. Kitteridge followed, they jumped into the car and peeled off.

"What is it?" Kitteridge asked again, grabbing the handle as the tires screeched.

"There was a paper in my pocket last night," Frankie said.

"Didn't recognize it. Figured it was something from the office.

I didn't look at it."

They reached Frankie's apartment building. Frankie ran up

the steps. Was about to unlock the door…

"Stop," Kitteridge barked.

Frankie froze.

Kitteridge signaled. Eyes. Gun. Watch everything.

They both unholstered. Opened the door slowly. Cleared

the place together, slowly. Carefully. Nothing seemed

disturbed.

Back by the entrance, Frankie lowered his weapon. So did

Kitteridge.

"There," said Frankie.

He pointed to the ceramic dish where he'd dumped his keys.

The paper was still there.

He grabbed some latex gloves from under the kitchen sink.

Put them on and without picking it up, gently unfolded it.

Same cut-up letters. Same style.

And it read:

I'm taking her tonight.

You'll feel it.

Like you felt Cathy.

Like the silence after your mother sank.

I've been cutting into you for decades.

Soon you'll understand.

Then I'll stop.

Frankie's chest tightened. The room spun.

He was too late.

He showed the paper to Kitteridge.

Kitteridge read it aloud, eyes widening. Almost fascinated.

"This is what we've been talking about," he said.

"How so?" Frankie asked, tense.

"He's obsessed with your pain. Like…"

"What?" Frankie snapped. "He's a psycho. A sick fuck."

He pulled his phone from his pocket and called it in. Made

sure the note would be collected as evidence.

He crossed the room and dropped onto the couch.

Kitteridge followed. Stood nearby.

Waiting for CSU.

"He is," Kitteridge said. "But he's also smart. Calculating.

This isn't impulse."

Frankie stared ahead.

"He's been doing this for decades," Kitteridge continued.

"And no one's come close to catching him."

He paused.

"He wanted you to see the pendant next to the victim,"

Kitteridge said. "He wanted to rip open an old wound."

A beat.

"He was probably watching you," he said finally. "When you found it. He wanted to see it. The pain on your face."

Frankie face didn't flinch.

"He probab…" He stopped himself.

"What?" Frankie asked.

Kitteridge didn't answer right away. He bit his lip. Looked off to the side, testing the thought before letting it out.

"You found that body in the alley because he wanted you to." He caught himself.

"Better to follow the evidence," he said. "Not guess."

"No," Frankie said. "I think you're right."

"That alley…" He continued.

"What about it?" Kitteridge asked.

"I pass by it every day," Frankie said. "On my morning walks. I never really noticed it, but…"

He trailed off.

"It can't be a coincidence."

"No," Kitteridge said, shaking his head. "It isn't."

He looked at Frankie.

"He knows your routine. Got pretty close. He's been following your movements."

A beat.

"Detective Rimler's too."

Frankie ran a hand through his hair, then rubbed the back of his head.

"Close enough to slip a note in my coat," he muttered.

"How the hell did he do that?" Kitteridge said, almost to himself.

Frankie stared ahead. "I don't know. Fuck."

"Think," Kitteridge said. "Any weird encounters? Subway maybe?"

Frankie's eyes snapped open.

"That's it," he said. "Someone bumped into me. On the stairs. Going down to the subway."

"CCTV," Kitteridge said. "Maybe we can trace his steps."

Frankie picked up his phone and called the precinct, asking to speak with the captain.

"Captain, I need access to subway CCTV footage from last night. I think that's when the perp slipped me the note."

"I'll call Transit Bureau. Ask for expedited access to the surveillance feed. You can head over as soon as CSU's done. They should be there soon."

Frankie could hear the precinct buzzing in the background. One of their own had been taken.

"Will do. Thanks," he said.

The captain continued, "Wait. I have an all-hands-on-deck meeting in an hour. I want you there."

"Yes sir," Frankie replied, then hung up.

CSU arrived, photographed the note in the key bowl, sealed it in an evidence bag, and left without a word.

Frankie and Kitteridge grabbed their coats, got in the car, and headed to the NYPD Transit Bureau.

In the passenger seat, Kitteridge kept rereading the note in his head. Tapped the end of a pen against his lips. Muttered to himself.

"Like the silence after your mother sank…"

Frankie's voice cut through, low and tight. "How would he know about something like that?"

Kitteridge didn't look at him. "Not hard to guess. But he brings it up to hurt you. You're the center of this. He's feeding off your pain. That's the point."

He paused, then added, "He probably watched the families of his other victims too. It's not just the killing. It's the aftermath. The slow unraveling. He toys with them. Maybe that's what he really enjoys."

Frankie's voice tightened.

"Whatever his reason. He has Emily."

A beat. Breath held.

"We need to find him. Now."

They pulled into the NYPD Transit Bureau, tires crunching across the private personnel lot.

A flash of their badges, a silent nod from the security guard, and the gate rolled open.

They drove up one level in the concrete maze of the parking

structure, found a spot, killed the engine.

Got out.

The air smelled like rubber. And city grime.

Rain still pouring. Fast. Heavy.

The sky so dark looked like it was midnight.

They crossed the lot.

Steps echoing.

Sharp. Hollow.

Each one louder than it should be.

A man waited near the entrance. Mid-fifties, buzzcut,

lanyard around his neck. The kind of guy who's been here

since dial-up internet.

Sergeant Luetti.

Quick handshakes.

No small talk.

They walked straight into the building, down narrow halls

to the surveillance room, chilled, humming with static and

LED screens.

Luetti gestured to the wall of monitors.

"We were able to spot you… and the guy who bumped into

you. But he's smart. Real smart. He stayed in the blind spots

the entire time. Got to you without ever showing his face."

Frankie leaned in. Jaw tight.

"What about the entrance and exit? Can we pick him up on another feed?"

"Maybe," Luetti shrugged. "But it's gonna take canvassing. You'll need your team… Store by store. Block by block. Hope he slipped somewhere."

Frankie nodded.

"Alright," he said.

"Let's look at it."

Screens lit up.

Mikey, the tech guy, hit a few buttons on the keyboard, then leaned back in his chair.

"There it is," he said.

The footage rolled. People going down the stairs.

"This is you there," Luetti said, pointing at the screen. "And this is your guy riiight… there. Bumping into you. Split second."

Frankie leaned in, jaw clenched. "Rewind a little… There. Stop. Look."

"What?" Luetti asked.

"Right there. A reflection." Frankie tapped the glass.

"Oh, shit. Mikey, zoom in."

They leaned forward. Mikey who was sitting on an office chair by the controls froze the frame, expanded it. A faint shape appeared in the reflection of a glass panel. Not clear, but there. A face.

Frankie pulled out his phone, searched for Edward Allen Milton, held the image beside the screen.

Kitteridge squinted. "Hard to tell."

Frankie's voice rose. "We're wasting time. We need to find Edward. Now. I don't care if it's circumstantial. Emily is out there."

Kitteridge stepped forward, voice steady of a man stating facts he'd rather not believe.

"Oakland office confirmed he's in the Bay Area. He couldn't have bumped into you, grabbed Rimler, then flown back across the country."

Frankie froze.

Blink.

Like someone yanked the floor from under him.

He hadn't considered anyone else. Not really.

Kitteridge pressed on. "We have a profile. He's on camera. Twice. We're closing in."

Frankie's jaw tensed.

"Not fast enough."

He stared at the floor.

Processing.

A second passed. Maybe two.

Then his eyes shot up.

"What if he didn't enter through this station?"

Luetti jumped in. "We checked the train cams. We didn't see your guy getting off."

"How far back did you go?" Frankie asked.

"Just the last couple trains before you showed up."

"Then we need to check the whole day."

Luetti scoffed. "That's hours of footage. We're stretched thin, bubba."

Kitteridge said, "I'll get my team on it. They'll use AI. Less than an hour."

Luetti blinked, leaning toward Mikey. "What the fuck is AI?"

Kitteridge handed over his phone. "This is our tech team lead. He'll walk you through it."

Mikey nodded, took the call, and started typing. After a moment, he handed the phone back.

Kitteridge pressed it to his ear. "This takes priority. We have an abducted detective. I want full eyes."

"What are we looking for?" the tech asked.

"White male, tall, forty to seventy. Strong build. Walks with purpose."

"Seventy?" Frankie muttered.

Kitteridge raised a finger signaling him to be quiet.

"Check all feeds. Closest stations too."

"Got it."

Kitteridge ended the call.

Frankie looked at him. "Now what?"

"Now we wait," Kitteridge replied.

"Captain wants me at the precinct for the all-hands meeting,"
Frankie said. "I'm heading there now." Kitteridge followed.

Back at the precinct, the all-hands meeting was already
filling up. Rumors about Rimler were flying. Detectives and
uniforms crammed into the briefing room. Tension hung
heavy.

Everyone loved Emily.

Everyone was restless.

Everyone wanted to move.

The captain stepped up; hands raised for quiet. No one
listened.

He slammed the table. "SHUT THE FUCK UP."

Silence.

"Earlier today, and I don't have the exact time, you can check
your notes, Detective Silva and Agent Kitteridge conducted a
welfare check on Detective Rimler. She was not home. They
did, however, find a note. It read: 'TOO LATE.'

Silva was also slipped another note the night before. The
contents confirm our suspicions. Detective Rimler has been
abducted.

This is tied to yesterday's murder. And we may be dealing
with a serial killer."

He scanned the room.

"We canvas Rimler's neighborhood. Every building. Every window. Some nosy old lady saw something. This is Brooklyn. Someone always sees something."

Frankie pushed through the door mid-meeting. Captain turned to him without missing a beat. "Anything from Transit Bureau?" he asked.

The reply came quick.

"We need to canvass the area between Atlantic Avenue–Barclays Center and Grand Army Plaza. Suspect could have entered the subway from any station in that stretch."

"Good." Captain continued. " Subway canvass starts there. Look for anything. White male, strong, suspicious. I don't care if he was just buying a fucking pretzel. If he looks off, follow up."

The captain scanned the room. Eyes sharp. Voice sharper.

"You wanna add anything?" He turned to Frankie.

Frankie stepped forward. Jaw tight.

"He doesn't look like a killer. Looks like a middle-aged to older gentleman. Well-dressed. Well-mannered."

Kitteridge appeared behind him, cutting in without missing a beat.

"We're tracing Detective Rimler's phone, we'll know more about her movements last night. Pinpoint where she was, when the signal died. Once we have that, we'll push out an APB."

The captain didn't blink.

"We don't have time. We don't have leads. We only have boots."

A pause.

"So put yours on the ground."

He took a breath.

No one moved.

"What the fuck you waiting for?"

"Let's go. Go. Go."

They all dispersed quickly, splitting into smaller teams that huddled around their leads, receiving last-minute instructions. Then the groups scattered, breaking into pairs, sprinting toward their vehicles.

Sirens lit up the borough.

Brooklyn was awake.

And hunting.

Frankie and Kitteridge walked out of the meeting and made their way through the crowded parking lot. Every unit was heading out at once. Engines revving. Radios crackling.

Frankie unlocked the car.

"I've been cutting into you for decades," Frankie said under his breath, again. Like the words might give something up if he kept repeating them.

He slid into the driver's seat. "What does that mean? How

has he been cutting into me for decades?"

Kitteridge exhaled slowly. "I don't know. Maybe he's talking about the pain you've felt. Taking credit for it."

"No. He didn't say you've *felt* pain. He said *I've been cutting.* Like it's been deliberate. Ongoing."

Kitteridge didn't answer.

Frankie turned to him. "What?"

Kitteridge looked out the windshield. "You're too close to this. Way too close. I don't think it's smart for you to keep leading it."

"Who else should? You said it yourself, I'm the center of this."

"Exactly."

Frankie let that sit for a second, jaw tight. Then: "Look. I get it. Different case, different time, maybe I'd agree. But this? This gives me an edge. I *feel* him. I can catch him."

Kitteridge muttered, "Maybe."

Frankie kept going. "It's an FBI case now anyway. Crosses multiple states. I'm just support."

"Yeah. Right," Kitteridge said. Flat. Not buying it.

They drove in silence, broken only by the hammering rain and the rhythmic whining of the windshield wipers as they drag back and forth.

Frankie cut through the tension. "We need to go back. To

his childhood. His mother's death. His sister's too."

"You still think it's Edward?" Kitteridge asked.

"Yes," Frankie said. No hesitation.

Kitteridge shook his head. "How? He's in Oakland. Thousands

of miles away. What, he teleported?"

"Private jet, maybe… I don't know… Still working it out,"

Frankie said, eyes on the road, mind racing faster than his

words."

Kitteridge sat still, eyes forward, mind processing all the

facts and evidence. Edward was a solid

suspect… But flying across the country twice in under 36

hours to pull this off?

A stretch.

Could a private flight go unlogged? Quiet enough to dodge

attention? He wouldn't trust a pilot to keep secrets. Unless

he flew himself. That would make it all possible.

Easy enough to check. FAA records. Licenses. Logs.

The rain hit harder. Wipers squealed.

Then his phone rang. He answered without hesitation.

"Special Agent Kitteridge."

A pause.

"Uh-huh… uh-huh."

The call dragged on. Kitteridge scribbled notes in a small

pad, face unreadable.

"Tiffany… Got it. Do we have her file? Great. Could you

forward it, please?"

He hung up.

Quiet for a second as he finished scribbling. Then looked over at Frankie, who was driving them back to Emily Rimler's apartment.

"Final report came in on Edward. Full records. CPS included."

Another pause. Then:

"Turns out Edward's father, Theodore Milton, was abusive in his first marriage. First wife called the cops once. Said she was sure he was going to kill her. There was a hospital visit later. The daughter, five years old, broken arm, bruises."

He exhaled, checking his notes.

"She was pulled out of school after that. Official line was homeschooling."

Frankie didn't say anything. Just kept driving. Knuckles white on the wheel.

Kitteridge spoke, eyes on his notepad. "Not long after, the wife was dead. Ruled a suicide. Nobody looked too closely. Couple years pass. He remarries."

"Wait a minute." Frankie cut in. "What were the circumstances of the suicide?"

Kitteridge flipped a few pages. "Umm… drowned in her bathtub. Pills and alcohol in her system."

Frankie's face went hollow. All the color drained.

Kitteridge's voice grew distant, muffled in Frankie's ears.

"Can't be… it can't be…" Frankie kept saying.

"Silva? You ok?" Kitteridge's voice finally broke through, clear now.

"My mother… she… no… it can't be." Frankie could barely form words.

"What about her?"

"My mother died in similar circumstances. She drowned in her bathtub. Pills. Alcohol. The ME couldn't say if it was suicide or an accident. No sign of foul play. But then the note

Like the silence after your mother sank."

Kitteridge put a hand on his shoulder. "First wife died before Edward was even born. Shitty coincidence is all. And killer said *sank,* not *drowned.* He's choosing his words carefully."

Frankie's voice was low. "Maybe he drugged her. Forced the pills down. Then put her in the tub and watched her sink…"

Neither of them spoke for a moment.

The idea hung there, heavy.

Frankie stared at the screen a moment longer, then said quietly, "Keep going."

Kitteridge nodded. "Alright. A couple years pass after Theodore Milton's first wife's suicide. He remarries. Daughter's about seven at this point. New wife gives birth to a son about a year later. Edward."

He glanced at Frankie.

"Spitting image of his father, by the way…"

Kitteridge shook his head. "No reports after that. Nothing official. Clean record. Kid grows up normal. Family's successful. Philanthropic even. Until…"

"Eleven years later. The daughter, Edward's half-sister, is found in the woods by the lake. Throat slit. No suspects. No leads. Family mourned quietly and moved on."

He turned back to Frankie.

"Since then… No trouble. Just wealth. Influence. And a spotless public image."

Frankie stared ahead. "No trouble… if no one's looking…"

A brief silence followed. Just enough to process the latest information.

Then Frankie continued, "Edward's asking us to investigate his sister's murder?"

"Maybe," Kitteridge said quietly.

"Can we get access to her file?"

"Yes." Kitteridge answered. "It's being sent to me as we speak."

Frankie pulled the car to the curb and they stepped out.

Frankie looked up at the gray sky. The rain had paused, just for a moment. Then he turned back to Kitteridge. "I think he saw his father abuse his sister. First wife was gone. Nobody around to call the cops. No one looked. No one helped. His mom was submissive. Just happy to be rich. Turned a blind eye. And Edward? Just a kid. Small. Powerless."

Kitteridge nodded. "I wouldn't be surprised if the old man forced him to take part."

"Or made him watch," Frankie said.

Silence.

"Kid grows up. Starts reenacting it."

Frankie looked Kitteridge in the eye.

"That tracks."

His phone rang as they walked past officers canvassing Emily's building. He answered it, sharp and clipped.

"Detective Silva."

He listened. Said nothing. Then: "Thank you."

He hung up and looked at Kitteridge.

"We have a match on the fingerprint. Sophia — the missing girl. Went missing Christmas Eve.

Print from her keyboard matches the one left on the pendant.

He has her."

Kitteridge's face tightened.

"He's daring us to do something about it."

Frankie nodded.

"That's not all, lab results came in.

Bleach on the body.

Blood matches the victim.

Multiple healed fractures.

She was abused. For a long time."

Kitteridge's eyes widened, gears turning.

"How long?"

Frankie's voice dropped. Flat.

"Years."

Kitteridge echoed it. Processing.

"Years…"

Frankie nodded. Grim.

"That makes sense! When he's dormant, not hunting, he's holding a captive. He finds one he wants. Keeps her. Tests her. If she's the right one, she stays. If not…" He doesn't finish.

Kitteridge's eyes flicked to Frankie. Almost lit up. A breakthrough. But then he saw Frankie's face. Something in it changed. Hollowed out. And he remembered. Frankie's sister might be one of the killer's victims. Her body was never found.

based on this new finding, signs of long-term captivity, healed fractures, she'd most likely been kept. Maybe for years.

Kitteridge's voice lowered.

Barely a whisper.

"I'm sorry."

He didn't say for what. He didn't have to.

"He kept her…" Frankie said quietly. "He… kept her? Cathy…"

"We don't know that," Kitteridge replied.

"I've been cutting into you for decades. That's what he means." Frankie's voice cracked. "He kept Cathy. Maybe for decades? No… can't be. That's impossible."

But he didn't sound convinced. He needed it to be wrong. His mind was already retreating, pushing the thought away. His body stayed still, but everything inside him was screaming.

"I told you, you're too close to this, Silva," Kitteridge said. Firm. Unflinching. "He's toying with you. He wants to hurt you."

"Bring it on," Frankie said through clenched teeth.

He can't fool Kitteridge. As tough as he wants to seem, he's hurting. Bad. And Kitteridge can see it. Every word, every breath, every silence, it's all pain, barely contained.

Frankie, trying to move forward, trying to sound steady, said, "The victim is in her late twenties, early thirties. So she couldn't have been his captive the whole time he was dormant. There must be others. Either never found or never connected to him."

"Agreed," Kitteridge replied. "FBI's already cross-referencing cold cases with a similar M.O. We'll know if anything matches soon."

He sighed hard, eyes narrowing. He wanted to help Frankie. Knew detective instincts could crack cases wide open. But Edward Milton…

As preposterous as it sounded, he had to run it through.

Test the logic.

Try to poke holes in it.

Stress-test it.

See if it held.

"Alright," he said. "I'll bite. Let's build a timeline. Tell me what you think happened."

Frankie's frown deepened.

"Alright. He flies to New York to dump a body. Let's say he owns an estate here. Maybe under a shell company. Maybe inherited. That's where he kept our vic. He kills her, does the deed, dumps the body early Sunday morning. Then flies back to Oakland. Makes sure he's seen. Normal day."

"What about his wife and kids?" Kitteridge asked.

"Either they're used to him disappearing or he tells them he's got business. Something they don't question."

"Okay," Kitteridge said. "Go on."

"Sunday afternoon he flies back to New York. Slips the notes. Abducts Emily. Stashes her at the same estate. Then flies back to Oakland again. Only times he's missing are late afternoon and overnight. Not unusual enough to draw attention."

Kitteridge stared ahead.

Didn't say anything.

Not yet.

"So if your theory's right…" Kitteridge finally said. "Detective Rimler's alone. In captivity. Right now."

Yes." Frankie's voice was tight. The weight of it hit him all at once.

"We need to find her. Now.

And we need Edward in custody."

Kitteridge stared at him, quiet. Still processing. But the pieces were starting to fit. Not neatly. But enough to see the shape.

He exhaled through his nose, pulled out his phone, and stepped aside, dialing.

The call dragged. Kitteridge paced slowly, voice low.

Nodded. Argued. Paused to listen. Argued again.

Frankie waited by the car, watching the rain sheet across the windshield.

Finally, Kitteridge hung up. Face unreadable.

"They're not buying the whole thing," he said.

Frankie cursed under his breath.

"But," Kitteridge added, "I convinced them to interview him, at least… He'll be held for maybe 2 hours max." He looked at Frankie.

"They'll call us once they have him," Kitteridge added.

"Alright, let's get to work. See if we can place him near Emily's building," Frankie said, already moving. He held out a printed photo of Edward he'd pulled from an online search.

"This man, did you see him around here last night?"

Most shook their heads. A few barely looked.

Doors closed just as quickly as they'd opened.

No one recognized him.

No one saw anything.

And time kept slipping.

Media showed up, of course. Cameras. Questions. Shouting. They swarmed Frankie, but he just grunted and kept walking.

Kitteridge stepped in. "This is an active investigation. We can't discuss it."

They pushed through, exhausted every lead they could find.

The footage the FBI team had been combing through finally came back. Nothing.

No sign of the guy in the hoodie. No footage of him entering any station.

It didn't make sense.

Despair started to creep in. Quiet. Heavy.

Then Kitteridge's phone rang. He answered fast. Listened. Nodded once.

"Edward's in custody," he said, tilting the phone slightly

away from his mouth. "they're on their way to the office."

He asked to be patched in to observe. They agreed.

He looked at Frankie. "Let's go."

They got back in the car and drove to the precinct.

Parked, what felt like the millionth time, and walked in. Past

busy desks, neon lights above their heads, ringing phones…

The precinct was alive. Humming with pressure.

Detective missing. All hands on deck. Everyone moving.

Everyone helping.

Even O'Malley was on the phone, taking down a tip.

Not his usual asshole self. Voice low. Focused.

Saw Frankie. Just gave a nod and turned back to the caller.

No one was joking. No one was leaning back in their chairs.

One of their own is missing…

Frankie and Kitteridge cut through the noise, reached

Frankie's desk.

Kitteridge opened his laptop. Logged in. The screen lit up.

The signal came through and they got patched into the live

feed.

Edward sitting alone in a metal chair. In front of a metal

table. Cold room. No agents yet.

He looked calm. Collected.

Not fidgeting. One leg crossed over the other.

Leaning back. Waiting. Confident.

Frankie leaned in. Eyes locked on the screen. Studying

every shift in posture. Every blink. Trying to psychoanalyze

a pixelated shape.

Then it happened.

Edward looked up. Right at the camera.

Right at Frankie.

Held the stare for a beat. Calm.

Then looked away. Like it meant nothing.

Just like the gas mask perp.

Frankie froze. Chills surged up his spine and settled like pins in the back of his neck.

It was him. He could feel it.

Edward knew. He was watching. And he was taunting him.

Frankie felt it deep in his chest.

This was personal now. Him versus Edward.

His heart thudded like a fighter stepping into the ring. A

warrior about to charge.

His grip tightened on the back of the chair in front of him,

knuckles whitening. Laser focused. Locked in.

You're not getting away with this, he thought.

You killed my sister. My mother died because of you. You took

Emily. You tortured them all.

This ends with me.

Finally, an agent enters the room.

Chapter 12
Captives

Basement.

Damp. Smells like rot.

Mold festers on the walls.

Air thick. Wet.

Silent.

Soundproof.

Chains dangle from the ceiling.

Rusted hooks at the ends.

Rust mixed with dried blood.

Hair stuck to them. Bone fragments clinging.

They sway slightly.

Creaking in the stillness.

Remnants of an evil that visits here.

A stained mattress rots in the corner, soaked with years of suffering.

The air is thick, damp. Smells like blood, piss and shit.

A single bulb hangs from a frayed cord above. Flickering. Humming.

In the center of the room stands a thick wooden post.

She's chained to it.

Arms wrapped around like she's hugging it. Ankles bound.

Completely exposed. Naked. Shivering.

Her face is fully wrapped in duct tape. All but two tiny holes, carved where her nostrils are.

Each breath is a struggle. Each second, a fight.

Claustrophobia gnawing at her.

Terror keeps her awake.

He visits every few hours.

Urinates on her. Whips her. Rapes her. Then leaves.

Every few hours, the basement doorknob creaks and like

Pavlov's dog, she whimpers. He comes down the stairs.

She's fully exposed. Immobile.

She feels his urine on her back, her legs.

She trembles. Just how he likes it.

He violates her while she slips in and out of consciousness.

The basement doorknob creaks.

The captive shivers.

Nowhere to hide.

She hears footsteps.

Then a thud and a whimper.

Another girl. Dragged in. Groggy. Drugged.

Could barely lift her head. Tries anyway.

Sees the captive.

Going in and out of view as the single light sways.

The bulb swings.

She catches a glimpse.

Sees her bound.

What the fuck.

Her heart pounds.

Breath shrinks.

Light fades.

Returns.

She sees more.

Naked.

Shaking.

A chilling sensation runs up and down her spine. She almost

pees herself.

Dark again.

Then light.

She sees the face.

Completely duct-taped.

Terror floods through her system, unchecked. Unregulated.

It takes over before she can even breathe.

Complete horror-induced paralysis.

She is tough.

But not enough for this.

A man walks down the basement stairs, calm and casual,

like this place is just another room in his house. He doesn't

rush. Doesn't speak. Just moves with the quiet confidence of

someone who knows no one will stop him.

He mutters a few words.

Too low to hear.

Like he's talking to someone.

Or maybe to himself.

He frees the captive from the post, grabs her by the shoulder, and kicks her across the floor. She slides on the concrete, skin tearing as she goes. She doesn't scream. Doesn't fight. Just folds into herself, arms pulled in, knees to her chest, shackles biting into her skin.

No bearings. No sense of time. Pain is the only truth she knows.

Then he grabs the new one.

She whispers a scream.

"No… no… no… Why are you doing this??"

In her head, she is screaming.

Thrashing.

Fighting.

But her body is drugged.

Useless.

All it gives him is a whisper.

But even that is too loud for his liking.

He punches her in the stomach.

Full force.

She crumples. Gasping.

He binds her to the post.

Another punch.

Lower. The kidney.

She can't breathe.

Then, duct tape.

Across her face.

No air. No holes.

She thrashes.

Convulses.

He watches.

Smirking.

Hard.

Then he finally pokes the holes.

She breathes. Barely.

He strips her from the waist down.

Leaves her clothed on top.

The contrast makes her feel more naked.

More exposed.

She gets violated.

Her legs are bound.

Speaks as he works.

"You can stay as my captive… or I cut you up like cattle."

His voice:

Whiny. Weak. High pitch. Butchering words.

He talks like a clumsy accountant with taped eyeglasses.

The kind who packs tuna sandwiches and labels his fruit so

no one takes them. The kind who eats alone, afraid someone

might sit too close.

The kind of voice that tells you

he's never been laid.

Never will be.

Except he's not clumsy.

And he's not weak.

He continues:

"I sever your limbs while you scream.

Slit your throat.

Dump you like the fucking trash you are.

Or…

You stay here. With me.

You'll have some good days.

Days without punishment.

Live upstairs.

TV…"

"HMM mmm," she mumbles. Face duct taped.

He leans in.

"What?"

"HMM mmm," she growls louder, shaking her head violently.

"Hmm mmm. Hmm mm. Hmmm mm."

He grabs his knife.

Slices a small hole near her lips.

She spits the words out.

"Fuck you. Kill me.

"I'd rather have…"

She struggles to inhale. Already out of breath.

"…my limbs severed…" Still fighting. Voice rasping.

"…every day while I scream…" A gasp. One last breath.

"…than spend one more minute here with you."

Another gasp.

Tough gal.

Not for long.

He leans in.

Close.

So close she can feel his breath through the duct tape.

Hot. Damp.

Smells like licorice.

He wants her to hear him.

Wants his words to crawl inside her.

Finally, he speaks.

"The ways I am going to hurt…"

Bam.

She interrupts him.

'Rudely'.

Headbutt to the nose.

Crunch.

Breaks.

"Fuck you," she spits.

He screams in pain.

Staggering.

She lifts her head.

Breath ragged.

"Do."

Inhales.

"Your."

Breathes again.

"Worst."

Across the room, the captive on the floor stiffens.

She cannot see.

But she hears his scream.

Feels the fury that follows.

The new girl hurt him.

And for the first time in a long while…

She feels something.

Goosebumps.

Joy.

Strange feeling.

He clutches his nose. Blood streams through his fingers.

Breathing hard. Animal rage.

Then silence.

He calms.

Smiles.

Almost pleased.

She gave him a reason.

He walks away. She hears his footsteps.

Can't see a thing.

Face still duct-taped.

Then…

A sound. Something heavy dragged across the floor.

The captive hears it too.

Flinches.

He moves toward her.

Slow. Deliberate.

The sound that follows…

Not words.

Not human.

Pain.

Pure and raw.

Screams escape the small hole he carved in her mask.

Screams through shredded breath while he rapes her with

a bat. Violently.

When it stops, she sags against the post.

Whimpering.

"Kill me," she cries.

"Kill me…"

He smirks through the blood, nose still leaking down his lip.

His voice stays whiny, out of place in the horror he creates,

like a child playing villain in a school play. He leans in, eyes

gleaming with something close to joy.

"Let's play a little game," he says. "It's called *Would You Rather*.

Would you rather I kill you… or kill her?"

He points at the captive on the floor. Still. Barely conscious.

"Kill me," she says without hesitation. "Kill me."

He tilts his head.

"And keep torturing her for years?"

That lands.

She stammers.

The trap snaps shut.

"I'll let you think about it," he says.

Then turns away.

Still smiling.

Still bleeding.

Faces the captive on the floor.

Walks toward her.

She recognizes that walk.

The *I'm about to do my worst* walk.

She trembles.

Flinches back.

He grabs her by the hair.

Violent.

Drags her across the floor.

Yanks the duct tape from her face.

Hair rips.

Skin with it.

Her eyes take time to adjust.

When they do, she sees the new girl chained to the post.

Horrific.

He punches her in the stomach.

She crumbles. Gasping.

Then he lifts her by the legs.

Hooks them.

Right through her Achilles.

Onto the rusted chains.

She screams.

Keeps screaming.

Until her voice breaks.

She hangs.

Swinging.

He grabs the whip.

Starts.

Doesn't stop.

Keeps going until he can't breathe.

Then drops it.

Carries her off the hooks to the table in the corner.

Blood-stained wood.

Old. Heavy.

Spreads her limbs.

One by one.

She tries to scream, but no sound comes out.

Her throat's too raw, her voice long gone.

He locks each limb in leather straps.

Chains tight.

Then he walks back to the new girl.

Removes the tape from her eyes.

Tapes her mouth shut.

Her eyes adjust.

The table comes into focus.

She sees the captive.

Strapped down.

Limbs stretched.

The table has piping along the edges.

Drainage tubes.

Running down into buckets.

Then he returns.

Wearing a plastic coat.

Pushing a stainless steel cart.

Carving knives on it.

Bone saws.

All laid out.

Clean.

Ready.

He grabs the hose, turns the valve. Freezing water slams into her body. She jerks against the restraints, a broken scream trying to push past the duct tape. Too weak to fight, too alert to fade out.

He clips on the spinning scrub head, lets the pressure drive it, then starts scrubbing. Hard. Efficient. Like he's done it a hundred times.

Her skin opens. She cries out. He doesn't blink.

Then comes the bleach. He pours it slow, deliberate, across the raw flesh. Lets it sit. Lets it burn. She writhes, strapped down, helpless.

He hoses her again, rinsing away the blood, the skin, the dignity.

He empties the buckets with care, pouring the thick runoff directly into the floor drain. Not a drop spilled. He moves with habit, like it's routine. Like it's necessary. Then he sets the buckets back in place beneath the drainage pipes. Everything exactly where it belongs.

Precise.

Practiced.

Perfect.

The new girl stays tied to the post, body aching, brain fogged. She blinks against the low light. Everything feels slow. She still can't remember how she got here. Not clearly. But that guy… He looks familiar. Somehow.

She tries to follow his movements.

But her head won't clear.

Then he's gone. Next door maybe. Another room? Hard to tell. The captive still stretched out on the table.

She hears footsteps.

Then the water starts.

Shower. Running hard.

Ten minutes. Maybe more.

Then silence.

Another set of footsteps.

Closer this time.

Then a door slams.

And then…

Nothing.

The new girl exhales. Slowly. The tape across her mouth is loose. Damp. She works her jaw until it slips away.

She turns toward the table. Toward the woman.

"Are you okay? What is happening?"

The captive barely moves. Her head shifts. A slow shake. No.

"What the fuck is going on? How long have you been here? We should try to escape."

"Shut… up," the captive mutters. Voice dry. Barely there.

The new girl blinks. Confused.

Then she thinks she understands.

"It's okay," she whispers. "He left. I heard him leave."

Silence.

Then the captive speaks again.

"He likes to trick.

He likes to test.

We can't talk."

"Has he done it before? Tricked you like that? Does he have

cameras down here?"

Silence.

Then,

"I don't know," she said. "I could never tell."

He didn't.

Surprisingly, he never used cameras. He liked the real thing.

The smell. The stench.

Too arrogant to believe anyone could escape. Never felt the

need.

"Has he brought others?" the new girl asks.

A pause.

"There's two of them," the captive says.

"Two girls?" the new girl asks.

Unclear.

She's slipping. In and out. Trying to say as much as she can

before it's too late.

"He's gonna kill me tonight," the captive says. Her voice

thin, stretched tight over pain.

She's still strapped to the table. Barely conscious. Eyes half-open. Breath ragged.

The new girl doesn't know what to say. Her mind races, but nothing lands.

What the fuck is happening.

What is this place.

How is this real.

She manages to speak.

"Don't think that way. You don't know for sure," the new girl says, trying to sound steady, like hope is still something they can hold.

The captive shakes her head. Weak. Barely breathing.

"You don't understand…"

She coughs. Swallows hard.

"If I die… I'm free…"

She catches her breath.

"But… then it's you." Her voice breaks in the middle. She rests for a moment, pulling in what little air her lungs will allow. Her eyes stay open, locked on something that isn't there.

She breathes.

Then finishes.

"You become his slave."

A fact.

And a curse.

She coughs. Blood.

Barely breathing.

She closes her eyes. Her body's failing. Every breath harder than the last. Whether it's tonight or tomorrow, she knows she won't survive much longer. Something inside her is giving out.

She starts mumbling names, like she's talking to people in the room. People who aren't there. Maybe never were. She even smiles once. The kind of smile that breaks your heart to see.

She stared at the ceiling, lips cracked, whispering nonsense only she could understand. "Butterflies…" She said.

A pair of moths fluttered near the lightbulb, dusty wings dancing through the dark.

She smiled, eyes glassy. In her mind, they were butterflies. Free. Weightless.

She imagined herself rising like that one day.

Free.

The new girl watched, still paralyzed by terror.

But she is tough.

She is tough.

She keeps saying it in her head like a prayer. Like armor.

"Listen," she whispers. "You are not getting killed tonight. We need to fight. We can get out of these shackles. Let's think."

No answer.

"Hey. Hey, stay with me. Listen. Tell me about yourself, okay? What's your name? Where you from?"

Nothing.

"Shit… Hey!" Her voice cracks. "Can you hear me?"

Silence.

Still.

Cold.

Like death's already in the room.

Scratch that.

Death never left the room.

She's on her knees now, slumped against the wooden post. Arms wrapped around it like a child clinging to a tree in a storm. Ankles shackled. Naked from the waist down.

She's bleeding from the savage rape. Wet. Pee cooling against her skin.

Every breath is work.

Every inch of her body screams.

She has no idea what time it is.

Could be dawn.

Could be next year.

She drifts.

Comes back.

Drifts again.

She wakes to the sound of a loud, wet cough. Sharp and raw, like something tearing loose inside a dying animal. Her eyes blink open, slow and confused. Everything hurts. Her head. Her legs. Her ribs. The cold has settled into her bones.

Then she hears it again.

The girl on the table.

Alive.

Coughing.

It snaps her upright. Not much, but enough.

"Hey," she calls out, voice trembling. "What's your name?"

The girl gurgles blood. Tries to breathe through it. Chokes it down. She draws whatever strength she has left.

"Mary" she says. "My name is Mary…"

"How long you been down here Mary?"

"I don't know. Years…"

The words hang in the air.

Like rot.

The new girl's heart drops.

Years.

Of this.

Her stomach turns.

Eyes burn.

Oh sweet death, come deliver this person, she thinks.

Please.

"Every girl he brings him…" Mary's voice is barely a whisper, wet with blood. "He asks me… if she should replace me… or if he should kill her."

She coughs. Blood splatters across her chest.

It takes everything she has to keep talking.

"He wants me to choose…"

She trembles. Eyes unfocused. Body failing.

"I couldn't let anyone… go through what I went through."

Another cough. Longer this time. Her whole body shakes.

"So… I tell him not to replace me."

A pause. A breath.

"I tell him to kill them."

The words hit like ice. A slow, creeping shock climbs up her spine and wraps around her throat. She thought she was tough. Strong enough to survive anything. But now, hearing this… hearing what Mary chose, what she's endured…

She realizes.

She doesn't know what tough is.

Mary does.

Tough is years in hell.

Tough is choosing to get tortured so others don't suffer.

Tough is still breathing after that.

Mary, she thought to herself. The name echoed in her chest like a weight too heavy to hold. Then she said it out loud, needing Mary to hear it.

"Mary," she whispered. "You're a hero. You're an angel. You're a saint."

She blinked through tears. Voice steady, breaking only at the edges.

"Don't fight anymore. I'll be okay. I'm tough. I swear I'm tough."

A pause. A breath.

Go in peace. Go to sleep. You've had enough. Go rest now," the new girl whispered. Her voice was steady, but her heart wasn't. "Don't worry about me."

Mary knew.

Whether she fought or not, her time was up.

Seconds left.

Maybe less.

She looked toward the voice.

Blood on her lips.

Eyes soft.

She managed eleven final words.

Then exhaled.

One last time.

And she was gone.

Her head fell gently to the side.

Finally.

At peace.

The door opens. Then shuts again.

He's back.

The new girl freezes. Her heart races, pounding in her
throat. Fear spreads across her skin like cold sweat. Sticky.

Inevitable.

Footsteps.

Then the basement door creaks.

Shuts behind him.

She watches him walk down the stairs. Calm. Blank.

No words. No sounds.

He walks straight to Mary.

Stops. Looks.

Takes one glance and knows.

She's dead.

He knows death.

He walks to a closet by the wall. Opens it. Pulls out a plastic
suit. Full cover. Even his shoes. He puts it on without a word.
Then grabs a saw.

He drags over a rolling stool, settles beside the table like
a man preparing for routine work. No hesitation. He picks
up the saw and gets to work, carving through flesh and bone
with the kind of precision that only comes from repetition.
No rush. No pause. It takes hours.

He never stops.

When it's done, he threads the needle.

Thick twine. Coarse and stiff.

Sews her legs where her arms should be.

Arms where her legs were.

Botched. Grotesque. Wrong.

Then he slices her throat.

Stitches it shut.

He carves a smile into her face, slow and deliberate, like he's drawing a final insult. Then he stitches it shut with the same rough twine, sealing it into something cruel and permanent.

"There," he mutters.

He turns.

Walks to the far wall and wheels over a large, custom-built barrel. The inside is lined with a clean tarp, fresh and waiting. He flips Mary onto it, face down, her limbs still sewn wrong, her mouth grinning against its will.

Then he disappears into another room behind the basement wall.

She hears it. Car doors. A heavy thud. Doors slam shut. Engine starts. Garage door lifts.

The car drives off.

Silence follows.

She breathes. Still here. Still next.

She's more alert now. The pain is still there, gnawing at her from the inside, but her mind is clearer. She thinks of Mary.

Her voice. Her final breath. Those six words.

She inhales. Exhales. And gets to work.

She twists, grinds, shifts her weight. Minutes blur into

hours. Her wrists are raw. Ankles bleeding. She hasn't had

water in over a day. No food. No rest. Her stomach cramps.

Her mouth tastes like rust.

Eventually, she collapses.

Body giving out.

Mind barely hanging on.

Darkness.

Then noise.

The garage door groans open. A car pulls in. Basement door creaks.

She hears him before she sees him. Heavy steps. Breathing heavy.

He drags another woman behind him.

She blinks hard.

Tries to sit up.

He yanks the woman by the arm and punches her hard in

the stomach. She folds. He drops her to the floor like garbage,

then walks over to the girl still tied to the post. Her face is

exposed now, the tape loose from earlier.

Without a word, he grabs a fresh strip. Wraps her face.

Tight. Full.

Only two small holes left to breathe.

Then he turns and leaves.

No words.

Footsteps crunching on the dirty floor. A door creaks, then

closes behind him.

Complete. Deafening. Silence.

The woman groans, eyes unfocused.

She looks at the girl on the post, trying to make sense of what she's seeing.

She can't. It's too much.

The human brain wasn't built to process that kind of horror.

Her limbs tremble as she tries to move. Disoriented. But something in her refuses to stay down. She blinks hard, locks her eyes on the girl at the post, and starts crawling.

Each inch costs her. But she keeps going.

She reaches the post, one hand dragging the other. Her breath is shallow, her voice cracked, but she forces the words out anyway.

"Don't worry… I'll get you out. I'll get you out…"

She leans her head against the post, tries to steady her voice.

"I'm a cop… I'm a cop…"

She tries to say it again.

"I'm a co…"

Then collapses. Face down. Out cold. Breathing shallow.

Chapter 13
The interrogation

AGENT YOUNG: "Thank you for coming, Mr. Milton. We appreciate your cooperation. I'm Special Agent Young."

EDWARD: "Of course. Happy to help. What's this about?"

YOUNG: "Do you remember Cathy Silva? She went missing in '97. Last seen at your house party."

Edward leaned back slightly.

"Cathy Silva," he said. "Wow. I haven't heard that name in ages. Always felt bad about that. Went missing after leaving my party."

A pause.

"Was her body found?"

"What makes you think she's dead?" Agent Young asked.

Edward was caught off guard. He stammered.

"I just… assumed."

Agent Young held his stare for a beat, then continued.

"No. There's an active case in New York. Details are limited, but there may be a connection. We were hoping you might remember anything about Cathy. About that night."

"I didn't really know her," Edward said. Calm. Measured.

"I knew her friend, Inez."

"Cathy," he continued. "She seemed nice. Kind. I always felt bad she went missing after my party."

He paused, reflective but composed.

"She'd just been accepted to Berkeley, if I'm not mistaken. Impressive. Bright girl."

Another beat.

"Had a future."

"Where did you know her friend," the agent said, glancing down at his notes. He found the name, then looked back up. "Inez. Where did you know her from?"

Edward let out a low whistle.

"Pretty much my whole life," he said. "Our parents were friends. Always were. We knew them forever. Used to vacation together sometimes."

He paused, then explained further,

"I mostly hung out with her brother. David. He was a bit older than me, but… you know… we got along."

"Got it," Young said. "What do you remember about that night?"

Edward shuffled in his seat trying to get comfortable in vain.

"Oh god… it was over twenty years ago," Edward said. "A typical high school party. I don't remember much. Music. Too many people. Nothing out of the ordinary. At least not that night. Well…"

He paused like he just remembered something.

"Well what?" Detective Young said, leaning closer.

"Nothing," Edward said, smiling. "Someone keyed my car that night, that's all."

He shook his head, like it was silly.

In New York, Frankie's eyes lit up as he watched the interview on the screen. A rush of adrenaline hit him all at once. He grabbed Kitteridge's arm, squeezing hard.

"We got him," he said under his breath.

Kitteridge turned to him, startled.

"What just happened?"

Frankie smiled, eyes fixed on the screen.

"I got you, motherfucker."

On the screen, Detective Young tilted his head.

"Oh?" he said. "You make any enemies that night?"

"Who knows," Edward said, still smiling. "I don't recall getting into any tiffs with anyone, but people will people, you know."

Detective Young let out a small chuckle.

"Yeah," he said. "People will people."

A pause.

"I remember hearing the news the next day." Edward Continued. Serious now. "Cathy went missing."

"Do you currently own any property in New York?" Young asked.

Edward's brow lifted. Trying to make the connection.

"Am I a suspect?"

"We're gathering information," Young said. "Trying to eliminate you as a person of interest."

"I don't understand," Edward said. "Did you find something that connects me to this?"

"Not directly," Young said. "But you might have details that help us. Your cooperation would mean a lot."

Edward paused. His eyes narrowed slightly.

"Am I free to go?"

"Yes," Young said.

Edward glanced at his watch. Thought about it. Then exhaled.

"Alright," he said. "What was your question?"

"Do you own property in New York?" Young asked.

"I don't," Edward said. "But our company does. We have a warehouse out there. Haven't used it in a while."

"When was the last time you were in New York?" Young asked.

Edward hesitated. Then smiled faintly.

"Sounds like I need a lawyer."

"We're just trying to rule you out," Young said.

"Why do I need to be ruled out?" Edward asked.

"Because of the Cathy Silva connection," Young said. "We're crossing some T's. Dotting some I's. That's all."

Edward shifted in his chair.

"We were all in New York last weekend," he said. "Meetings in the city. One of our acquisitions is about to go public."

"Who's we?" Young asked.

"Board members. Myself. My father. A couple of investors."

Frankie's eyes snapped to Kitteridge.

"Did I just hear that right?"

Kitteridge didn't answer. He leaned closer to the screen,
eyes fixed, not willing to miss a word.

"When did you get back?" Young asked.

"Sunday morning," Edward said. "We flew out around seven.
My father stayed behind to wrap up a few things before the
IPO."

"Which airport?" Young cut in.

"Private," Edward said.

A beat.

"Out of Brooklyn."

Frankie scoffed, more to himself than anyone else.

The phone on his desk rang.

Kitteridge grabbed the laptop and stepped to another desk.

Frankie picked up the call. His expression shifted, eyebrows
narrowing, jaw clenched.

He hung up slowly, eyes locking on Kitteridge.

"They have DNA," he said.

"What?"

"They found a dried blood spot. On the twine. Not the
victim's."

Kitteridge picked up the phone, eyes still locked on the

screen. It rang a couple of times. On the live feed, they watched Agent Young glance at his cell. He excused himself and stepped out of the room.

Young answered. "Kitteridge, what's up?"

"Ask him if he's willing to volunteer a DNA swab. Just say it's to rule him out."

"He's not gonna agree."

"I know. I want to see how he reacts."

"Alright."

Young walked back into the room. "Sorry about that."

Edward nodded. "Did you get everything you need? I really have to go."

"Almost done. Thank you again for your time. Just one last thing. Would you be willing to do a cheek swab for our records? It won't take long. Helps us eliminate you completely."

Edward smiled. "Sure. If you think it'll help."

Frankie's jaw slackened. Kitteridge's eyes went wide. The floor felt like it dropped out from under them. For the first time, they had a real shot at material evidence. One way or another, they'd finally get an answer.

"I don't get it," Frankie muttered.

"He's volunteering his DNA without a fight," Kitteridge said, still staring. "He must be sure he never left any trace behind."

"We got you now, fucker," Frankie said under his breath.

Edward shifted in his seat. "On second thought… I'd prefer you go through my lawyer. With a warrant. Best to go through the proper channels."

"Motherfucker…" Frankie growled. "He's toying with us."

Young stuttered, caught off guard. "Oh… yeah. Certainly. Thanks again for your time, Mr. Milton."

"Anytime," Milton said, smiling.

"Oh, Mr. Milton… almost forgot," Young added as Milton turned toward the door.

"Were you close with Tiffany?"

Edward stopped mid-step. Turned back. "Tiffany?"

"Your half-sister."

Edward looked at him, steady. "Yes. I was close with my *sister.*"

He stressed the word, *sister*, like there was no half about it. She *was* his sister.

"She helped raise me," he said, voice stern. "Until she was killed."

No flicker. No crack in the mask. Just that same calm, measured tone.

"Anything else, Agent?" Edward asked.

"No," Young said. "Nothing else. Thanks again."

He led Edward out of the interrogation room.

In New York, Frankie and Kitteridge watched Edward leave

through the live feed.

Kitteridge turned to Frankie, urgency creeping into his voice.

"So? What was it?"

Frankie didn't take his eyes off the screen.

"My best friend from back then was at the party," he said. "At the time, he claimed he didn't see anything. I always suspected he did. Just a gut feeling."

He paused.

"I called him yesterday. He admitted he keyed a rich kid's car. The host's. Edward's. Said he was caught."

Kitteridge's frown deepened.

Frankie continued.

"My friend, Mo, says that Edward came out of the bushes. Disheveled. Like he'd been in a fight. He saw Mo key the car. Then he just went back inside. Like nothing happened."

Another beat.

"And get this," Frankie said. "White SUV."

Kitteridge closed the laptop. Stood up. Took a slow loop around the room, eyes flicking left and right, working through it.

"Is your friend willing to sign an affidavit?" he asked.

"Yes," Frankie said. "I'm sure he will."

"He declined the cheek swab," Frankie added, letting it land.

Kitteridge nodded.

"Not unusual. Most people don't hand over DNA without a warrant."

A pause.

"But…"

Frankie got it immediately.

"We can get one with Mo's affidavit."

"Yes," Kitteridge said. "Probable cause for a buccal swab and a property search."

He went quiet for a moment.

"What is it?" Frankie asked, noticing the shift.

"One thing stood out," Kitteridge said.

Frankie glanced at him.

"He loved his sister," Kitteridge said. "He didn't kill her."

Frankie's jaw tightened.

He didn't respond.

Just stared ahead, lost in thought.

A knock on his open office door cut through his thoughts.

"Detective Frankie Silva?"

Frankie looked up. "Yeah, that's me."

"Evidence box came in from cold case. It's downstairs. Gladys signed for it.

"Rachael Cohen," Frankie muttered, the name flashing in his memory. He stood, grabbing his coat. "She was local. From Brooklyn. This must be her evidence box."

Kitteridge perked up. "Let's go."

They made their way down into the archives basement.

Cold, quiet, footsteps echoing off the stone and concrete. The air smelled like dust and forgotten time.

Gladys sat behind the thick glass window. No attitude today—just concern. Her face softened when she saw them.

"Paypuhwork's ready," she said, slidin' the clipboard across. "Sign right theyah."

Frankie signed.

She handed him a slip of paper. "Row sixteen, shelf B. Already pulled it. Badge?"

Kitteridge held his out. She copied the info, buzzed them through.

As they pushed open the heavy metal door, she called out. "Hey, Silva."

Frankie turned back.

"Get this fucka', will ya?"

He nodded. "Yes, ma'am."

And they disappeared through the heavy door into the cold belly of the archives. Rows of steel shelves stretched out like skeleton ribs, everything dim except for flickering fluorescents overhead. The air was still, heavy with the scent of dust, cardboard, and old stories.

Each step echoed on the concrete, their shoes clicking in

unison as they passed box after box labeled in fading ink.

Years. Victims. Numbers. Lives.

"Row sixteen, shelf B," Frankie muttered. "Here." He

pointed.

They stepped closer. He reached for the box. It was tiny.

Much smaller than expected. Too small. He held it a moment

before opening, like it might breathe or bite. Then carefully

peeled back the lid.

Inside: a stained scarf. A silver watch. That's it.

"We should retest the scarf for DNA," Kitteridge said.

"Science is a lot more advanced today."

"Agreed," Frankie said. "Run it against Edward's. If we get

the warrant."

Kitteridge nodded in agreement.

They closed the box and set it back on the shelf. Then

walked out of the graveyard of evidence and past Glady's

desk.

"Ya found what ya was lookin' fo'?" she asked, eyes still on

her paperwork.

"Thanks," Frankie said, not answering the question.

"You'll get 'em next time…" she muttered, tapping a stack

of papers even on the desk before spinning in her chair and

filing them in a cabinet behind her. "It's the little things that

get ya."

"Yeah…" he said, not really hearing her.

Then he paused mid-step.

"It's the little things that get ya," Gladys had said, almost to herself.

But it hit him like a brick.

He turned to Kitteridge.

"Berkeley," he said.

Kitteridge looked at him. "What about it?"

"Edward. He said she got into Berkeley."

"Yeah?"

Frankie's voice was low. Steady.

"She'd been going to community college," Frankie said. "We got the letter that she'd been accepted to UC Berkeley after she went missing. No one knew. Just me and my mother."

The noose was tightening on Edward. They could both feel it. Still, something made Kitteridge hesitate. He wasn't rushing to conclusions.

He nodded slowly.

"Your mother could've told someone. A friend. A neighbor. Word gets around. It's not a slam dunk."

Frankie shook his head.

"She didn't. She barely spoke after Cathy disappeared. She didn't even open the letter at first. I did."

The silence that followed was different. Heavy. Intentional. A pause meant to stop the argument before it started.

Kitteridge kept going, trying to make it make sense.

"So if even Cathy didn't know she got accepted, how would he have come across that information? If neither you nor your mother told anyone?"

"I don't know," Frankie said. "Maybe he broke into our home. Saw the envelope…"

He stopped mid sentence.

"Oh fuck," he said quietly.

"What?" Kitteridge asked, already bracing.

"The scarf," Frankie said, voice low. "I knew I'd seen it somewhere."

He pulled out his phone hands shaking and scrolled through an album of old photos. Pictures he had taken of the originals. Preserved.

Swiping fast. Then he stopped. zoomed with his fingers, "There."

He held it up. A photo of Cathy and Inez in Cathy's bedroom. Laughing. Late afternoon light cutting through sheer curtains. Posters of *Alanis Morissette* and *Buffy* on the wall. Beaded lamp on the nightstand. CD tower by the bed. And on the back of a chair, the scarf.

Hanging beside a mess of yarn and a half-finished friendship bracelet.

Kitteridge leaned in. Quiet now.

"That's the same scarf from Rachael Cohen's evidence box,"

he said. Completely taken aback.

"The little things," Frankie said, tapping the phone against

his other hand

Chapter 14
Legacy

It's freezing down in the basement. The kind of cold and mold

that gets in your bones. Soaks your lungs. Makes you sick.

Wet. Smelly. Death lives here. Evil festers here.

How many women were held here? Tortured. Dismembered.

The girl tied to the post is coughing. Hard. A wet cough.

Six words. She remembers Mary's six words.

Post Bottom Weak Help Next Girl

She understood now. The bottom of the post was weak. If

she kept at it, kept trying, one day it would give.

From what she tried so far, it didn't even budge. Not even a

little.

All the work Mary did wasn't for her.

It was for the next girl.

And the next.

And the next.

A legacy.

Each girl passing it down until one finally breaks free.

Grabs the bat.

Kills the fucker.

The cop lady stirred. Groaning. Right beside her.

It was freezing. She was shivering.

Her eyes opened slowly, scanning the basement. She could

barely move.

She looked at the girl tied to the post.

Got up. Slow.

She reached out with her cuffed hands and peeled the tape

off the girl's mouth then eyes and face.

The girl took a deep breath.

"You're a cop?"

"Yes."

"We need to get out of here," she said, voice trembling. "He

killed another woman down here. Cut off her limbs… then

stitched them back on. Real psycho."

She hesitated. Eyes darting. Breath shaking.

"He raped me," she added, barely audible. "With a bat."

The cop lady stood up slowly. Something wasn't right.

Why wasn't she chained up?

She went straight to the girl strapped to the post. Tried the

cuffs, the shackles. Nothing gave. The metal was solid, rusted

deep into the concrete. But she peeled the tape off her mouth.

Then she explored. Every inch of the place.

The basement was massive. Like a dungeon.

She found the meat grinder first. Industrial size. The smell

stopped her cold.

Thick. Metallic. Cadavers.

What is this place?

Why are we here?

She tried the door to the garage. Steel. Bolted. No keypad,

no handle. Just a slab of metal that wouldn't move.

She walked back to the girl. "What's your name?"

The girl opened her mouth, but didn't get the chance to answer.

The door creaked shut upstairs. Heavy. Deliberate.

He was back.

They heard his steps descending, slow, calm, like he had all the time in the world.

His nose was wrapped in a fresh bandage.

He saw the girl chained to the post, duct tape peeled off her mouth. His eyes flicked to the cop.

She looked terrified.

Young. Fresh out of the academy. Still had the shine of training on her.

She'd pulled him over for a busted tail light. Routine stop.

He had a bloody nose…

and a body in the back of the van.

She asked him to step out.

Calm voice. Just protocol.

He nodded. Compliant.

She turned slightly, angled toward the radio on her shoulder.

Something was off. White van, bloody nose, that smell.

She wanted backup. Just in case.

That's when he hit her.

Quick. Clean. Right in the throat.

She dropped, gasping.

Before she could reach for her weapon,

he already had it.

He shoved her into the van.

Next thing she knew,

She was in the basement.

"Looks like you earned yourself another punishment," he

said. Almost happy.

The cop stood. Tried to hold her ground. Instinct more

than anything. No plan.

He drew his gun and shot her in the head.

"Don't really need you," he said.

That was the cop the officer had joked about at the Silvas'

apartment.

"Probably partied too hard," he'd said.

She didn't party too hard.

She almost caught a serial killer.

He dragged her body to the meat grinder.

Spent hours cutting her up.

Piece by piece.

Threw the parts into the grinder.

This is how he gets rid of the ones he doesn't want to display.

The kills that aren't ritual.

He's perfected this routine.

Done it before.

Obviously never caught.

Never suspected.

The girl chained to the post could hear it.

The wet sound of butchering in the room next door.

Couldn't cover her ears.

Couldn't stop the nausea.

She wanted to be tough.

Thinks maybe she can make it out.

But deep down, she knows.

This is where she dies.

Then it hit her.

Today is Christmas.

Or maybe the day after.

Hard to tell anymore.

She'd gone to a party on Christmas Eve.

Someone she knew had abducted her.

Dumped her in a basement.

Not more than five miles from home.

She'll never see her mother again.

Never hug her brother again.

Her name was Catherine.

Cathy.

Cathy Silva.

For the first year, she broke every bone in her body trying

to weaken the post.

Kicked. Slammed. Twisted herself bloody.

It held.

At some point, he took her out of the basement. Locked her in a cage in the back of a van.

Drove for days. To New York.

Fed her like a dog.

She pissed and shat in that cage.

After about five days, he pulled her out.

Dragged her into another basement.

Worse.

Colder. Wetter.

Filthier.

All that work. Wasted.

New post. New hell.

Everything he does, he does to break you. So you can truly become his slave.

He wanted to be closer to Frankie. Closer to the thrill. To his pain.

He began following him. Exhilarated by the secret he carried. Watching Frankie grieve, knowing he still had his sister. Alive.

He did that for years.

But she didn't give up.

Started over.

Sick. Feeble. Emaciated.

Still, she picked at the new post.

Every day, a little more.

When she realized she wouldn't be the one to break it,

she carved those six words into the wood.

She used a shard of her own tooth…

from when he punched her so hard, three snapped.

She'd laughed at him.

"All you got? Pussy."

He couldn't break her.

The more he punished, the more defiant she became.

"Do your worst," she'd say.

Tough gal.

Put most men to shame.

When she finished carving the words, she etched two final

letters underneath.

CS.

And then, a name.

His name.

She'd recognized him.

The man who killed her.

The man who would kill again.

She left his name behind.

Just in case someone ever came looking.

Then she gave in.

To the pain.

To the pneumonia.

To the infection.

She stopped fighting.

"Butterflies…" she whispered.

She thought of Mary. Of that first night.

Of the way she'd looked at the ceiling, dazed, dreaming of

butterflies.

Maybe she hadn't been delusional after all.

Maybe she'd seen it coming. Freedom.

One last breath.

There.

Like the butterflies.

Mary's butterflies. Then…

Into the grinder.

And on to the next girl.

Rachael Cohen. He brought her in a few days earlier. He

knew Cathy wasn't going to last much longer.

Cathy had whispered it to her in the dark.

Keep hitting the bottom of the post.

One day, it'll give in.

Rachael listened.

She carried the legacy.

Mary's legacy.

Cathy's.

A silent chain of resistance passed from one broken soul to the next.

She kept at it.

Every day.

Until the post began to shift. Just a little.

Rachael met her fate in 2010. But not before passing the message down to the next girl, Silvia Rojas.

A whisper in the dark.

Keep hitting the post.

One day, it will give.

It has to.

And so Silvia took her place in the cold.

Chained.

Starving.

Picking at the wood with bleeding fingers.

Nine more years passed.

She was no longer the new girl.

She was just broken.

Bones like twigs.

Spirit eaten away.

But the post.

The post was finally weak.

Mary's legacy was finally paying off.

Before she could finish the job, he came down again.

Older.

A little slower.

But still strong enough.

Still a monster.

He stretched her out on the table.

Arms and legs wide.

Poured bleach to burn the evidence.

To cleanse his sins.

But his body betrayed him. He was sick. Cancer.

He knew he wasn't going to last much longer. He wanted to finish his masterpiece before his body gave out. He had plans for Frankie. He needed to set them in motion. Now.

He coughed. Didn't feel it. Didn't see the speck of blood that landed on the twine. Wasn't as attentive as he used to be. Too excited about what he had in store.

He flipped her onto the wheelbarrow.

Face down.

Tarp below.

Just like Mary.

Cathy's pendant in his pocket.

He drove to the alley before dawn.

Gas mask on.

Dumped the blood.

Dumped the body.

Placed the pendant like a calling card.

Stared. Looked at the camera.

Then vanished.

Came back.

Suit pressed.

Hair slicked back.

Standing tall.

Proud.

Watched from behind the yellow tape.

Rain falling in sheets.

Cold, hard needles from a sky that can't stop crying.

The alley sealed in caution and dread.

Hazmat suits moving slow and careful, like ghosts cataloging

a nightmare.

Frankie's there.

His eyes locked on him like magnets.

Following his every move.

Voice low. Talking to the officer. Then he kneels. Shoes

soaked.

He watched from the distance.

Felt it in his chest.

The rush.

The climax.

This is what he came for.

What he's been waiting for.

Frankie's fingers hover over something small.

Almost missed.

The pendant.

Cathy's pendant.

He lifts it with a pen.

Stares.

His face changes.

Confused.

Across the alley, the killer's breath caught.

He watched from the dark, stinking passage.

Rain poured over his fedora.

He didn't mind.

Didn't even notice.

He savored the pain blooming on Frankie's face.

A smirk slipped out before he could stop it.

He loved hurting the people close to his victims.

He enjoyed the whole experience, the trolling, the hunt, the

kidnapping, the torture, the kill, the family's sorrow.

He felt the power in all of it.

But this was his masterpiece. Cathy.

The truth.

That she had been alive.

For years.

Same city as her brother.

He had stopped looking.

While he lived, she withered.

While he slept, she trembled.

He had stopped searching for her. He was only searching

for answers.

She stopped breathing.

And the killer watched.

Smiling in the dark.

Pain layered on pain.

Just the way he planned it.

Just the way he likes it.

Savoring every painful moment.

Schadenfreude.

Then he saw her.

Detective Emily Rimler. Frankie's partner.

A part of his torture plan.

He'd followed them before. Planned it all.

He wanted to be closer to Frankie.

Closer to the thrill.

He was excited to close the loop.

Close the cycle.

With Frankie.

He had plans for him.

Tailed them from the murder scene to the precinct. Waited.

Watched. When Frankie finally left, deep in thought, the killer

followed at a distance. At the subway entrance, he closed the

gap and, in one smooth motion, slipped the note into Frankie's

coat pocket. Then he sped up, heading down the stairs ahead

of him. Frankie was still walking slow, distracted. The killer

struck up a casual conversation with an older woman, just a

stranger, but he spoke like they knew each other. On camera,

it wouldn't raise suspicion. Near a blind spot, he flipped his

tailored jacket inside out, pulled a hidden hoodie from beneath

his shirt, and covered his head. Then he turned and walked

back up, fast. At the top of the stairs, he bumped into Frankie

on purpose. Just a guy in a hoodie. Not the well-dressed man

who had vanished into the crowd. He knew where the cops

would look. Then he headed to Emily's apartment.

Emily unlocked the door and stepped inside, drained. She

dropped her bag, slid the holster off her shoulder, and tucked

it into the drawer of the console table by the entrance. Her

badge came next, unhooked from her waistband and placed

gently beside it. She collapsed onto the couch, pulled the band

from her ponytail, and let her hair fall loose. A quick rub of

her aching feet, then she got up and headed to the kitchen.

Popped open a cold drink. Turned on the TV. Noise helped.

Her mind was racing. Ran a hot bath. Let the water rise.

Then, the doorbell.

Who could that be?

She walked quietly to the door and peeked through the

peephole. A bouquet of flowers nearly filled the frame, hiding

most of a well dressed man in a suit.

She opened it, cautious but polite. "Hi," she said, managing

a smile.

"I'm sorry to bother you," he replied warmly. "I think I've

got the wrong floor. My daughter, she's pregnant. Just found

out. I'm surprising her." He held up a piece of paper. "Is this

the right address?"

Emily leaned forward to read it. caught off guard by how

ordinary he looked. Too late. He moved quickly. Instinct.

He'd done it dozens of times. A punch to the gut knocked

the air out of her. Then a handkerchief soaked in chloroform

pressed to her nose and mouth. She went limp. He closed

the door with a quick back kick and lowered her to the floor.

Smooth. He tidied the apartment so there was nothing out of

place. Not one thing. Except the mirror. He hung it upside

down and slid the note behind it.

Then he lifted her over his shoulder, carried her down the

fire escape, loaded her into the van, and drove

When her eyes opened again, she was tied to a post.

In a basement.

The air was thick with rot.

And misery.

Chapter 15
The Arrest

Brooklyn Precinct. 2019

An eyewitness could place Edward disheveled that night. A white car spotted near Cathy's building. Same as Edward's.

The scream. The Berkeley comment. The scarf.

It was enough to move for a warrant.

Frankie and Kitteridge had the scarf rushed to the lab. DNA testing would take time, but the chain of custody was clean enough to proceed.

They went back to Frankie's office to work on the warrant request. Sat at his desk.

Chinese takeout containers were scattered across it. Neither of them touched the food.

The preliminary report from the alley came in.

Cause of death: septic shock.

Dozens of wounds. Left to rot. Skin breaking down.

Infection in the blood. Pneumonia. UTI. She hadn't eaten in days. Her stomach was empty.

She died slowly.

Her name was Silvia Delgado. Disappeared from San Francisco in 2010. Nineteen years old. College student in Oakland. Took BART into the city one Friday night. Got off at Powell Station.

Never seen again.

Now, nearly a decade later, she turned up dead in a Brooklyn alley.

Years in captivity.

Dragged across the country.

Then thrown away.

They had a theory. No direct evidence. Circumstantial at best.

If the lab found something on the scarf, maybe, just maybe, they'd have a shot.

The results from the blood droplet on the twine came back.

Not the victim's.

Male. Caucasian. O-negative.

Frankie stared at the report.

"He bled."

Kitteridge nodded.

"And left us a piece of himself."

Now they had something.

"Hey!"

The sudden voice made both men jolt. O'malley peeking through the office door. "I got someone on the line. Says she had a weird encounter with a guy going down the subway stairs. Same station. You need to hear this."

Frankie and Kitteridge were out of their chairs before he finished the sentence, following him to his desk. He tapped the speaker button.

"Thanks for holding, ma'am," he said. "I've got Detective Silva here with me. Would you mind going over it one more time?"

The woman's voice came through the speaker, a little annoyed. "Yeah, like I was saying… I was going down the stairs like I've done for the past five years, minding my own business."

"Around what time was this?" Frankie asked.

"Same as always. Eleven twenty-five. I catch the eleven thirty train. I work nights as a receptionist in Kings County Hospital."

"Thank you. Please, go on."

"Like I said… I was going down the stairs when this gentleman, very well-dressed, actually, starts walking next to me. Talking like he knows me."

"Like how?" Kitteridge asked, leaning in closer to the phone.

"I don't know. He laughed, like I'd just told a joke, and said something like, 'You crack me up, Silvia. How's Cathy doing? Give her my best, please.' I thought he was just senile or confused. I mean, I don't know. But then I saw you were looking for any info on a white guy from that night, near that station, and I figured maybe it helps."

Kitteridge's eyes shot to Frankie. His voice came quick, charged with sudden energy. "It helps. Very much. Thank you, ma'am. We appreciate it." The line clicked off.

"Call Luetti," Frankie barked at O'Malley. "NYPD Transit

Bureau. He'll help. Give him the time, tell him to send the footage over."

Kitteridge held up a hand. "We have it. From earlier. FBI had it logged. I can pull it up from my laptop."

"Let's go," Frankie said.

The three of them rushed back to Frankie's office. Captain walked in a moment later, hovering behind them, silent but watching.

"Alright… eleven twenty-five, north entrance," Kitteridge muttered, fingers flying across the keyboard. "Here we go."

The footage rolled.

"There. A gentleman laughing," Kitteridge said. "Lady looks confused."

He hit pause.

All four leaned in. Took a good look… then three leaned back.

Frankie didn't. "I think I saw this guy. Here. At the precinct. Suit and all. Didn't catch the face, fedora tilted low. Making a cup of coffee… but I think it was him."

The captain stepped back, already moving.

"I'll get forensics to close the kitchenette and dust for prints. We'll check CCTV. Track his movements inside the building."

"Does it look like Edward to you?" Kitteridge cut to the chase.

Frankie nodded slowly. "Yeah. I think so."

The captain squinted at the image; jaw locked in his usual frown. He stepped back.

"Well, get off your fucking asses and go get him."

Frankie lifted his head and exhaled hard.

"Yes, sir."

They grabbed the affidavit and warrant papers, slid them into a file and headed out.

In the hallway, they saw Detective Mendez.

"Silva!" she called from down the hall.

He raised a hand and kept walking toward her.

When he reached her, she rubbed his arm briefly. Grounding. Familiar.

"How you doin'?" she asked.

"Alright," he said.

She glanced at Kitteridge. "Hi."

"Detective Mendez," Frankie said. "Missing Persons. This is Agent Kitteridge. FBI."

"Nice to meet you," Kitteridge said.

"The fingerprint," Mendez said. "Belongs to my missing person. Sophia."

"Yeah," Frankie said. "Sorry I didn't loop you in sooner."

"It's okay," she cut in. "I was called right away. Any leads? Anything I can tell the family?"

"No," Frankie said. "Nothing should be shared yet. But we do have a suspect. Solid. We're on our way now for a warrant."

"Keep me in the loop, Silva."

"I will," he said as he started walking again. "I promise."

They got into the car and pulled away.

Both stared straight ahead.

Not a word.

The stakes were too high. They were close. They could feel it.

No need to talk it through anymore.

They just needed the warrant.

And Edward in custody.

They pulled into the driveway and climbed the stone steps, boots heavy against the damp concrete. A colonial home sat quietly under the night, soft porch lights casting long shadows across the front yard.

Frankie barely knocked.

The door opened before his knuckles landed a second time.

Judge Fatima Rashad stood there, already in a headscarf and robe, eyes sharp even at this hour.

"Come in," she said, stepping aside. "How are you, gentlemen?"

"Better once we make the arrest," Frankie said.

She gave a knowing nod and led them into a tidy kitchen. Wood floors. Low light. The table was cleared, a pen and reading glasses already waiting.

"I assume you have cause," she said, sitting.

Frankie handed over the file. Kitteridge stepped forward.

Judge Rashad adjusted her glasses and picked up the affidavit, a stack of stapled pages still warm from Frankie's hands. Kitteridge stood across from her, steady.

"Page five," he said. "Lab report from the most recent dump site. Blood droplet found on a piece of twine used to bind the victim. Male. Caucasian. Blood type O negative. DNA profile extracted. No match yet, but clean and viable."

She flipped to page five. Skimmed it. Said nothing.

"Page six," Kitteridge continued. "CCTV stills from the subway. Timestamp places Detective Silva entering the station at 11:24 p.m. One minute later, a man enters. Similar height. Build. Gait. The footage isn't crystal clear, but it's enough to raise flags."

Judge Rashad tilted the page toward the desk lamp. Her brow creased.

"The man initiates a conversation with a woman on the stairs," she read. "Refers to her as 'Silvia.' Then says, 'How's Cathy? Give her my best.' Cathy, as in Cathy Silva."

She looked up.

"That name wasn't public. Correct?"

"Correct," Frankie said. "Never released. Cathy, my sister, disappeared in 1997. Last seen leaving this man's party. That detail is on page three."

Judge Rashad looked at him over the rim of her glasses.

"Sister."

She flipped back. Read silently. Her lips tightened.

"Page three also," Kitteridge said. "A pendant belonging to her. Cathy. Found next to the most recent victim's body."

"And the agent?" Judge Rashad asked, still reading.

"Rimler," Frankie said. "Detective. NYPD. My partner."

"She's missing," Kitteridge added. "Last seen driving home from Brooklyn Precinct. A note was found at her apartment."

He tapped the affidavit.

"Page seven."

Judge Rashad flipped the page. Her eyes moved fast.

She looked up at both men.

"This still doesn't tie directly back to your suspect," she said.

"There was a witness," Frankie said quickly.

He glanced at Kitteridge for help.

"Page eight," Kitteridge added.

The judge looked back down. Flipped again.

Silence.

She read. Then shook her head.

"This eyewitness isn't even certain," she said. "*Thought* it was the host. Not positive."

"It's him," Frankie said. "He owned a white SUV. Same type seen in our building parking lot. Same type mentioned by Melissa's friends before her abduction. He knew about Berkeley."

"We're requesting a buccal swab," Kitteridge cut in. "And a full search warrant. We believe he's responsible."

Judge Rashad leaned back slightly and removed her reading glasses.

"So," she said, "you believe he has her in Oakland."

"We believe he owns property here, Your Honor," Kitteridge said. "Many of the victims were from the West Coast. We're confident we'll find evidence linking him to those disappearances. And something that tells us where he's holding her in New York. The DNA will tie him to the most recent murder."

Judge Rashad hesitated.

"I can approve the buccal swab," she said. "Not the property search."

"Your Honor," Frankie started to protest.

"If," she interrupted firmly. "If the swab comes back a match, you return to me. You'll get your search warrant."

She jotted a note on the affidavit and slid it back across the table.

"Go."

Frankie took the signed warrant carefully.

"Thank you, Your Honor."

She met his eyes. She could see the disappointment. She understood it. But they had nothing concrete. Even the buccal swab was a stretch.

They moved fast. Gravel kicked up behind the tires as they sped off her driveway.

In the passenger seat, Kitteridge was already dialing.

"We got a swab warrant," he said into the phone. "Sending it now. Signed by a federal judge in New York."

The FBI team reached Edward's home in record time. A forensic agent took the swab. Sealed it. Bagged it. No small talk. It was rushed straight to the lab.

Edward stayed calm. Defiant. He slipped his hands into the pockets of his smoking robe and stood at the edge of the drive, watching the black SUV disappear down the hill.

No cuffs. No questions.

A rage sitting just beneath the surface, held in check.

Frankie drifted into his office and sank onto the small couch against the wall. Kitteridge dropped down beside him. The Captain joined them briefly, sat in Frankie's chair, and put his feet up on the desk.

They talked. Discussed. Tried to convince themselves that soon they would arrest him and get to Emily.

It didn't work.

The Captain stood, grabbed his coat without a word, and walked out into the night.

Kitteridge broke the silence.

"The DNA's being rushed," he said quietly. "We should have

results by morning."

Frankie didn't answer.

He just sank deeper into the couch.

Noise slowly crept back into the precinct. Faint at first. Then sharper.

Keyboards clicking. Phones ringing somewhere in the distance.

Frankie stirred. Blinked his eyes open. Looked around, confused. Second night in a row falling asleep on a couch.

His neck was stiff. His back sore.

He sat up, rubbed his face with both hands, and looked around again.

Kitteridge wasn't there.

He looked to the window.

Clouded over. Gloomy, dark sky. Like it was a mood ring.

He stood, moved slow. Shuffled to the restroom.

Used it. Washed his hands. Splashed his face with cold water.

Then walked out heading toward the kitchenette.

Still taped off. Forensics hadn't cleared it yet.

He let out a grunt and turned around.

Kitteridge stood there, holding two coffees.

"Morning," he said, voice dry.

Frankie took one. "Thanks. Really needed this."

Kitteridge didn't smile. Just nodded, and they both started walking toward the desks.

"Lab sent the report," Kitteridge said.

Frankie tensed. "And?"

Kitteridge hesitated. "It's not a complete match."

"What the hell does that mean?" Frankie asked as he sipped his hot coffee.

"They couldn't extract enough for a full sequence from the droplet. Sample was too degraded. But the blood type matches."

Frankie stopped abruptly. "Wait. He's O negative?"

Kitteridge stopped a few steps ahead, looked back, and nodded. "He is."

Frankie exhaled. Slow. Started walking again.

"Son of a bitch."

"That's not all," Kitteridge said.

Frankie looked up mid-sip of coffee.

"I checked for any tickets on the white SUV," Kitteridge said. "From back then."

Frankie's eyebrows lifted as they approached the desks, slicing through the chaos of the station.

Kitteridge raised his voice to cut through the noise. "July tenth. Nineteen ninety-nine. He got a citation. Parking in a restricted ranger spot. After hours. Eugene, Oregon. Hendricks Park."

Frankie's heart dropped. The noise of the precinct faded for a second. Phones ringing. Sirens outside. Keyboards clicking. Then it all came rushing back. Louder, somehow.

"That's the same park they found Melissa's body," he said. Feeling like they cracked the case. His intuition had been right.

Kitteridge nodded. "Yep."

"He dumped her body. And got a parking ticket doing it. And no one connected the dots," Frankie added. Eyes wide. Voice tight. Something underneath it. Horror. Rage. The beginning of clarity.

"Do we have enough to arrest him?" Frankie said. Waiting. Finally. For confirmation that he'd been right all along.

"You bet your ass we do," Kitteridge said. "Team's on the way."

Frankie's jaw tightened. Finally. This was the closest he'd ever been.

Kitteridge nodded again. "If the judge signs off, we can move on extradition. If he's our guy, he'll be in New York before the weekend."

Frankie exhaled.

It was four a.m. in Oakland. Federal black SUVs carved their way through the winding hills of Oakland, engines humming like a threat. The convoy came to a stop outside a massive estate perched above the city. A wrought-iron gate blocked the entrance, towering and still.

Agent Young stepped out, warrant in hand, the other resting on the grip of his service weapon. His vest read FBI. His face read fuck around and find out

He walked up to the intercom and pressed the button.

"FBI. Open the gate. We have a warrant."

A pause. Then the gate groaned to life, swinging open slowly.

Young got back in and the SUVs surged up the long drive, circling a marble fountain before screeching to a stop. The front door was already open. One of the staff stood back, expression blank.

Agents swarmed in.

Edward Milton appeared at the top of the stairs, descending in a tailored suit. Calm. Smirking.

"Agent Young," he said. "Long time no see."

"Miss me?" Young said. "You have the right to remain silent."

Edward's smile faltered. He looked past Young, down the stairs, where his wife had just appeared.

"Call the lawyers," he said.

Young cuffed him and handed him off to another agent, then turned to direct the search.

Agents fanned out through the house. Upstairs. Downstairs. Behind hidden doors and locked cabinets. Floorboards pried up. Books yanked from shelves.

They were looking for anything. A trace of blood. A shred of clothing. A photograph. Something that tied him to the killings. Or led them to Emily.

The mansion was spotless.

Mrs. Milton stood in the foyer, arms crossed, watching them dismantle her home piece by piece.

When the search was over, agents filed out one by one.

Boots tracked dust and debris across polished floors.

The mansion looked like a crime scene.

Just not Edward's.

Young lingered at the door, taking one last look.

Then he turned and stepped out.

It was time to talk.

"Understood," Kitteridge said, then hung up.

He looked at Frankie who was waiting, tense, hoping the FBI team would find something in Edward's mansion.

A trace of Emily. A trophy. Anything.

Kitteridge shook his head. Not clear if it meant *no evidence* or *no hope*.

Either way, it hit the same.

"He's in custody, at least. We'll be patched through again," Kitteridge continued as he veered toward Homicide's office, "Like last time."

While the search was being conducted, Edward was left alone in the interrogation room. Disoriented. Agitated. Furious.

"I'm not saying a word until my lawyer gets here," he said. "This is absurd."

They let him sit. Stew in it.

By the time his attorney arrived, Edward was seething. But quiet.

Agent Young finally came in. He opened the door and stepped inside, slow and deliberate. Tired from the search. Disappointment written all over his face.

He was holding a file.

He sat down, opened it, and got straight to it.

"We have a preliminary blood type match from a victim in New York," Young said. "You were in the city last weekend. Can you account for your movements?"

The lawyer cut in. "Are you charging him?"

"Not yet."

"Then he's free to go."

"No. He's in federal custody for at least forty-eight hours. Unless he cooperates. If he provides a solid alibi, we have no reason to hold him."

The lawyer opened his mouth to protest, already launching into legal jargon about rights and detainment protocol.

Agent Young didn't let him finish.

"You don't seem to grasp the gravity of this situation. We

have a missing NYPD detective. We have blood on a body that matches your client's rare blood type. A necklace found near that body belonging to a girl who vanished at his party. And evidence connecting him directly to another victim. Your client is not walking out of here. He's being extradited to New York. And when that hits the media, a CEO under investigation for murder, that IPO of his won't just tank, it'll burn."

The lawyer glanced sideways at Edward.

Agent Young leaned in, voice sharp. "Start talking. Now. I'm out of patience."

Edward looked at his lawyer who gave him a nod. He exhaled. "What do you want to know?"

Frankie, staring at the screen, leaned in. laser-focused.

"Start with your movements. Where were you last weekend?" Said Agent Young.

"I flew into New York on a private jet. Friday night. Stayed at the Plaza. Saturday morning, I had a meeting. Then dinner in the city. Back to the hotel that night. We had breakfast in the morning, then flew out Sunday morning around seven or seven thirty."

Frankie looked at Kitteridge. A look that said, *did I hear that right?*

"Who were you with?"

"My father. He's the chairman and president. A few investors. My lawyer can provide a list."

"Anyone who can confirm you were in your hotel room?"

"I mean… it's a hotel. I'm sure they have cameras."

"We'll check." He looked at an agent standing to the side and gave him a nod. "What's the name of the hotel again?"

"The Plaza." Edward replied with a smirk.

"On it," the other agent said and left the room to go check on the CCTV.

Agent Young continued. "You received a ticket in 1999. July 10th. Do you remember?"

Edward scoffed, leaning back on his chair. "No, I do not remember 1999. That was 20 years ago…"

"It was in Oregon."

"No. I've never gotten a ticket in Oregon…"

"How can you be positive?"

"I went to school in Seattle, I would pass by Oregon driving back home from college but I don't remember ever getting a ticket there. Plus, July? What would I be doing in Oregon in July, I would be home. I graduated in 99 actually so I moved back to California already by then…"

"Well you received a citation July 10, 1999 for parking in a Ranger only spot."

"Yeah, that's impossible," Edward said.

"We're going to have to let a jury decide then," said Agent

Young. "Your blood type found on the victim. Cathy disappeared from your house. Another victim dumped in the woods. You receive a ticket at the exact spot she was discovered."

"What?" Edward says. "Look, you got it all wrong. I have nothing to do with any of these. Cathy. I don't know what happened after she left the party. I have never gotten a citation in Oregon and my blood type is not that rare. Millions of people have that blood type. You got it all wrong. I am telling you."

Captain walked into the office. Frankie and Kitteridge were watching the feed, following every move. He hovered behind them.

"Sumbitch confess yet?"

Kitteridge gave a slight shake of his head. "No."

"Let's move this to the conference room," Captain said.

Kitteridge grabbed the laptop, not even looking where he stepped, and followed them out. He placed it on the oval table and connected it to the big screen on the wall. Then they all sat down, eyes locked on the interrogation.

"He's good. Real good," Frankie said. "I almost believe him."

Agent Young left the interrogation room, letting Edward stew. It was early morning. They'd woken him around 3 a.m. No coffee. No food. Sleep-deprived and off balance. That's how they wanted him, disoriented. Off his game. More likely to slip.

In the meantime, Agent Young called Kitteridge.

"What do you think?" he said.

"He's good," Kitteridge replied, echoing Frankie's earlier comment.

"Yeah… but he'll slip."

"Press on Tiffany again," Kitteridge said.

"Planning on it. I'm gonna let him marinate a bit longer first."

Edward sat there with his lawyer for a while, genuinely, by

all appearances, trying to figure out how he got a ticket in Oregon.

Agent Young walked back in, sipping a coffee. He sat down,

holding a folder.

He opened it, pulled out the photos of all the victims, and

slid them across the table toward Edward.

His lawyer objected immediately. Edward looked away.

Then came the last photo. Tiffany. His sister.

Edward glanced at the file. Just for a second. Then he looked

up at Agent Young.

"You think I killed my sister too?" he said. "When I was

eleven?"

"Do you remember the day she was killed?" Young asked,

coldly ignoring the remark.

His lawyer leaned in. "You don't need to answer…"

Edward held up a hand, stopping him before he could finish,

eyes still locked on Agent Young. His voice was firm. No

hesitation.

"Like it was yesterday."

"Run me through it," Agent Young said, leaning forward.

Edward exhaled. "We were at our lake house over Christmas break."

"Christmas," Frankie muttered. "Tiffany was the first."

Kitteridge didn't react. Eyes forward. Focused on Edward as he continued.

"We had visitors. My dad's business partner at the time. His wife. Kids…"

He paused. Swallowed hard.

"We took the sled that day. Tiffany was teaching me how to slide. She taught me a lot of things. She was kind. My dad wasn't the nicest. Neither was my mom. But Tiffany… she always took care of me."

He looked down at his hands.

"We came back up the hill. I was tired. I went upstairs to nap."

A pause.

"I don't know how long I slept. I woke up to my parents arguing about Tiffany. Something about her being disrespectful. Missing dinner. Not telling anyone where she'd gone. My mother always found things Tiffany did annoying."

His voice dropped.

"My dad left. Then he came back not long after. Red in the face. Shaken." A breath. "He went straight to the phone. Called 911."

Edward blinked a few times.

"I didn't understand. Cops were everywhere. I couldn't

make sense of it."

A beat.

"My sister was dead?" He swallowed.

"She'd just been teaching me how to sled."

Another pause.

"I was confused. Nobody told me anything." He stopped, emotion

rising in his throat.

"I'm sorry, I just… I haven't relived these memories in so

long. You think you moved on, but… you never really do."

He leaned back, lost in it for a moment.

Then he straightened up. Regaining composure.

"He's good," Captain said as he stood and headed for the door.

"Keep me updated," he added. "I've got a meeting with top brass."

Edward, voice shaking, adjusted his position in the chair and

continued.

"Eventually, I found out how she died. How gruesome it was.

One of the other kids visiting us at the lake house told me. He

was older. Helped me process it. We went back home. Cops

never found any evidence. My father sold that lake house. We

never set foot there again."

Edward looked shaken. Like pain was crawling back up

from somewhere deep, buried for decades.

His lawyer glanced at him, then turned to Young.

"We're done here. You've got no proof. No probable cause.

My client is clearly distressed."

"Okay," Agent Young said, calm. He waved to an agent by the door. "Take him to his cell."

"I'll have him out in an hour," the lawyer snapped.

"No. You won't," Young replied. "He'll be on a plane to New York in an hour. Paperwork just came through."

He stood, collected the photos and the file then paused, and added with a hint of mock sympathy,

"Maybe they'll buy his emotional performance," the lawyer said. "You know how New Yorkers tend to be. Sensitive."

Young and the lawyer went back and forth, voices overlapping, but Edward wasn't listening. He stared down at the table, brow knotted, jaw tight.

Then it hit him.

The frown vanished suddenly and his head snapped up.

Eyes wide.

"Wait!" he yelled.

His voice cracked as the words spilled out.

"I remember now. The ticket. I know what happened."

He sucked in a sharp breath, almost choking on it.

"Oh my god," he shouted. "Oh my god. I can't believe it."

He looked between them, shaking.

"He… he killed my sister."

Young's jaw dropped. The lawyer stared at him, stunned.

In the conference room, Frankie and Kitteridge shot to their feet and rushed to the screen. Frankie ran his hands through his hair, gripping the back of his head, exhaling hard.

Kitteridge stood frozen. Eyes wide. Heart pounding.

The case had just blown wide open.

Chapter 16
The beginning. 1985

A huge mansion sits on a massive estate. The kind where you

can get lost walking. The kind that could be used to shoot a

horror movie. Isolated. Cold. It exudes money and secrets.

The kind you want buried forever.

The estate stretched for acres. Trees as far as the eye could see.

There was an old well. A tunnel system from over a century ago.

Spooky. Forgotten.

At the edge of the property sat a basement.

Locals said it was used for slaughtering animals back in the

1800s. At least, that's the official story.

Rusty chains still hung from the beams.

The walls were damp with mold.

The air felt wrong.

Evil lived there. You could feel it. Evil still lurk here.

Inside the mansion were more rooms than one could count.

More rooms than anyone would ever need.

Cold. Not just physically. Cold in a way that seeped into

the soul.

To the children, it was a prison.

An older boy. A younger girl. Siblings.

Their innocence was stolen in slow motion.

The mother was strict. The kind that smiled in front of

guests, then slapped you across the face for laughing too loud.

Blind loyalty to her husband. Worshipped him like a god.

Feared him like the Devil.

They'd play like children do. Loud. Running. Chasing each other through the halls.

Didn't matter.

She'd find a reason to hurt them.

Running with shoes on. A toy left out.

Whip across the back. Leather belt.

No warning.

The father was gone most of the time. That was a blessing.

When he was home—it was bad.

Real bad.

He'd call for the daughter.

Do things.

Things no one talked about.

Things the staff pretended not to hear.

Then the boy.

Forced him to watch.

"So you can learn," the father would say.

This went on for years.

The girl endured it.

The boy absorbed it.

Something in him cracked. Permanently.

It became normal.

The sounds. The crying. The smells.

It was just life.

He didn't know any different.

Eventually, he started torturing animals around the estate.

Birds at first.

Then rabbits.

Then stray cats.

Curious at first. Then deliberate. Then ritual.

He followed girls home from school.

Didn't touch them.

Just watched.

Imagined.

Played it out in his head.

Then his first kill. Tiffany.

It was Christmas break 1988. He was fourteen.

They were on vacation with his dad's partner's family. Big lake house in Lake Tahoe. Woods all around. Tiffany was there. Older. Gorgeous. The kind of girl who turned heads without trying.

He had a crush on her for as long as he could remember. He watched her more than anyone else. Followed her with his eyes. Counted the minutes she was near.

He told himself she liked him too. Convinced himself. Read into every glance, every smile. Built a whole story in his head.

She was kind to him. Patient. Laughed when he asked if she wanted to hang out. Said he was sweet, but he was only fourteen.

That's when something snapped.

He punched her in the stomach. Hard. Just like his father

used to hit him.

She dropped into the snow.

He put her on the sled, dragged her deeper into the woods,

picked up a rock,

and crushed her skull.

But it wasn't enough.

He walked calmly back to the house. Entered through the

back. Went into the kitchen. Grabbed a knife. No one noticed.

Then he walked all the way back.

She was still alive. Crawling. Gurgling.

He got on top of her and slit her throat.

Afterward, he threw the knife into the lake. Went back to

the house. Took a shower. Changed his clothes. Stayed in his

room.

Downstairs, everyone was drinking, laughing, passing

plates. No one noticed he was gone.

When Tiffany didn't come back by nightfall, they started

searching.

They found her in the woods.

David was still upstairs. Sitting in bed. Pretending to read.

No one suspected him.

A few years later, the father got sick. Lung cancer. It was

fast and brutal. He died in that same house. Alone in his bed.

No one cried. No one said goodbye.

The daughter was finally free.

She buried it all deep.

Tried to live.

Best to forget.

The wounds didn't heal. But they closed. Enough to
function.

The boy kept reliving his first kill. The fantasy became
unbearable.

He didn't resist.

He embraced them.

Started hunting.

At the edge of the property was that old basement.

The one no one talked about.

The one with the chains.

The smell of rot in the walls.

He made it his place. His temple.

The first time he abducted someone, he was seventeen. He
killed her. Buried her under the floor. He quickly realized
it wasn't the killing that satisfied him. It was the pain. The
control. The helplessness in their eyes.

So he brought another one. Kept her for a while. She died
too.

He learned quickly how to push just far enough to inflict

the worst pain without killing them.

He'd pick his prey and follow her for days, sometimes weeks.

Learn her schedule down to the minute.

He knew where she bought her coffee, which bus she took,

what time she walked home.

He waited. Watched. Practiced his smile. When the

moment came, he offered her a ride. She hesitated, but his car

was nice. He was clean, polite. Young. She got in.

The next time she opened her eyes, she was tied to a post.

No one ever came looking.

It wasn't just the physical pain he enjoyed. It was what

happened after. The moment they lost hope. The moment

they stopped believing they'd ever be found. That was when

it got quiet. And he didn't like that.

So he played with her mind. He untied her sometimes. Gave

her food. Let her shower. Told her he was letting her go. Gave

her clean clothes. Told her it was over. Then took it all away.

Tied her back up. Hurt her worse than before. It became a

system. Reward, revoke, destroy. Over and over.

It went on for years.

She stayed down there. Alive. Damaged.

He fed her just enough to keep her breathing.

Just enough to keep her pain fresh.

No one dared go near that basement.

Not the staff. Not the family.

The estate itself felt cursed.

His mother rarely left the house.

His sister spent most of her time at her best friend's place.

She hated that mansion. Can't blame her.

And that best friend became his fixation.

Something about her gnawed at him.

She was beautiful, but that wasn't it. It wasn't "something"

about her. It wasn't one thing. It was everything.

Her hair. Her nails. Her smile. Her teeth.

The way her cheek folded when she smiled.

The way her thumb hugged her other fingers.

No one in their right mind would notice any of this.

To him, she was perfect.

She reminded him of someone.

Like her, she was perfect. To him.

Not to love.

To hunt.

To fantasize about hurting.

And somewhere, buried in his wiring,

Was a sickness.

A need to destroy girls who looked like that.

He'd been around her before.

School. Family visits.

Always watching.

He once asked her out.

She said no.

Polite. Kind.

But it still felt like a blade to the chest.

After that, he couldn't sleep.

Couldn't eat.

The thought of her consumed him.

He had to have her.

Not for love.

Not for lust.

To own her.

To break her.

To make her scream his name in pain.

Christmas Eve, 1997.

They were at the same party. People drinking. Music
echoing through the halls.

She wanted to leave early. Said she was tired.

He knew which car she was getting a ride from, so he messed
with it. When it wouldn't start, she walked out alone.

He followed her.

Caught her near the tree line. Hit her in the head. Dragged
her off the path and hid her in the woods. Then he walked

back.

Came face to face with Mo, who was keying an SUV.

Shit.

He was going to get caught. He needed to deal with this.

But he also needed to get back to the party. Fast. Like nothing

happened. His alibi would collapse otherwise.

Mo, startled, walked away quickly, got Salah, and left.

He stayed a few more minutes. Laughed at a couple of jokes.

Said he was tired too. Made sure people saw him leave alone.

He borrowed a car from a friend. Didn't want to use his.

Returned to the woods.

She was starting to come to. He hit her again. Carried her

to the white SUV. Careful. Making sure no one was around.

Then drove out.

He passed Mo and Salah as they were pulling away. They

had parked on the side street.

So he followed them.

To Mo's building.

Gun in his waist. He needed to deal with him before he

could say something to the police. He wasn't sure what Mo

had seen. But he had seen Mo before. Knew exactly where he

lived. Same building as Cathy.

His sister, Inez' best friend.

He sped up, trying to get there first.

Mo dropped Salah off first. That helped.

He parked near the entrance of Mo's building and waited.

Eyes fixed. Determined. No one was going to mess up his plan.

He was too deep in thought to notice Cathy waking up.

She reached for the door handle. Slowly. Then yanked it open and bolted. Head pounding. Dizzy. She could barely stand, let alone run.

He chased her. Caught her by the hair.

She screamed. Loud. It echoed.

Her brother heard it.

But how could he have known.

Fuck.

He pulled the gun and pressed it to her temple as he dragged her back to the car.

One word and you're dead.

She had double vision. Concussed. She complied. Got back into the SUV.

He sped out of the parking lot just as Mo was pulling in.

Mo would never know that Cathy saved his life that night.

He joined the search the next day for a reason. In case he found something. He went back to the spot where he had taken her. If they ever found his DNA there, he would already have an explanation. He was helping.

That's when he saw it.

Her earring. Bloody.

He knelt by the bushes near the driveway. His hand went into his pocket. The earring dropped inside as his fingers closed around a dime.

He stood and held the dime out.

"False alarm."

Chapter 17
The Reveal

"Wait!" Edward said suddenly.

His voice cracked. "I remember now. The ticket. I know what happened." He gasped. "Oh my god… I can't believe it. He… He killed my sister."

Agent young looked seriously at Edward then his lawyer.

He leaned in "Who?? Who killed your sister?"

"David… David. He did it. He killed my sister"

Frankie and Kitteridge shot to their feet and rushed the screen. Frankie ran his hands through his hair, gripping the back of his head, exhaling hard.

Kitteridge stood frozen. Eyes wide. Heart pounding.

"Who is David?" Kitteridge asked.

"Inez brother." Frankie whispered. Could barely breathe.

"Who?" Kitteridge asked.

"Inez was my sister's best friend. We practically adopted her… But what makes him think David did it?"

Edward looked confused, still trying to piece together information that didn't make sense. Or maybe he didn't *want* it to make sense.

"My dad's partner's son," he said slowly. "The one we used to vacation with. The one who was there when Tiffany died. The one who told me about the gruesome details…"

Young leaned in. "What makes you think he did it?"

Edward took a breath. "Because… summer of '99. I had just come home from college. He borrowed my car for a week. I didn't think anything of it. I used my mom's car that week.

Later, my father got a ticket in the mail and paid it. Gave me

hell for it."

He paused.

"It didn't register. I didn't even remember being there. I

had no clue where or when the citation happened."

His voice got quiet.

"It was him. David."

Back in the conference room, Frankie and Kitteridge were

already making moves.

"He must be in New York," Frankie said.

"I'll get the team to check if he owns any property in the

city," Kitteridge replied, as they both started heading out.

"Frankie, wait," Kitteridge said.

The Captain was walking in. "What's going on?" he asked.

Kitteridge didn't get the chance to say what he had in mind.

Instead, he addressed the Captain's question.

"Edward Milton just identified a potential suspect," Kitteridge

said. "We're going to locate and apprehend him."

"I'll get SWAT ready to move," Frankie added.

"This is what I wanted to talk to you about…" Kitteridge

said. "You're sitting this one out."

"The hell I am!" Frankie said, frowning. "FBI is benching

me? Now?"

"No one's benching you," Kitteridge said. "You shouldn't

have been allowed anywhere near this case in the first place. When it comes to arrest and interrogation, we need this by the book. We can't risk losing a conviction."

Frankie looked at the Captain, searching for backup.

But the Captain nodded slowly. Agreeing.

"Emotions could run high," the Captain said. "It's better if you stay out of it."

"That's not happening," Frankie said. "I'm coming, no matter what any of you say."

The Captain looked at him, surprised. Frankie Silva had never disrespected him. Not once. Not ever.

Kitteridge jumped in. "You're already not thinking straight."

Frankie started to push back again, but the Captain cut him off.

"Frankie!" he barked. The tone stopped everything cold.

He never called him by his first name. Ever.

Frankie looked down and off to the side. Tried to process what this meant. That he wouldn't be the one arresting his sister's murderer. Or the man who took Emily.

"You did more than enough," Kitteridge said laying a hand gently on his shoulder.

"We're arresting him because of you. Let's do this right. For Cathy."

Frankie exhaled hard. Gave in.

Kitteridge nodded, tapped his shoulder. Then looked to the Captain and gave a nod.

The Captain nodded back.

Kitteridge took off sprinting, already dialing.

The hunt for the real killer had just begun.

The hunt to free Emily.

Frankie walked back to his office. The bullpen was buzzing, but in his head, it was silent. He stood in front of the board, eyes locked.

Inez's brother. He thought to himself…

Inez…

Eyes widened. He grabbed his phone and dialed her. They hadn't spoken in a long time. She was a big-shot lawyer now, based in D.C. Huge success. Always humble. With a childhood like hers, she turned out alright.

She picked up. "Frankie?"

He wasn't expecting that. Stuttered a little. "Hey, Inez. How are you?"

"I'm alright, how are you? Yes, you can put those folders there, thank you," she said, clearly giving instructions to someone on her end. "Sorry about that, we've got a big deposition. Gotta prepare. What's going on, Frankie boy?"

He smiled at the nickname. She and Cathy used to call him that. Simpler times. God, how he wished he could go back. Just twenty-four hours in 1996. Before everything.

"Umm… Inez, I'm working on a case. I can't say much, but

I need to ask you some questions. Can you help me?”

“Sure. Not sure what I can help with, but of course, Frankie.

Anything for you.”

“Thanks, Inez. Umm… does your family own any property

in or around New York?”

“Umm… sorry, what?”

“I know. I know how that sounds. But please… I’ll explain

everything later. I swear. If you care about me… if you ever

cared about Cathy… please just answer my questions.”

“Frankie, you’re scaring me. What’s going on?” she said,

snapping her fingers at an assistant to leave. He heard the soft

click of a door closing.

“Inez, please. I promise I’ll explain everything. Just not right now.”

“Okay, okay,” she said, lowering her voice. “No, we don’t

own any property in New York. We sold everything a while

ago. David took care of the sale.”

“Who’d you sell it to?”

“A company… I’m not sure. I don’t remember the name, but

I remember it was a company. David said they were tearing it
down.”

“Do you have the address?”

“I’m so confused, I…”

“Inez,” Frankie cut her off. “I’ll personally sit down and

explain everything to you. I promise. But I need that address.

And I need you not to mention this conversation to anyone.

Especially David.”

"I'll text it to you. I don't have it on hand… I'll need to check my records. Maybe it was in an old email."

"Pronto, Inez. Please."

"Okay, okay… Please be careful, Frankie boy. I trust you. I don't know what this is, but please…"

He hung up. Tried Kitteridge. No answer.

Minutes later, the text came through. The address.

Followed by another message:

Please, Frankie… what's going on?

He put the phone in his pocket. Bolted out of the precinct and into his car.

At the FBI office, Kitteridge and a team of seasoned agents were combing through everything tied to David. Focused on a Northeast connection. They pulled DMV records. His Bay Area mansion came up as the listed address. Kitteridge informed the Oakland field office. They were locked and loaded, speeding to the property within ten minutes flat. But they didn't stop there. They kept digging. Real estate records. Asset transfers. He'd liquidated most of what the family inherited.

"There," Kitteridge said, pointing at the screen. "They had an estate upstate. New York."

An agent tossed a pencil on his desk and leaned back. Frustrated.

"Sold in 2007."

Kitteridge leaned in.

"Oh, do not despair. Not… just… yet," he said. "Look at the buyer. There. Stillwater LLC. Run a search."

The room went silent for a beat.

"Registered to David Miles," one agent read out.

"There it is!" Kitteridge shouted. "He sold it for himself!"

He bolted out of the computer room, radio already in hand, sprinting toward the tactical wing where the field team was already booted up, ready for the go.

"We got him. Let's move! go, go, go."

The judge had been on standby. As soon as the address came through, the search and arrest warrant was signed. No delay.

FBI SUVs tore out of the city toward the old estate. Inside the convoy: rifles checked, safeties clicked, Kevlar vests cinched tight. Comms active. Eyes focused.

In the lead vehicle, the team lead gave the rundown.

"We have an abducted Detective. Presumably on site. We clear the estate, we take the suspect alive. Repeat: **alive**. Shoot only if necessary, aim for the legs. If we lose him, we may never find Detective Rimler."

"Roger that," came the response.

The convoy pushed forward. Gravel flying behind them.

One shot away from ending it … or losing everything.

Chapter 18
Closing In

Frankie was driving frantically toward the address Inez had emailed him. Their old estate. The one David sold.

His hand clenched the wheel. Eyes fixed. Face blank.

He feared he might do something stupid.

No, not feared. He was certain.

The second he saw David, he was going to kill him.

But first… Emily.

He gritted his teeth. *I need to free Emily first.*

He reached a deserted road. Night now. Full moon. He killed the headlights. Drove slow.

Pulled up to the estate. Shut off the engine.

Got out of the car quietly. Gently closed the door. No noise.

Unholstered his gun. Ran toward the house.

Checked all the entry points. The place looked abandoned.

Then he heard it. A thump. Faint. But he knew he heard it.

The doors wouldn't budge.

He circled the perimeter, looking for any windows. Every single one was covered in forged iron.

Alright. No more waiting.

He aimed at the doorknob. Finger just about to squeeze the trigger when he heard it…

Gravel shifting. Tires.

Cars approaching.

He looked back.

Under the full moon, the shape of black SUVs emerged.

FBI.

"Shit," he muttered, holstering his gun.

He stepped out, hands up. *Don't fucking mistake me for the
perp*, he thought.

All weapons were aimed at him.

"Lower your weapons, lower your weapons!" Kitteridge
shouted as he rushed up.

They listened.

"Silva?!! What the FUCK!"

"Listen," Frankie said. "I know his sister, alright? We grew
up together. She gave me the address. Said it was sold. I
decided to check it out."

"Why didn't you call it in?"

"Didn't wanna waste resources. In case it didn't lead to anything."
Kitteridge didn't buy it.

This wasn't about leads. This was about revenge.

The tactical team lead walked over, hands hooked through
the straps of his Kevlar vest, watching the standoff unfold.

"What the hell is going on here?" he said. "Y'all gonna stand
around dancing all night, or can we go do our damn job?"

Kitteridge stared at Frankie for a second longer, jaw tight,
then let it go. Too late now. Frankie was already here.

"What did you see in there?"

"House is impenetrable. Iron-covered windows on the

ground floor," Frankie said. "I heard a thump, northwest corner. Might be the basement."

He glanced toward the upper floors. "Our best bet is the second floor. No iron on the windows. Or one big bang through the front."

The team lead looked up at the narrow frames. "Nah, too risky. Small windows. We'd get picked off one by one."

"I can go alone," Frankie said. "Scout."

"No," Kitteridge snapped.

"That's a good idea," the team lead said.

Kitteridge looked at him, ready to argue, but the lead had already pulled Frankie aside and started going over the plan. Kitteridge had no choice but to give in.

"Go in clean. My team will be downstairs. Don't waste time. Open the front door. Watch your back. We'll clear the house once you're in."

Frankie nodded.

The lead then turned to the group.

"Alright. Last check. Officer presumed held captive on-site. Detective Silva will be so kind as to invite us in. We go in clean. Clear every room. Watch your lines."

He turned to one of his agents and gave a sharp hand signal. The agent broke off in a sprint toward the tactical van, grabbed a collapsible ladder, and nodded to Frankie. Both of them ran low and quiet to the dark side of the house.

The ladder went up.

Frankie climbed fast. Knees popping. Adrenaline high.

He broke the window low and quiet. Cleared the shards
with his coat and the back of his gun. Slid inside.

FBI held position below. Silent. Waiting.

Lead whispered one final instruction. "Flank wide. Sweep
fast. We take him alive."

Guns raised. Positions taken. It was time.

It was taking longer than expected. The FBI lead was
starting to get nervous. Kitteridge too. The team was getting antsy.

Fuck, Kitteridge thought. *Did he go full rogue on us?*

The team lead, gun forward, glanced sideways at Kitteridge.

Kitteridge muttered, "Come on, Silva."

He took a small step back, about to look up—

Click.

The door unlocked.

Relief all around. The team lead gave quick hand signals.

Agents moved, flanking the house. The search for Rimler
began.

"Clear!"

"Clear!"

"Kitchen clear!"

The whole house was cleared. Frankie kept searching for
a basement entrance. He tapped on the floor with his feet,

listening for hollow sounds.

"Shhh," Frankie said, holding a finger to his lips.

Kitteridge stepped closer, confused.

"I hear a phone ringing," Frankie said.

Kitteridge paused, then nodded. He hears it too

"Anyone see a phone?" Frankie called out.

"Here!" an agent shouted from across the hall.

Frankie ran, holstering his weapon. Kitteridge followed.

They stopped in front of the old landline phone, ringing on

a small table.

Both stared at it. Then at each other.

Kitteridge held up his phone, showing Frankie he was recording.

Frankie grabbed a napkin, wrapped it around the receiver,

and lifted it between his ear and Kitteridge's phone.

"Hello," he said, eyes narrowed.

A whiny voice on the other end of the receiver.

"Made yourselves at home, have you?"

Frankie signaled to Kitteridge. Two fingers to his eyes, then

toward the corners of the room.

Cameras.

Kitteridge caught on, turned to the tactical team lead, and

passed the message.

The team spread out, scanning the walls, the ceiling.

Frankie stayed on the line.

"Where's Emily?"

"Oh, she's comfortable, don't worry…" His voice came out whiny, nasal. He took a loud breath, then continued, nonchalantly, "Baby's okay too."

Frankie's blood drained from his face. Everything spun a little.

Couldn't be.

"Oops… did I ruin the surprise?" David said, mockingly. "I thought you knew. My fault."

"You motherfucker," Frankie growled through clenched teeth, voice low. "If you touch one hair on her head…"

David cut him off.

"Oh, spare me. You couldn't protect her. Just like you couldn't protect your sister. Cathy."

He laughed. That same high-pitched, nasal laugh.

"Listen. I'll make you a deal. A real one. I'll give you a chance to be the man you always wanted to be."

Frankie's grip on the phone tightened.

"If you leave that house, now," David continued, "I'll release Emily," he said, voice thin and smug. "She'll walk to you. Unharmed. Still carrying your child. You get to be a father. Build your little family. I'll vanish. No trace. You'll never hear from me again."

Frankie didn't say a word.

"But if you decide to stay and keep searching," David said,

"I'll meet you in the front yard. You can take me in, no fight. But she dies the same instant. Her and whatever she's carrying."

"You sick…" Frankie started.

Click. He hung up.

Kitteridge replayed the recording.

It was audible. Faint, but clear enough.

He rewound the last part again, listening closely.

Frankie stood beside him, arms crossed, jaw tight.

"He wants to hurt you." Kitteridge said, firm. Certain.

"He's enjoying this."

The phone rang again.

Frankie picked it up the same way. Napkin. Careful.

David's voice slithered through.

"Oh, one more thing. If the FBI disables the cameras… she dies."

A pause. Then that voice again.

"I kept Cathy, you know… For years."

Frankie's fingers tightened on the napkin.

"My own slave," David continued. "Tortured her daily. Raped her daily."

He spoke like poison was dripping from every syllable.

Each word deliberate. Foul.

Like he wanted it to rot in Frankie's ears.

"I moved her from Oakland to New York when you did.

Wanted to be close to you."

Another pause.

"You moved on. That's what killed her. I told her you stopped looking. She cried so hard. Then died. Heartbroken. Her savior failed."

He chuckled.

"She used to say it, you know. 'My family will find me. They'll know it's you.'"

He laughed harder.

"Oh man… sorry. It's just… so funny."

A wheezing breath.

Another burst of laughter.

"All that time, you guys were searching everywhere. With Inez! And she was in the basement. Our basement!"

He giggled like a child.

Deeper. Meaner.

"Our house!"

Hysterical now.

"Hahahahaha!"

Then the laugh broke into coughing. Violent. Uncontrollable.

Wet and rasping. Like something is rotting inside him.

And then silence.

Like he was waiting for Frankie to break.

Frankie stood frozen.

The receiver trembled in his hand.

"Just open the door," he said, almost whispering.

"Step outside and I will meet you in less than five minutes.

Then you can do whatever you want with me."

A pause.

"And Emily…"

A sharp sound followed.

Chk!

The kind of noise you make to mimic a throat being slit.

Frankie closed his eyes. Jaw clenched.

His grip on the phone tightened.

Click. David hung up.

It didn't register. Frankie was still holding the receiver.

Staring. Frozen.

Kitteridge stepped in. Took the phone from him carefully,

using the same napkin. Set it down on the table.

"He's trying to get in your head, Frankie," Kitteridge said,

fast, almost shouting. "This is what he wants. This is his

finale. His masterpiece. You walk out that door, you give him

everything. Don't do it."

Frankie didn't move. Just kept staring.

He wants you to come after him. Wants to die by your hand,"

Kitteridge added. "So you'll live the rest of your life in prison

because of him. Blaming yourself for Detective Rimler. You

would be his last captive. Even after death."

The tactical team lead approached, standing beside them.

He spoke through clenched teeth, barely moving his lips. No emotion. Nothing a camera could catch.

"Hill by the edge of the estate. Looks man-made."

Kitteridge's eyes widened. "What makes you say that?"

"Vent pipe sticking out the top… I think."

"You think?" Frankie asked.

Kitteridge moved slightly to the window, trying not to draw attention. Peeked out. Took a moment, then stepped back.

"Looks like a pipe…I don't know." He said.

"Hard to tell from here," the team lead replied. "But it's not just a bump in the land. That shape's too clean."

"I think he's right," Kitteridge said. "That hill's more like a buried structure. Probably connected to the house underground through some kind of tunnel."

Frankie glanced toward the window but didn't fully turn his head, careful not to raise suspicion.

"I can meet you in less than five minutes," Kitteridge said.

Frankie looked at him, confused.

"He said, 'I can meet you in less than five minutes,'" Kitteridge repeated.

Frankie got the point. "He's close."

"Very close," Kitteridge replied, nodding toward the hill.

Frankie turned to the lead. "How would we do this? He's

watching us."

They froze. The information had to land clean.

If David saw them move, he'd kill Emily before they reached him.

Silence.

"Sir!" a SWAT operator shouted. "Someone's out there!"

The sky was just beginning to lighten.

That's when he saw it.

"He's sprinting to the structure!" the operator yelled.

Frankie threw the back door open and bolted outside, the team lead and agents right behind him.

David had been watching them the whole time.

When SWAT breached the house, he'd been close, just not close enough. He'd pulled up the camera feed on his phone, tracking every move while making his way back on foot.

Once near the property, he kept low, hidden in the trees, still watching.

Then he heard it over the feed. They'd figured it out.

The hill wasn't a hill at all. It was a covered basement.

He realized his window was closing.

If they got to Emily first, he'd lose his leverage.

So he ran. Full sprint. Straight for the hill.

Frankie behind him, running as fast as he could. David went out of view.

"Fuck," Frankie muttered, picking up speed. Almost there.

The agents were closing in behind him.

He reached the hill. Ran around it.

No door. No entrance.

"What? Where the fuck is it!" Devastated, he dropped to

his knees, feeling frantically for an opening. Dirt covered his

hands and face

Then they heard it.

Gunshot echoing.

Birds scattered.

The echo cracked through the trees.

Through the dawn sky.

Through Frankie's chest.

"No, no, no…" he gasped, as he dug harder. "Emily…

Emily…"

Gun out. Jaw clenched. Heart slamming. Tears flying.

In his mind, Emily had just been shot. What else could it be.

He needed to get to him.

He needed to kill him.

Agents caught up.

"Quickly!" he yelled. "Look for an opening. Look for an opening!"

Frankie knew it then and there. On his knees. Searching.

David's master plan worked. He would be his captive forever.

Because as soon as he saw him, he would kill him. Nothing

and no one would stop him. He would execute him. Point

blank. In the face.

"Here!" someone yelled.

Frankie jumped up and ran. Like a madman.

"Look," the team lead said, pointing.

A clean cut in the ground. Like a hatch disguised as earth.

An underground entrance, covered in fake grass.

David had built himself a house right into the hill, and

beneath it, a basement of horrors.

"Stand back," Frankie yelled.

He pulled out his gun, took aim at the hinges.

Suddenly, the door budged. It started opening. Slowly.

Frankie took a couple of steps back and pointed his gun,

finger on the trigger, ready to pull. Droplets of sweat followed

the etched lines on his forehead, sliding down through the

dirt. His eyes full of tears and rage.

Kitteridge came charging up behind him, breathless.

"No, Frankie, don't! That's what he wants. Don't do it,

Frankie!!"

The words echoed behind him.

None of it registered. Nothing got through. His ears rang.

His muscles locked. There was no movement left in him

except his trigger finger.

The second he saw his face, he was going to shoot.

Damn the consequences.

Chapter 19
Emily In the Basement

Detective Rimler, Emily, opened her eyes. Groggy.

Tied to a post in a basement.

She tried to focus. Tried to piece together what happened, but the ringing in her ears made it impossible to think. If it could just stop. For. One. Second.

Her stomach hurt. Her head throbbed.

She'd been hit. Or maybe dropped.

She looked around as much as she could. Torture chamber. Chains. A bloody table. Mold. Rot.

She was in his world now.

Think, Emily. Think.

She yanked hard at the handcuffs. Not strong enough. Her wrists were already bleeding. She was kneeling, so she tried to stand. Slowly.

Let her cuffed hand guide her up the post. Her head felt like lead.

She leaned on the post. Caught her breath.

Alright… why am I here?

What does he want from me?

I don't fit the profile.

Just a hostage? Just in case?

Where is he?

How long have I been out?

That's when she felt it.

At first, with her forearm against the post.

She turned around it and tried again.

Now with her hands…

Letters.

Her head was still ringing, pain radiating through her skull.

Focus, Emily. Focus.

She ran her fingers across the post's surface. Slow. Careful.

Felt each groove. Felt the spacing.

Six words.

Okay.

First word.

She traced her fingers again. Four letters.

First letter… a line, then a triangle… half circle?

P. Next letter. Circle.

O.

Then… sharp angle. S.

Then a cross. T.

P-O-S-T.

A chill ran down her spine.

Someone had carved this. Someone speaking to her from

the hereafter.

One of the girls.

One of the others.

She closed her eyes, took a deep breath, and kept going.

Fingers steady.

Hard to decipher. Almost impossible.

She exhaled hard.

"One of the victims risked everything to carve this.

I will decipher you."

Back at it.

"Yes. That's a W for sure. Next, B… maybe E?

W-E-A-X…

Oh shit. Weak.

Last letter has to be a K.

WEAK.

POST WEAK.

Girl… whoever you are…

You are an angel.

My guardian angel.

I feel your presence.

I feel your love.

I feel your protection.

I will not let you down. I will get this."

She hears the door open. She can't let him see the letters.

The door creaks as footsteps approach.

"Hello, Detective," he says in a whiny voice. "Don't worry.

I'm not going to hurt you."

He liked giving false hope.

Made the pain hit even harder.

That voice. She remembers it. Whiny… Where had she

heard it before?

She couldn't focus. Her head still pounding.

"I wonder what Frankie's going to feel about this…" he said with a smirk.

That voice. That smirk.

Third degree…

The kitchenette!

Back at the station. Old-school lawyer type. Pressed suit. Fancy fedora. He was right there.

Brazen.

"What do you want?" she asked.

"Hmm…" he replied, thinking. "What. Do. I. Want…"

He tilted his head, letting the words linger.

"I want to test people. I like giving them choices… seeing what they choose."

He stepped closer.

"I like to help people discover what they're really made of, you know?"

He smiled faintly.

"Frankie will have a choice to make. Either spare me and get to you… and your…"

He stepped in closer and touched her belly.

"Baby," he said.

She flinched so hard she nearly stumbled back.

She was stunned. No one knew.

"How did you," she started.

He cut her off with a smile.

"Or he kills me and never sees you again. Or the baby."

He smiled again, proud.

His masterpiece was almost ready. Narcissistic prick.

"I hope he kills you," she said. "Scratch that. I'm certain he will kill you."

"If he chooses to kill me, I will grant him that," he said. "But he would have to accept that I kill you first."

He looked at her, reading her every thought. "If he gets me first, then… you… rot… here." he sing-songed.

Ugh. Just hearing him made her want to throw up.

She really hopes Frankie kills him.

She won't rot here. She'll find a way.

He left. Finally.

She goes right back to feeling the letters. Trying to decipher them. It's not easy. Backwards letters. Etched in pain.

She has to take a break. Her head. Her whole body.

She kneels, hugging the post.

And passes out.

Concussed.

When she finally woke up, she had no idea how long she'd been out. But she was parched. Head still pounding. A little dizzy.

She went right back to feeling the letters.

D or O? A…

Wait.

This isn't the same set. These aren't the six words from

before.

This is different. Two words only.

She felt up along the post until she found the original set.

Okay, she thought. Got it. Six words up here. Two separate

ones down below.

She slid her hands back down.

Labored breathing. Cold sweat.

The mold smell thick in her nose.

She heard a moan.

Far end of the basement.

The darkest corner.

She froze.

Listened.

Nothing.

A minute passed.

Still nothing.

Maybe she imagined it, she thought. Went right back at it.

"Alright. D or O, already got that. Then A. Then definite V.

O-A-V…

No. D-A-V.

David.

Yes. Next letter is a line. I.

Tracks.

And D.

David.

Who's David?

That your name, whiny prick?

Next, M. I. L. B… no, E. Then S.

David Miles."

She froze. Eyes wide.

"I know your name now.

Come on, Emily. You can do this. His victims endured much

more.

Come on.

Pull yourself up.

Come on."

She screamed, teeth clenched, and pushed off the floor.

"AHHH…"

She stood, arms reaching upward, hands back on the top

carvings.

Post. Weak. B…

O… easy. Let's go.

T. Yes. Another T. Got it.

Bottom.

Post. Weak. Bottom.

Her heart started beating fast.. Post is weak at the bottom!

Next...

She kept at it, line by line, letter by letter. Took an eternity.

Or maybe it just felt that way.

But when she finally recited the full message, it hit like a truck.

POST WEAK BOTTOM HELP NEXT GIRL.

She started bawling.

Whoever carved that, gave everything. Not for themselves,

but for the next girl.

For her.

She shook the post. Felt it.

The bottom was giving in.

With every yank, her head lit up like an electric shock to

her spine.

No. I will not give up.

This is for you, whoever you were.

I will get him. In your name.

She kept at it. All night. Never stopped.

Eventually, she passed out.

She woke up to cold water dumped on her. Gasped. He was

there, staring at her.

He handed her some water. Let her barely drink. A couple

slices of cold cut and a piece of bread. Then he left.

That was all she needed.

Energy. Just enough.

She got back to work.

Yanking. Kicking.

Pulling with everything she had.

Pushing like a footballer at practice.

She barely paused to breathe.

Then she heard it again.

A faint moan.

Darkest corner of the basement.

Something was there.

In pain.

Definitely.

Then it happened.

The plaque screwed into the floor gave in. Concrete had

been poured over it, but the cracks spread.

She stomped on it. Hard. Again. Again.

It broke.

She yanked the post. Pushed harder.

It helped that it wasn't screwed into the ceiling. That gave

her a chance.

One last pull.

She climbed it, arms and legs wrapped around as it tilted.

And finally, it gave.

The bottom plaque split in half.

The post fell backward with Emily on it.

A big thud.

It echoed through the basement.

Frankie heard it.

She took a second to gather herself. Got up.

Arms still tied around the post, she followed it down to the

edge and worked her looped hands free.

She looked down.

At the letters.

She could read them now, instead of just feeling them.

There they were.

There was a "**THE**" and some kind of circle or diamond

etched before the word **POST**.

Maybe Cathy had meant to write *the post is weak at the bottom*

at first.

Then decided it was too long.

No need for all the extra words.

There was also the killer's name.

And below it, the third set she hadn't noticed.

Initials she never thought she'd see carved into wood.

C S

She knew it.

Cathy Silva saved her.

Her eyes teared up. Her heart burned.

She scanned the basement. Quickly. Looking for weapons.

There were plenty.

Saws. Knives. All kinds of butchering tools.

She grabbed a saw, propped it between her knees, braced it

on the wooden table, and worked the cuffs until they snapped.

Then she grabbed a hammer. And a knife.

Head still pounding, she went straight toward the sound of

the moan. Moved slow. Careful.

Couldn't see much, but the moaning was clear now. Easy

to follow.

As her eyes adjusted, a shape began to form, a woman.

Naked.

Closer now. The woman looked young. Tied up. Face

duct-taped.

Emily stepped closer and the girl flinched, terrified.

"It's okay," Emily whispered softly. "It's okay. I'll get us out

of here. I'm a cop."

She reached for the tape. The girl flinched again.

"It's okay," Emily said once more. "I got you. I got you, baby

girl."

She took the tape off as gently as she could.

The girl was shivering.

Emily cut the ties and reached for a tarp nearby, wrapping

it around her shoulders.

"Here," she said quietly. "You're safe now." "What's your

name?" she asked.

"Sophia," the girl wheezed.

Emily smiled holding the girl's freezing hand.

"Of course," she said. She pressed on her arm gently. "Hi, Sophia. I met your mother. I'm getting you out of here. I promise."

Sophia could barely speak.

Emily didn't need to ask.

he could already imagine the unspeakable things that monster had done to her.

But he was coming back.

Mr. Whiny.

And she was ready for him. She thought to herself as she adjusted her grip on the hammer.

Suddenly, commotion outside. Running feet. Getting closer.

Emily put Sophia back in the corner and pressed a finger to her lips. Stay quiet.

She took a second to gather herself. Drew a deep breath, tightened her grip on the hammer, and tiptoed toward the entrance.

The door creaked open as she neared it. A beam of light cut through the dark, his shadow framed in the middle of it.

He stepped in fast, pushed the door shut, and pressed his ear against it, listening. Then he turned toward the stairs…

He was met by a hammer coming straight for his head.

She missed the mark. Double vision. Still, it landed hard

enough against his shoulder to throw him off balance.

He reached for his gun with his left hand, but she lunged,

fighting to rip it from him.

She was weak. Exhausted.

He wasn't.

He slammed an elbow into her nose and kicked her off.

She hit the ground hard, bleeding from the face, didn't move.

He stared at her for a second, vengeful. Like a predator

savoring the moment before killing its prey.

Then he stepped down slowly. Calm. Confident.

Got real close to her face. About to say something cheesy

with his whiny fucking voice.

He didn't get the chance.

She drove the knife she'd been hiding straight into his neck.

His surprised face froze in time.

She summoned everything she had left, shoved him off,

hard, and sat up, groaning.

Didn't trust he was dead. Cop instinct.

She grabbed the gun fast. Knife stuck in his neck, eyes fixed

on her. Gun pointed at him. He moved. Barely.

Loud bang.

She shot him in the head.

The sound rippled all the way outside the basement.

"Die, motherfucker."

She shuffled back to Sofia.

"Come on," she said. "He's dead. You're safe."

Sofia, in disbelief, barely whispered, "What about the other one?"

Completely out of it.

"There is no one else," Emily assured her.

She helped her up, and they walked carefully past the body.

Sophia pressed herself into Emily.

Seeking protection.

Even from a monster who was already dead.

They climbed the stairs. One step at a time.

Emily opened the door slowly.

Blinding light.

Both squinted, raising a hand to shield their eyes.

As their vision adjusted, guns were pointed at them.

On the other side of the hatch, Frankie saw the door move.

He took a couple of steps back and pointed his gun, finger on the trigger, ready to pull.

Kitteridge came running. "No, Frankie, don't! That's what he wants! Don't do it, Frankie!"

None of it registered.

The second he saw David's face, he was going to shoot.

Come what may.

The door opened fully.

Frankie's grip tightened. His aim adjusted.

"Don't shoot."

A hoarse female voice.

His heart skipped a beat.

Two women appeared. Bleeding. Terrified. Clinging to each other.

Frankie dropped his weapon. Fast.

Emily collapsed.

He holstered his gun as he ran forward, catching her just in time.

Eyes wide.

Heart pounding.

He looked down into the basement and saw David in a pool of his own blood.

Knife lodged in his neck. Bullet hole in his forehead.

"We got him," Emily whispered. "We got him."

Agent Kitteridge rushed over and helped Sophia.

EMS had been on standby. They quickly made their way to the scene.

Kitteridge guided Sophia to the medics, who wrapped her in a thermal blanket and placed her gently into the ambulance.

Frankie sank to the floor with Emily in his arms. He held her tight, like she might disappear again if he let go. He couldn't stop whispering it, "I'm sorry. I'm so sorry."

"I thought you were dead," he said. "It's all my fault."

Emily stirred, opened her eyes.

"Frankie."

"Shh," he said. "Let's get you checked out…" Then he looked back "Can I get some help here?"

"Wait," she whispered. "Listen… Cathy saved me. Cathy saved me."

He blinked. Confused. Maybe she was still in shock.

"Need some help here!" he called out.

Emily gripped his arm. "You need to see. You have to come see."

She tried to move but faltered. He caught her. Kitteridge rushed to her other side, and the two of them guided her gently down into the basement.

The team lead followed, eyes sweeping the room as they descended.

"Holy shit," he muttered.

Emily stepped toward the broken post, unsteady but determined.

"You did this?" Frankie asked.

"Cathy did," she said. "Look."

Confused, he crouched beside her, eyes scanning the wood.

Etched in deep, uneven lines:

THE then some sort of circle diamond shape

POST WEAK BOTTOM HELP NEXT GIRL

DAVID MILES

He fell to his knees. Traced the words with his fingers.

"Cathy," he breathed. "What did he do to you…"

Emily leaned beside him, wrapping her arms around his shoulder.

"She was a hero, Frankie. I'm alive because of her."

For the first time, Frankie finally understood what had happened to his sister.

It was worse than anything he'd ever imagined.

And he'd imagined the worst.

EMTs lifted Emily carefully onto a stretcher and wheeled her out.

Frankie followed, staying close as they carried her up from the basement.

Her hand reached toward him.

"I'm right behind you," he said, trying to comfort her.

"I'll meet you at the hospital."

He watched the ambulance drive off then he and Kitteridge

walked back toward the car. They peeled off their vests, sweat soaked and covered in dirt. Neither of them spoke right away.

They sat on the hood.

Frankie looked back at the estate one last time. Pulled off his vest, shook the dust from it.

"I guess it's over," he said.

"I guess so," Kitteridge replied.

He offered his hand.

"It was an absolute pleasure working with you, Frankie."

Frankie took it, shook it firmly.

"You too…" He paused, then chuckled softly. "Actually, I don't think I know your first name."

Kitteridge laughed, the tension breaking just a little.

"It's Thomas. My friends call me Tommy."

Frankie smiled, tired but genuine.

"Nice to officially meet you, Tommy."

Kitteridge smiled back.

"Ditto, Frankie."

"How old are you anyway?" Frankie asked, half-joking. "You even allowed to be out this late?"

"Hardy harr," Kitteridge said, rolling his eyes.

They kept talking. Joking. Letting the adrenaline bleed off into laughter.

Frankie and Kitteridge finally said their goodbyes as the sun broke through the last gray clouds on the horizon, warming the air just enough to feel alive again. Frankie had one important phone call to do but first he called Detrective MEndez told her they found her missing girl and asked for a favor. If he could please be the one to call the mom. MEndez agreed. She knew he needed that.

Miss Galanis woke the way she always did now. Half asleep.

She hadn't had a full night's rest since her daughter went missing. Just tossing. Turning. Sleep coming in pieces, chased away by the same demons every time she closed her eyes.

What was happening to her daughter.

Where she was.

If she was cold.

If she was hurt.

If she was still alive.

She lay in bed, awake in the dark. Waiting for the sun so the day could start again. Crying. Studying photos. Calling the police. Begging for updates.

It had been freezing cold for weeks. Months, it felt like.

This morning was different.

As the sun crept through the window, she felt warmth. Real warmth. Something close to hope. It made her uneasy. She didn't let herself trust it.

The sky was clear. She could hear birds chirping. The light felt kind.

She didn't let herself enjoy it.

She got out of bed and started walking toward the window, almost without thinking. A day like this had to be looked at. Had to be checked.

Halfway there, the phone rang. Loud. Violent.

She froze. Then ran for it.

Her hands shook as she picked up. Please God. Please God.

Spare me.

"Miss Galanis?" a voice said.

"Yes. This is she."

"This is Detective Silva. I met you before. With my partner,
Detective Rimler."

"Yes," she said. She sat on the edge of the bed, shoulders
slumping. Tears came fast. She braced herself. Just say it. Get
it over with.

"Miss Galanis. We found Sofia."

Her breath hitched. She misunderstood. Thought he meant
her body.

Frankie continued. "She's at the hospital." He was about to
say which one when Miss Galanis cut him off.

"What?" She sat up straight, wiping her face.

He could hear the confusion in her voice.

"She's alive, Miss Galanis," Frankie explained. "She's been
through a lot, so she's being looked after. But she's alive."

The sound that came out of her was raw. Uncontrolled.

She dropped to the floor. The phone slipped from her hand.

Frankie said her name, but all he could hear was joy.

For a second, Frankie imagined what could have been if
that day had gone differently. The day Detective Shaeffer
knocked on their door with photos of bloody clothes. The
day his mother let out that sound and collapsed to the floor.

The day he split his brow.

He wondered how different everything could have been if

that knock had brought good news instead.

Cathy and Inez living together. Berkeley. Law school.

Maybe opening a small firm side by side.

He pictured himself somewhere else too. MIT. Engineering.

The life he used to talk about before everything narrowed

into this.

The thought was cut short.

Miss Galanis picked the phone back up. "Thank you," she

said. "Thank you. I can never thank you enough."

Frankie didn't know what to say. "I'm glad she's okay," he said.

"What hospital is she in?"

Frankie told her the name. She knew it. He could hear it in

her voice. She was already moving.

"I'll stop by the hospital later," he said, and hung up.

He could already picture her driving. Too fast. Crying.

Laughing. Alive with it.

And for once, that felt enough.

He took a moment to savor the feeling. One he had been

robbed of by the monster in that basement.

He looked up just as the forensic team pulled onto the wet,

muddy grass.

One by one, they walked down the steps.

Into the basement Frankie was still staring at.

The sun hung behind them as they descended through the

hatch in the floor.

Their shadows stretched across the bloody concrete, long

and distorted.

The sound of boots against the metal stairs echoed faintly,

swallowed by the evil that still lingered here.

They all felt it.

The air stood still. A vacuum.

Dark and damp and desolate.

Time didn't exist here. Not for the captives.

Day and night were only faint memories.

Just pitch darkness.

Deafening silence, broken only by the ringing in their ears.

A couple of floodlights were quickly set up.

As soon as the beams came on, the place revealed itself.

The post lay broken on the floor, David's body sprawled

perpendicular to it in a pool of blood. The M.E crouched

besides the body. Examining.

In the far northeast corner, a pile of stained clothes.

Bloody shoes — at least ten pairs.

A rusty barrel with a broken wheel.

Across from it stood a long sink, rusted and filthy.

Strands of hair hung from the side, matted and dark.

Above it, a pipe with a motorized vent that pushed stale air through the room.

The smell of piss and bleach finally had an image to go with it.

Weapons hanging on the wall. Knives. Rusty hooks. Strands of hair caught on metal.

They started cataloging everything.

The table in the middle was soaked in old blood. Crusted. Stiff.

The next room held two closets. Both full.

Boxes stacked high.

Photographs. Graphic.

Jewelry. Journals.

Each new discovery painted a clearer picture of what had happened down there.

The kind of picture no one wanted to see.

Frankie finally got off the hood of his car and shuffled to the door. He grabbed the handle.

Couldn't get himself to open it.

Took another moment. Deep in thought.

That's it?

It's over?

He looked to the side, toward the basement entrance. One last time.

Why can't he let go yet?

His grip loosened on the handle.

Maybe one last look, he thought.

He turned and made his way back into the basement.

Slowly.

He walked toward the post. Knelt. Stared at Cathy's etched

letters.

Flashes popped behind him as the forensic team photographed

the scene. Light. Then dark.

He ran his fingers over them. Tears poured from his eyes.

He couldn't let himself imagine what she went through.

Why?

What was the point of this?

He glanced sideways hatefully at David's body lying on the

dirty floor, a pool of blood spreading beneath him. Flashes

caught the blood-smeared face, then left it dark again.

The thing about monsters.

They don't look like monsters.

Not the way we imagine them.

No.

The worst ones look just like us.

The M.E. stood. Peeled off his gloves.

"Victim's deceased."

Frankie, still staring at the bloody face like it could vanish,

mumbled back, "No shit." Then scoffed. "victim."

For so long, Edward's face had been the one Frankie

accepted as the monster's. The shape of it. The way evil

settled there so easily in his mind.. The bovine residue. The

meat plant. The ticket. The white SUV that belonged to his

father. Theodore…

His train of thought stopped. Hard. Sudden.

He looked back at the post. Leaned in closer.

The etched letters.

THE

Then some kind of diamond or circle. Then

POST WEAK BOTTOM HELP NEXT GIRL

DAVID MILES

C S

He held the stare.

Then his frown slowly cleared. His eyes widened. His heart

began to pound, fast and heavy, like he had just run a marathon.

A chill ran up and down his spine.

And it wasn't because of the cold.

Chapter 20
Theodore

He jolted up and ran out of the basement, dialing his phone.

A voice on the other end said, "Miss me already?"

Frankie was out of breath.

"He wasn't alone. He wasn't alone. He had a partner. He

had a partner!"

1975

Wool-pressed pants. Italian leather shoes. A perfectly fitted

button-up shirt. Sleeves rolled.

He leans over the tub and tests the water. Moves it between

his fingers, left and right. Sits back and stares down, wiping

his hands dry on a towel.

Murky suds.

As they settle, he sees it.

At the bottom.

Staring up with empty eyes.

His wife's face.

He holds the stare for a second. Then he walks out. Calm.

Slow. He drops the towel into the hamper and steps down the

stairs, still calm. Still slow.

He moves into the family room as the nanny runs upstairs

to the crying girl. She had just walked in. He doesn't acknowledge
her.

He sits on the edge of the long leather couch.

Reaches for the pack of cigarettes on the round side table.

Slides one into his mouth. Sets the pack down.

Picks up the Zippo beside the lamp. Lights it.

Draws a deep breath. Holds it. Then exhales a cloud of smoke.

He lifts the rotary phone and rests it on his lap. Spins the dial. Three times. Waits.

Another drag.

On the other end of the receiver, a voice.

"911. What is your emergency?"

"Help!" the man screams, sudden and wild, like something has possessed him. "My wife. My wife. Oh my God. Why, baby, why?"

"Sir, calm down. What's wrong with your wife?"

"She… she…" His voice breaks. "Oh my God. Why?"

"Sir. What happened?"

"She killed herself," he cries. "She drowned herself. Why, baby, why?"

One hour earlier.

A whimper behind a closed door catches her attention. She had just come back from visiting a friend. She wasn't supposed to be home for hours, but she wasn't feeling well. So she came back.

The house is quiet. Empty. But her husband's car is parked outside.

She slips off her heels and walks upstairs, calling for him. No answer.

Her heart drops. She moves faster. The bedroom is empty.

One door closed. She turns the knob.

Locked.

"What's going on?" she screams.

Silence.

The door opens. Her husband stands there. Putting his belt
back on.

Her daughter sits in the corner. Shivering. Crying.

"What did you do?" she says, her Italian accent thick, hands
flying to her face. "What did you do?"

He looks at her. Then back at the girl.

"What do you mean? Nothing," he says. " She was acting up.
I spanked her a little."

She looks at her daughter.

A thin line of blood runs down her inner thigh.

The girl presses herself against the wall, sobbing.

Before she can say anything else, he grabs her by the throat
and drags her into the hallway. Back toward the bedroom.

Only a few months earlier, she had called the police on him.
He had been abusive for most of their marriage, but recently it
had escalated. More violent. More focused on their daughter.
She had been planning to leave him. But leaving meant
losing everything. With no money of her own, she didn't
know how she would care for her child. She was afraid he
would never let her take Tiffany. Afraid of what he could do.

He was too powerful.

That morning, she had gone to a friend's house asking for help. She left Tiffany with the nanny. Her husband, Theodore, was supposed to be at work.

He wasn't.

He drags her into the bedroom. Rage fills his eyes. He throws her onto the bed and climbs on top of her. She screams. Kicks. Fights.

He grabs a pillow and presses it down.

He is strong.

She is small.

Pinned beneath his weight, she can barely move.

He doesn't stop until she's still.

Across the hall, his daughter is still whimpering.

He draws a bath.

And places his wife inside it.

He kept abusing his daughter for years.

He married again. Had a son. Edward.

He had a friend who did the same thing. David's father.

Inez's father. They understood each other.

David learned early.

One winter, during Christmas break, Theodore invited them to vacation with his family.

David became fixated on his daughter. Theodore noticed.

She had just threatened to go to the newspaper. To expose him. She knew the police were in his pocket. She knew what that protection was worth.

Around that time, Theodore had started taking young Edward with him on those trips. The strange ones. She understood what that meant.

She told him if he didn't stop, she would go public.

So he stopped.

But he made a plan.

He began feeding David small things. Spread out. Never obvious.

She would never go out with someone like you.

She thinks you're a loser.

She says you're a virgin.

Time passed.

Then he flipped it. Again, spread out.

I think she likes you, kid.

She has a crush on you.

Says you're strong.

David listened.

The obsession deepened.

When David finally asked her out, she laughed. Not cruelly.

Just enough. She was eighteen. He was a boy.

He killed her.

Theodore saw it. From a window.

He didn't stop it.

He understood immediately what it meant. That act freed

him from being exposed. And it bound David to him. Bound

David's father too.

David grew into the monster he was always going to be.

Theodore was there through it. Visiting. Watching. Abusing.

Choosing.

Sometimes he chose the girls himself.

He saw Cathy with Inez. Told David what to do.

David didn't hesitate.

Years passed. Theodore aged. David moved to New York.

The visits didn't stop. They just changed shape. Business trips.

Conferences. Acquisitions. Reasons that sounded clean on

paper.

Theodore never got his hands dirty.

David abducted. Held. Tortured.

Theodore visited.

Did what he came to do.

Then left.

Cathy never recognized him.

But one night, when she was barely conscious, David said

his name.

Theo.

Theodore struck him across the mouth before he could

finish.

That was all that came out.

Theo.

She heard it. Heard the slap.

No, she thought.

No one gets away with this.

So, on the last day of her life, she etched his name into the wood.

Theo

For someone to see it.

For someone to do something about it.

Someone. She didn't know it would be her brother.

Chapter 21
The last stand off

Frankie's eyes stayed on David's body. He replayed the pieces. The ones that fit. The ones that didn't.

Throughout the investigation, he had been certain it was Edward. The residue. The plant. The ticket. The white SUV registered to Edward's abusive father, Theodore.

He stopped. Blinked.

Theo… dore.

He looked back at the post.

THE etched above the other words.

The shape after it wasn't a symbol. Not a diamond.

It was an O.

THEO.

The realization hit all at once. His pulse spiked. Cold slid up his spine, sharp and immediate.

He jolted out of the basement and dialed.

"Miss me already?" the voice said.

Frankie could barely breathe.

"He wasn't alone. Son of a bitch wasn't alone. He had a partner."

Kitteridge was on the other end of the line. He checked his rearview, cut across lanes, and double parked. Hazards on.

He rubbed his eye. Fatigue settling in.

"What makes you say that?" he said softly, humoring Frankie more than anything.

"The post," Frankie said as he got into his car. "The etched

words." He held the phone between his shoulder and cheek
and started the engine. "It wasn't *the post weak*. It was THEO.
Then *post weak*."

He peeled off the property, the forensic team and news vans
shrinking in his rearview.

"Theo," Frankie said again. Stressed.

Silence.

Then it hit all at once.

"Son of a bitch," Kitteridge said, fully awake now. "Theodore.
Edward's father."

"Yes," Frankie said.

Another beat. Letting it settle. Letting the pieces lock.

"He's in New York," Kitteridge cut in, already checking his
mirror as he cranked a hard U turn. Horns blared behind him.

"Yes," Frankie said. "At the **The Plaza Hotel**. I'm on my way
now."

"Meet you there."

The call ended. Both pushed the gas harder.

Frankie called the Captain on the way. He was at the
hospital, waiting for Emily to arrive. The waiting room was
packed with NYPD. The place felt like a circus.

The Captain could barely hear him.

He stepped outside, jaw tight.

"You sure?" he said.

A beat.

He looked back through the glass at the waiting room. All NYPD.

He nodded to someone inside. The man jogged over. The Captain spoke to him briefly.

Then orders went out.

SWAT was called in for rapid deployment.

A dark blue van cut through Manhattan traffic, siren wailing.

An NYPD patrol car ran ahead, clearing the way.

Inside the van, vests were tightened. Magazines seated.

Eyes forward.

The same guys who had been at the property.

They were going to close this chapter.

They were ready.

Patrol cars and a SWAT van flew into the entry and parked directly in front of the hotel. Doors were already open.

SWAT rushed the lobby as tenants shrieked. A few let out short screams.

Police officers fanned out around the building while the SWAT leader ran for the elevator. Two followed. The rest secured the lobby.

They already had the room number.

The FBI got it.

The elevator dinged.

A scared old woman with a tiny dog stepped out.

Big dogs stepped in.

Doors closed.

Last weapons check.

The doors dinged open.

SWAT poured into the hallway. Flashlights mounted to rifles. Comms live.

The leader crouched near the door. Signaled.

The breacher charged and sent the door flying off its hinges.

They rushed in, clearing the room.

Theodore was in bed. Jolted awake.

They cuffed him as he cursed them.

Down the elevator. In his robe. Undignified.

The entire lobby watched. Phones out. Filming.

This will be on the ten o'clock news tonight.

Frankie and Kitteridge both got the call. Theodore had already been booked.

SWAT was too fast.

They will meet at the precinct.

Frankie pushed through the busy station.

Applause followed him down the hall.

The guy who saved their sister in arms.

It didn't phase him.

He cut through the noise and stepped into the room beside the interrogation suite.

Looked through the two way mirror.

There he was.

Theodore. Still in his robe.

Kitteridge was already there.

They stood shoulder to shoulder. Almost touching. Eyes

locked on him.

"How do you want to do this?" Kitteridge asked.

Frankie stayed quiet.

"We tell him we have evidence."

"Do we?" Kitteridge asked.

Frankie shook his head.

"Not yet."

Theodore's lawyer walked in.

The captain followed into the adjacent room.

Stood with them.

"We can't hold him for long."

Frankie knew that. The more he thought about it, the

clearer it became. How hard this was going to be to prove.

An etched name that could be argued as "The." That was it.

Bovine residue? A judge would laugh.

They had one shot.

Get inside his head.

Force a confession.

But it couldn't be Frankie.

He shouldn't conduct the interview.

Both the captain and Kitteridge agreed.

Kitteridge rolled up his sleeves and left the room. Walked straight into the interrogation suite.

Frankie followed immediately.

The captain called after him. Too late.

Kitteridge shot Frankie a look.

Too late.

They both pulled out chairs and sat.

The lawyer spoke first. Calm.

"Are you charging my client?"

"No," Kitteridge said. "We have some questions."

The lawyer didn't hesitate.

"No questions. Charge him. Jail him if you want to hold him for twenty four hours. After that, he walks. Or he walks now."

He leaned back.

"No questions will be answered."

Firm.

The captain walked in just as Frankie was about to speak anyway.

"You're free to go, Mister Milton," he said.

The lawyer stood.

Theodore Milton stood.

Kitteridge and Frankie watched. Disbelief.

"You'll be hearing from us," the lawyer said.

"We're suing the department."

Then they walked out. Just like that.

Frankie stayed seated. Stunned.

The captain sat across from him.

"The DA asked us to release him. We have no probable cause.

Nothing on him. Just an etched word. Not even certain it's a

name."

"It's a name," Frankie said quietly.

His eyes dropped to his shoes. Not anger. Something else.

Empty. Like the fight had finally left him.

He stood. Squeezed Kitteridge's shoulder. Kitteridge stayed

seated.

"We gave it a try," Frankie said.

Then softer.

"If you'll excuse me, I'm going to check on Emily."

He walked out of the precinct. The noise around him dulled.

Muffled. Like he was underwater.

He drove straight to the hospital. Leaving it all behind.

Driving toward whatever came next.

He parked and went inside. NYPD still owned the floor. He

asked for Emily's room and walked there. Knocked gently.

Then stepped in.

She was asleep.

He pulled the folding chair beside her bed and sat. Eventually, he fell asleep too.

At first faint. Then sharper. Beep. Beep. Beep.

Frankie opened his eyes. The IV drip was sounding. Needed to be changed.

A nurse came in and took care of it.

Frankie rubbed his eyes and sat up. A blanket was over him. Probably the nurse.

Emily was awake.

"Hey," he said.

"Hey, sleeping beauty," she said, smiling.

"Not you too," he smiled back.

He took her hand. No hesitation. No games. His heart finally felt still.

"I love you," he said.

The nurse smirked.

Emily's heart skipped.

The nurse changed the IV and walked out with a smart remark.

Emily kept staring at him.

"Now's a good time to say something," Frankie said.

She chuckled. "I love you too, you dumb dumb."

Relief washed over him. He leaned in and kissed her. Her lips were dry. Chapped.

He looked at her belly. Then back at her. Too afraid to ask.

"The baby's fine," she said.

He pulled her hand closer and kissed it.

He spent the next few days beside her. She was kept for observation because of the concussion.

When she was discharged, she went straight to his place.

Eventually, they got their own. Bigger.

More test results came back in the weeks that followed.

The bovine substance on Cathy's jacket matched the residue found on the scarf. Confirmed as bovine gelatin. Likely from lip balm or something similar.

Didn't matter.

Families were notified. One by one.

They were spared most of the details. There was no need to cause any more pain.

Sofia Galanis swore there were two of them.

She said they were never there at the same time, but she could tell.

Different heights. Different smells. Different sounds.

That was why she had asked Emily back in the basement of horror.

"What about the other one?"

She knew there were two.

She just couldn't identify them.

She never saw their faces.

Didn't matter.

Theodore got away with it.

And Frankie seemed okay with that.

After he stopped reading the journals, he seemed at peace.

Case closed.

But no closure.

Not yet.

Chapter 22
Closure… Or Something Like It

Frankie wanted closure. He wanted to move on. To stop being

a prisoner. A captive of pain and regret.

So he decided to hold a memorial for Cathy in Oakland.

A way to honor her.

And also to heal.

Or at least to start the process.

Closure… Or something like it.

The memorial was held at a small church in Piedmont,

overlooking Lake Merritt.

A large poster stood at the front. Cathy. Big smile.

Gorgeous wavy hair. Big brown eyes.

Beside it, a smaller photo of their mother. Flowers arranged

beneath both.

Frankie stood near the pictures as people filtered in.

Emily was there. Inez. The Captain who had already retired

and his wife. A few of Cathy's high school friends. Mo and

his wife.

When it was time, Frankie stepped forward.

"Thank you all for being here today," he said.

He took a breath.

"It feels strange being back in Oakland. For a long time, I

avoided coming here. Every corner of this city reminds me

of my sister."

He looked down, then back up.

"We used to sneak out of school, take the bus down to Jack

London Square, watch the boats. Buy snacks in Chinatown.

Ride up to Berkeley. Walk around campus. Dream about

going there one day."

A pause.

"I'm here now with something I didn't think I'd ever have.

Closure. We finally know what happened to my sister. The

person who hurt her got what he deserved."

He swallowed.

"And from what we know, she didn't go quietly. She fought.

She helped other women down there. In that basement."

He turned slightly and gestured to Emily, her hands resting

on her visibly pregnant belly.

"Her courage saved my partner. At work. And in life."

Emily wiped at her teary eyes. Frankie kept going.

"For a long time, I couldn't accept love. It felt like a

betrayal. Like moving on meant leaving behind the people

who mattered most."

He looked around the room.

"But I know now my mom and my sister would have wanted

me to live. To be happy. To choose joy."

The church doors opened mid-sentence.

A man in his late fifties stepped inside. Quiet. Track jacket.

Chain. Walking like he owned the place.

Tony.

From back in the day. One of the neighborhood guys who showed up when word got out Cathy was missing. The one who leaned in and whispered in Miss Silva's ear. The one who waited for her half nod. The signal. **Attack.** Then dragged a drunk out of a bar for running his mouth.

That Tony.

He slipped into a back pew, calm. Watching.

Frankie saw him. Paused. Gave him a nod.

Tony returned it.

"I lost my family," Frankie continued. "But standing here today, I see I still have one."

He glanced at the photos. His smile softened.

"May you finally rest in peace. I love you."

He stepped down and sat beside Emily as others came up to speak.

Inez approached the podium.

She talked about how Cathy saved her life. How she was the best friend you could ever dream of. She spoke briefly about the abuse she endured growing up. About her father. About her brother, David.

Her voice shook as she said she had always considered Cathy more of a sister than her own blood ever felt like.

"Your friends are the family you choose. I chose Inez." She said.

She looked at Frankie. Told him how sorry she was. Said

she wished it had been her instead.

When the memorial ended, people slowly filed out.

Frankie introduced Emily to Mo. They had kept in touch after that phone call, just like they promised. Life pulled them in different directions, but somehow they found their way back to each other.

And they made an effort to stay.

Mo introduced his wife. The two women fell easily into banter, warm and quick, like they'd known each other longer than they had.

Frankie watched them, quietly relieved.

Mo had ended up with someone kind.

He deserved that.

The next day, he and Emily stopped by Lake Merritt on their way to the airport. He and Cathy used to hang out there. All the time. It was their escape. They'd walk around the lake, feed the ducks, talk about the future.

They felt bad about how hard their mom was working. And they'd make promises. One day, they'd be successful. Move out of Oakland. Maybe to the Hills. Somewhere peaceful. Safe.

Now, as if retracing those old steps, they walked the path in silence. A gentle breeze touched their faces. Ran its fingers through their hair. The warmth of the sun wrapped them in something that felt like compassion. A familiar scent passed

in the air. He could almost see it. Feel it.

He remembered his mom and Cathy. Laughing. Cleaning

the house.

Girls Just Wanna Have Fun blasting from the radio.

Early nineties. Loud house. Warm house.

Inez was there too.

Part of the family now.

She had finally found love.

Real love.

Away from all the abuse.

He stared, like it was right in front of him.

He had been in heaven and never knew it.

You don't realize you were there until you fall from it.

He opened his palm. Emily's hand found it without looking.

She held tight, wrapped herself around his arm.

"I love you," he said.

Her heart skipped.

"I love you too, Frankie."

"I'm ready," he said.

She looked at him. Questioned the words with her eyes.

"I'm ready to move on."

He let go of her hand and walked toward the lake's edge.

Stared at the ducks. The way the water caught the sunlight.

"I love you, Cathy," he said. "Thank you for saving my

childhood.

Thank you for being the hope I needed most.

I'm sorry I didn't find you.

I'll live with that my whole life.

But I know you.

You're looking down at me right now saying—

Don't make this about you, Frankie boy."

He smiled through the tears.

"Until we meet again, sis…"

He took a breath.

"I love you, Mom.

Thank you for raising me the way you did.

For all your sacrifices.

For being both father and mother.

You did an excellent job.

I just wish I'd had the chance to repay you.

I'm sorry."

He grabbed Emily's hand and they walked on. Crossed the

street. Headed downtown.

They passed an electronics store on the way to the public parking lot
where they'd left the car.
Emily glanced inside through the window, then slowed. Frowned.
Stopped.
She pulled his arm. Frankie startled, looked at her. Then followed
her gaze.

The big screen TV in the window was tuned to the news.

THEODORE MILTON, OAKLAND MOGUL, FOUND DEAD AT 79

Emily's eyes widened. She looked at Frankie.

His face was blank. She couldn't read it. She didn't know if it was closure. Or vindication.

She started to pull him toward the store. He didn't budge.

Shook his head no.

She looked back at the screen.

FOUND DEAD IN BATHTUB. SUSPICIOUS CIRCUMSTANCES.

She looked at him again.

Nothing. Just an empty stare.

She held his gaze.

"What?" he said.

She couldn't ask.

Didn't want the answer.

They kept walking toward the parking lot. Quiet. Emily stunned. It would take a moment to shake the feeling.

They passed a trash bin.

Frankie reached into his pocket, pulled out a crumpled piece of paper, and dropped it inside without breaking stride.

A torn page from a journal.

At the top, a date.

Christmas 1997.

It detailed everything. Cathy's abduction. The scream. The search party.

At the very end, one line.

The line that made Frankie stop reading the journals. The line he'd been searching for, or something close enough to it. The moment he read it, he tore the page out and never looked back.

It read:

"Theodore visited tonight. Christmas night. Had fun with Cathy."

They kept walking.

Frankie pulled Emily into a side hug.

"You're my home now," he said.

Silence. A beat. Then she let it go. Whatever it was. She didn't need to know.

She rested her head against him.

"And you're mine," she whispered.

The End.